Ceiling and walls and floor vanished. She floated into his embrace and anchored herself there, his confidence wrapping securely around her, banishing the last of her fears.

"You have bewitched me," he said softly, grazing the pad of his thumb down her cheek. "Will you cast a spell for both of us now, Celia? Will you give me all your magic?"

"I will give you all I am," she whispered. "Please kiss me."

Gently at first, and then with deep, demanding passion, he promised with his kisses everything that was to follow. She felt his hand at her waist, and felt it move down, sliding over her hip, drawing her closer. Mindless, boneless, she melted into his body, glad of his strength. Needing it. Needing him . . .

By Lynn Kerstan
Published by Fawcett Books:

FRANCESCA'S RAKE
A MIDNIGHT CLEAR
CELIA'S GRAND PASSION

CELIA'S GRAND PASSION

Lynn Kerstan

FAWCETT CREST • NEW YORK

A Fawcett Crest Book
Published by The Ballantine Publishing Group
Copyright © 1998 by Lynn Kerstan Horobetz

http://www.randomhouse.com

Library of Congress Catalog Card Number: 97-94536

ISBN 0-449-00183-0

Manufactured in the United States of America

First Edition: April 1998

10   9   8   7   6   5   4   3   2   1

For Joel Hoersch, one of the truly nice guys,
and Doris Bailey, always a terrific friend.
Thanks, good buddies!

Chapter 1

Second only to marrying Lord Greer, this was beyond a doubt the most lunatic thing she'd ever done.

Celia knew, with blazing clarity, that she had slipped her own leash. Indeed, even while she had been preparing her makeshift costume, she'd repeatedly ordered herself to stop. But the rational part of her mind must have been closed for the evening, because here she was, risking everything she had set her heart on.

And all for the merest glimpse of a man.

He might not even be the *right* man.

All the same, how was she to know unless she got a closer look at him?

From her position by the door of the front parlor, she made certain the coast was clear. Then, lifting a tray laden with empty wineglasses, she stepped into the passageway and began to walk slowly toward the back of Lord Finlay's town house.

The double doors leading to the dining room stood open. She heard voices, laughter, and the clink of silverware against china. One voice, heavily accented, rose above the others. That must be the guest of honor, a Russian general come early to London for the victory celebrations.

He was on his feet, she noted as she dawdled past the door, his fringed epaulets and bejeweled medals glittering. Since the other guests had turned in his direction, she could see only the backs of their heads.

Rats! Celia sped to the servants' staircase, paused on the landing for a few moments, and then launched herself again in the direction of the parlor. This time her view of the dinner guests was blocked by a pair of footmen standing behind Lady Marjory, Lord Finlay's wife, who was ensconced at the end of the table closest to the door.

Celia made three more daring trips between stairs and parlor with equal lack of success. At this rate, she would likely wear a rut on the marble floor before catching a glimpse of her quarry. Arms aching, she set the heavy tray on a pier table in the parlor and reevaluated her plan. Obviously, it wasn't working. There were too many guests—thirty at least—and half as many servants in that dining room. On each of her passes, she had no more than three or four seconds to look inside.

Moreover, every time she ventured into the passageway, she faced the possibility of exposure. Her improvised maid's uniform, a black bombasine mourning dress with a lace-edged chemise pinned over it in lieu of an apron, would not stand close inspection, even though the house was swarming with temporary staff hired on for the evening.

Social ruin on her very first night in London? It did not bear thinking of. Worse, her conscience had begun to gnaw at her again. Only the most ungrateful of wretches would violate Lady Marjory's hospitality in such a fashion. She was monumentally ashamed of herself. Which did not prevent her from resolving to make one last trip past the dining room before calling it a night.

Taking up the tray, she charged into the passageway and all but collided with a startled footman. She jerked to a halt before running him down, but several glasses on the tray kept going without her. In dismay, she watched them shatter on the marble tiles.

"Mercy me," she murmured past the lump of horror in her throat.

In a swift motion, the footman seized the tray from her hands and swept her into the parlor, closing the door behind him. Then, to her astonishment, he bowed.

"Lady Greer," he said. "How may I be of service?"

Well and truly caught. "I suppose," she began haltingly, "you could clean up that mess in the hall."

"Yes, certainly." His neck and cheeks were an alarming shade of red. "But first, I'm afraid that Lord Finlay must be informed."

"That I broke a few glasses? Surely not." She took a deep breath. "I'll pay for them, of course. And he cannot wish to be disturbed while he is entertaining guests."

"It will be awkward, I agree. But the staff has strict instructions to report anything out of the ordinary. Immediately," he added, crossing to the bellpull. "Carver will know how to proceed."

She rushed after him, grappling his arm before he could summon the formidable butler. "Please don't. Truly, this is no more than an act of irresponsible foolishness on my part."

He stepped away and regarded her closely, uncertainty written on his round, pleasant face. "Lord Finlay is an important man, m'lady, and matters of state are conducted in this house."

Light dawned. "Good heavens, I'm not a *spy*! Well, not of the sort you are imagining," she added in strictest honesty. "How is it you know my name?"

"I held the horses when your carriage arrived this afternoon, and helped carry in your luggage. We were informed that Lady Greer would be staying for several weeks." He frowned. "But unless I am much mistaken, you were not expected until tomorrow."

Celia nodded. "It was insufferably rude of me to descend on Lord and Lady Finlay a day early, but the weather was fine and the road so good that we made excellent time. Perhaps I should have spent the night at a posting house outside the city, but it never occurred to me to do so. This is my first trip to London, you see, and I simply could not wait to arrive."

How absurd she sounded. How like the impulsive chit she had been when she married. She ought to have grown more wise, or at least more cautious, considering where her last major plunge into folly had landed her.

3

She dropped onto a chair. "Well, you may as well go ahead and turn me in. I deserve whatever happens, I suppose."

"It is none of my business," he said in a tentative voice, "but if you could possibly explain—"

"Oh, I can!" Did he mean to let her off the hook? Dear heavens, her fate was in the hands of a *footman*! She would have enjoyed the irony, were she not so furious with herself. "It is most embarrassing, though. I'm not altogether sure my tale will make the slightest sense to you."

A smile flickered across his lips. "Wait here if you will, m'lady, while I see to the disorder in the entrance hall."

Celia had only begun to regain her composure when he returned, a boar's-hair brush in one hand and a dustpan mounded with broken glass in the other.

"I was sent to tidy this room," he said, emptying the dustpan into a trash basket. "If someone enters, perhaps you will turn your back to the door and pretend to be helping."

She leapt to her feet and began gathering up sherry glasses. When he gave her an appalled look, she shrugged. "I've cleaned worse messes in my time, you know. Will you tell me your name?"

"Thomas, ma'am. Thomas Carver. My uncle is Lord Finlay's butler, and I mean one day to rise to that position myself." He gave her a conspiratorial smile. "As it happens, the first lesson he taught me was the importance of absolute discretion."

"You are a treasure, Thomas," she said sincerely. "Should I survive this misadventure with my reputation intact, I shall find a way to repay your kindness."

As they worked, gathering glasses and small plates, she made several stammering attempts to explain herself without revealing too much. But it was no use. Her skill at deception was, to put it mildly, nonexistent, and she generally resorted to the truth because no one ever believed her taradiddles.

"Lady Marjory was most apologetic, to be sure, but I could not be invited to the dinner party at such late notice. It would make the numbers uneven, you see, and spoil her seating arrangement. She kindly refrained from pointing out that my

4

wardrobe is wholly unsuitable for such fine company. I didn't mind terribly much at first. I had a tray in my room, which overlooks the street, and contented myself with watching out the window as the guests arrived. The thing is, Thomas, I thought I saw someone I knew. Well, I never actually met him, but I have private reasons . . . that is, I wish to make his acquaintance."

"Tonight?"

"Mercy, no." She held out her arms. "Looking like this? A demon must have possessed me, though, because I felt compelled to discover if he was really here, in this very house. If so, it would be an omen. A sign from heaven."

Thomas put down the plate he was holding and turned to her, confusion painted across his face.

He must think her demented, she realized. And perhaps she was. She was certainly behaving like the veriest bedlamite.

"I believe that I understand, m'lady," he said after a moment. "A matter of the heart."

Was it? she wondered. But how could it be? "Perhaps so, Thomas. In any case, I was determined to see his face in full light. It was shadowed by the brim of his hat when he left his coach and mounted the stairs, so I could not be positive of his identity. But something about him was uncannily familiar. The way he moved, perhaps."

She went still, a wineglass dangling from her fingers as she remembered the first time she had seen him. It was on his wedding day. . . .

Gently, Thomas plucked the glass from her hand. "You have convinced me, Lady Greer. Lord Finlay need hear nothing of this. But I expect you ought to return to your chamber now, for the ladies will soon retire to the first-floor salon. Indeed, the maids have doubtless begun to lay out the tea-and-coffee service. Perhaps I had better go ahead of you, to make certain no one is on the stairs."

With a sigh, still itching for one more look inside that dining room, she followed him to the door.

Hand on the latch, he turned again, his round cheeks apple red. "Not that this will be of interest to you, Lady Greer, but should *I* wish a closer look at the dinner guests, I would conceal myself in the maid's closet just down the passageway from the first-floor salon. With the door cracked open, one can enjoy an excellent view of anyone mounting the stairs. And later, to make my escape, I'd use the servants' stairs at the other end of the hall."

Celia burst out laughing. "Why, Thomas, I begin to suspect that *you* are a spy."

"I've a fondness for the young woman assigned to tend the rooms on the first floor," he confessed. "Sometimes we steal a kiss or two in that closet. So now you and I have exchanged confidences, ma'am. I trust both our secrets are safe."

He could not have found a better way to reassure her. Celia nearly planted a friendly kiss on his blazing cheek but recalled in time that she was Lady Greer. Already she had failed her first test, violating any number of civilized rules within hours of arriving in London to begin her new existence as a wealthy, titled widow.

"Thank you again, Thomas. I may just have a look at that closet. And I'll be very, very careful not to be discovered."

When Thomas gave her the sign that the passageways were clear, she scurried upstairs and into the closet. Sure enough, the view was excellent. But even with the door slightly ajar, the small room soon grew unbearably hot. She endured the stultifying atmosphere for half an hour, distracted by the sight of elegantly gowned ladies gracefully ascending the stairs and wafting into the salon.

After that, except for the occasional servant coming and going, nothing of interest occurred. The gentlemen, she understood, would converse over port and cigars in the dining room, possibly for hours, before joining the ladies.

Her attention was drawn to a closed door directly across the way. The view would be equally fine from that room, she thought. Even better, since the gentlemen would turn in that direction as they entered the salon, providing her a better look at their faces. From her current angle, she saw more backs than fronts.

When the passageway was temporarily deserted, she slipped across the hall and through the door.

She was in a study, she saw, a large one, with bookshelves along one side and an oversized oak desk filling half the opposite wall. Two wingback chairs were set before the hearth, and at the far end of the room, a bay window like the one in her bedchamber faced onto the street.

The room was too bright, though, lit by colsa lamps and several candlebraces. Fearing the light would draw attention to the slightly opened door, she snuffed the candles and all but one lamp before taking up her position. Gingerly, she cracked open the door.

Nothing happened for an exceedingly long time, if she discounted the movements of the servants. When her feet began to ache, she dropped to her knees for a bit, but still no gentlemen appeared. They must have taken root in the dining room, she thought when the mantelpiece clock chimed the passing of another hour.

She was sitting on the polished floor, half-asleep, her shoulder resting against the wall, when a loud, accented male voice shot her awake.

In groups of two and three, the men trooped up the staircase and turned into the parlor. Celia tried to stand, but her calves and feet were painfully cramped. She struggled onto her hands and knees, pressed her cheek against the door frame, and watched for him.

Suddenly there he was! Thank heavens she had stayed the course long enough to see him. Best of all, instead of turning directly into the salon, he paused at the top of the stairs to speak with Lord Finlay.

She looked her fill of him. And he was spectacular. No, that wasn't precisely true. Handsome, yes. Absolutely. But quietly so. His very stillness amid the bustle surrounding him impressed her enormously. Try as she might, she could *never* be still, let alone so poised and self-contained as the Earl of Kendal.

Item by item, she marked him top to bottom. Sleek, close-cropped hair, light brown. Well-shaped lips. Firm jaw. Wide shoulders, slim hips encased in formfitting black satin, hard calves under those white silk stockings—oh, mercy!

For seven years she had dreamed about him. Now he stood within a few yards, closer than he had ever been to her in real life, and her fantasies drifted away like smoke. In their place, a diamond-hard certainty took possession of her.

She must have him. She *would* have him.

But only for a short time, she amended hastily. In her experience, men should be taken in small doses. Never again would she permit a tyrannical male to control her life.

It occurred to her that this particular male was already directing her every move. Dear heavens, here she was before him on her hands and knees!

Her brain felt like egg custard and her body was heating up in the oddest places. She wished he'd proceed into the salon so that she could safely make her way to her bedchamber. Then Lord Finlay, his paunch bouncing as he made a wide gesture, turned in her direction and pointed to the door.

To her horror, both men started directly toward her.

There wasn't time to clamber to her feet. Celia scuttled to the only concealment within reach—the desk—and heard a loud tear as she inadvertently crawled up the inside of her skirt. She dove into the shelter of the desk's kneehole just as the study door swung open, sending a wide shaft of light into the dim room.

Chapter 2

James Randolph Elliott Valliant, Lord Kendal, was prodigiously bored.

It took precious little to bore him of late, he had reflected on his way to Lord Finlay's house in Curzon Street, and nothing had transpired during the interminable dinner party to change his mind. Even the mildly deranged guest of honor, a Russian general with an obsession for English poetry, could not hold his interest beyond the first few minutes.

Kendal had spent the evening making polite, tedious conversation with his dinner partners and wondering how soon he could take his leave. When the ladies withdrew, he tried to seize the opportunity to depart, but Lord Finlay was having none of his excuses. There were matters of importance to be discussed, he insisted, so Kendal was forced to endure the Russian's poetic ecstasies over port and cigars.

"Here's our chance," Finlay said nearly two hours later as they made their way upstairs to the salon. "Join me for a brandy in the study?"

"As you wish." Kendal glanced in the direction of the study door, which was slightly open. And unless he was very much mistaken, there was the tip of a nose silhouetted against the door frame.

It withdrew an instant later, but he caught a glimpse of white as whoever had been crouched behind that door moved away.

Interesting.

Placing his hand on Finlay's arm, Kendal turned to Lord Pace, who was passing through the hall, and spoke to him briefly about nothing of significance, deliberately allowing the intruder a few moments to conceal himself. A foolish caprice, he knew, born of ennui, and he'd not live to regret it should the man prove to be a hired assassin. In any case, he trusted what had always been a reliable instinct for danger, and for the proximity of an individual worth meeting.

In this particular case, he sensed trouble, although not of the lethal sort, and decided to handle it himself. First, however, Finlay must be permitted to conduct his business, after which he would be summarily shuffled out of the way. Kendal released his arm.

Slicing him a puzzled look, Finlay made his way to the study door and pushed it open. A single lamp glowed from a table at the far end of the room. "What the devil?" Grumbling, Finlay stomped around lighting candles while Kendal closed the door. "The servants know I expect this room in readiness at all times."

"Good help is hard to find," Kendal said, his gaze fixed on the curtains drawn over the bay window. The intruder could well be hiding behind them, although he would then be visible from the street.

Finlay aimed himself at a decanter of brandy on the sideboard. "If ever I doubted it, James, the past few hours in company with that Russian steppe hound have convinced me the war was easier than this peace is likely to be."

"Not for the soldiers," Kendal observed mildly.

"Yes, yes. I'm always forgetting you had a brother in the army."

"I still do, or so I believe." Kendal accepted a glass of brandy. "Mind you, I was sure he'd sell out when the Forty-fourth was dispatched to America, but he sailed with the regiment after all."

"Damnable business. Damnable. I've been too preoccupied with the French to protest this absurd quarrel with the Americans, but someone should have put a stop to it long ago. Instead, they're sending good English soldiers to quash a minor rebellion by a ragtag band of farmers and a poorly armed militia. At least *this* war, such as it is, will soon be over."

Less convinced that the Americans would be so easily

routed, Kendal made a slow, careful circuit of the room. There were few places to hide once he'd eliminated the bay window, and he quickly narrowed his search to the cubbyhole under Finlay's massive, paper-strewn desk.

"Do stop prowling, James. It is most annoying."

"Then tell me why you brought me here. It wasn't merely to elude Chirikov, I am persuaded."

Sure enough, he saw as he came around the desk, a dark shape was making itself small in the deep kneehole. Well, it was time to give him something to worry about. Lowering himself onto the leather-padded chair, Kendal leaned back and crossed his ankles atop the desk.

From underneath came a tiny squeak of dismay.

It was, he was reasonably certain, a female squeak. Or that of a young boy, but the faint scent of perfumed soap, redolent of honeysuckle, confirmed his first impression. He wondered if she knew he was onto her.

She would find out soon enough, but first there was the tiresome matter of ejecting Finlay from his own study. "You may as well spit it out," he said, lacing his fingers behind his neck. "Bad news has been stuck in your craw all evening. But I advise you to be discreet, William. With so many strangers crawling about the house, the very desks have ears."

There was a barely detectable gasp from the female.

"Oh, this is nothing to do with matters of security." Finlay pulled out his handkerchief. "Fact is, Castlereagh wants you to return to France. Tomorrow, if you can manage it."

"Unthinkable. I've been home precisely one day, and you're the one who recalled me from Paris."

"I wanted you here. But the foreign secretary overruled me this morning, and there we have it. He says you are needed in Boulogne, so to Boulogne you must go. As usual, you will have no official duties, but I expect you understand the situation well enough. Do whatever needs to be done, and try not to be too obvious about it."

Kendal did understand. The ruling princes, generals, and ministers of the allied powers gathering for the lavish victory celebration had already begun to assemble in the port town.

Within the week they would make the channel crossing aboard the *Impregnable*, captained by the Duke of Clarence. Apparently Clarence was finding the clash of egos and temperaments a bit more than he could handle.

Finlay mopped his forehead with his handkerchief. "Can't say I envy you. They'll all be posturing and jockeying for precedence, taking offense at perceived slights, and generally behaving like spoiled brats. I'd almost rather an invasion by Napoleon than Prinny's notion of a victory party, especially if General Chirikov is any sample of what we may expect."

"He is irritating, certainly. Why did he arrive in advance of the Russian delegation?"

"I daresay they had their fill of his blather and sent him on ahead. He wants to meet some English poets, by the way. Know any?"

"Not a one, blessedly."

"In that case, you are of little use to me until the circus arrives. Go to Boulogne, James. Soothe tempers, smooth waters, and keep our honored allies from going to war with one another. It will be good practice for the Vienna Congress." Finlay set down his glass. "I expect we should join the others before Marjory—"

"You must excuse me, William. If I'm to travel tomorrow, arrangements must be got under way. May I make use of your desk and writing materials for a few minutes?"

"Yes indeed. Ring for Carver if you require anything." He paused at the door. "Naturally you will send frequent reports from Boulogne, James."

When Finlay was gone, Kendal stood and went to lean against the closed door, in case Madame Spy decided to make a break for it. "You may come out now," he said, a pleasurable sense of anticipation vibrating under his skin.

There was a rustling sound, and the rap of bone against wood. Finally, a soft but distinct, *"Rats!"*

"Oh, I think not. For one thing, Lady Marjory would not permit them in her house. And for another, rodents cannot speak."

"Who said they could?" More rustling and thumping from

under the desk. "I'm trying to get out of here, but my hair has caught on something. A nail, I th—ouch!"

"Ah." He went to crouch by the kneehole and peered in. Little light reached to where she had curled herself, but he could make out the gleam of golden curls and a pair of enormous dark eyes.

Like a small animal cornered in a cave, she gazed nervously back at him. "It's too narrow in here, sir. I cannot reach whatever is gripping my hair."

"Then permit me." Dropping to one knee, he slid his arms alongside her head, his palms brushing her smooth cheeks as they went by. His forearms rested lightly on her shoulders as he felt for the tangled curl. Sure enough, it was knotted around a protruding nail.

This close to her, the fragrance of honeysuckle was distinctive. Also seductive, which struck him as prodigiously odd under the circumstances. Even odder was his surprising reluctance to move away from her.

"I am afraid," he said, his voice raspy, "that scissors will be required and a lock of your hair sacrificed if you are to be extricated."

"Fine. But do hurry. Both my legs have gone to sleep."

He could find no scissors in the desk drawers, but the small knife used for sharpening pens would do as well. Again on his knees, he slid his fingers through her hair and carefully sawed through the strands twisted around the nail. When she was free, he stood and moved away from the desk.

She emerged slowly, rose with a slight groan, and clung for support to the edge of the desk while she shook the cramps from her legs. Since she was careful not to look in his direction, Kendal was free to observe her closely.

Her uniform, if that's what it was meant to be, concealed most of her body. Still, the black dress fit her closely, outlining perfectly shaped breasts, a willowy waist, and the gentle, feminine slope of her hips. A connoisseur of the female form, he had rarely seen another so perfectly proportioned, or quite so suited to his particular taste. The top of her head would reach his chin, were they to embrace—

13

"I suppose you want to know what I was doing under the desk," she said, sounding more than a little put out at having to explain herself.

"Dusting?" he supplied helpfully.

She sighed. "That's a far better excuse than the one I was considering. But I don't suppose you'd credit any story I managed to devise on such short notice."

"In fact, I'd have expected you to come prepared with one."

"Well, I didn't. Had I been thinking in any coherent fashion, I would not be here at all. Could I persuade you to go away and forget I ever was?"

"Possibly."

She turned to face him, hope flaring in her eyes. They were the color of rich molasses, large and expressive, with dark lashes and brows. He wondered briefly if her hair had been dyed golden, but decided not. It shone naturally, and quite gloriously, in the candlelight. All in all, despite the swatch of torn lace dangling over her left ear and the wisp of a cobweb on her cheek, she was a remarkably beautiful young woman.

His gaze dropped to a spot just beneath her bosom, where her skirt had pulled from the bodice. Through a tear the size of his palm, he saw the filmy material of her chemise and, through that, a tantalizing glimpse of creamy skin.

The room had gone alarmingly hot of a sudden. Kendal wrenched his thoughts to the matter at hand. "Before permitting you to leave, I would first need to know who you are and precisely what you were doing."

"But those are the very things I don't wish to tell you, sir. If it helps, though, you may be sure that I am not a spy."

"Exactly *how* am I to be sure? You are most certainly not a housemaid." Stepping closer, he fingered a strap of muslin and lace pinned to the shoulder of her dress. "Unless I am much mistaken, this is a female undergarment masquerading as an apron."

A flush crept up her neck. "I never said I was a housemaid. Perhaps I merely have no sense of fashion. But if you must know, I am a house*guest*."

He had to give her credit for sheer nerve. Although clearly

embarrassed, she gave him back eye for eye, defying him to refute that declaration.

He realized that he was still clutching the filmy lace, his thumb a bare inch from the soft flesh at the side of her neck. Mouth dry, he let go and moved beyond the dangerous reach of her fragrance.

"Well?" Her chin went up a notch. "I am speaking the truth."

"Oh, I believe you," he said, unaccountably disoriented. "I'm also certain that Lord and Lady Finlay have no idea how you are spending the evening."

Alarm flashed across her expressive face. "Do you mean to tell them?"

"Is there some reason I should not?"

"Yes, indeed. I would find it exceedingly m-mortifying," she said earnestly. "And betraying me would thrust Lord and Lady Finlay into an awkward situation, which they do not deserve."

"On that count, I heartily agree. Perhaps we need not draw them into this affair, but only if you can satisfy me that they have no reason to hear about it."

He wondered where his diplomatic skills had fled. He sounded like a bloody Grand Inquisitor.

She was clutching at her skirts with both hands.

Deliberately, he gentled his voice. "I have no wish to betray you, my dear. Simply tell me the truth."

She gazed at a point over his shoulder. "This is my very first day in London, sir, and I am, not to put too fine a point on it, the veriest country yokel. So there I was, alone in my bedchamber and missing all the excitement, which as you can imagine was not to be borne. At length, I contrived this amateurish disguise and crept downstairs, hoping for a glimpse of the fashionable dinner guests. And most particularly, what they were wearing," she added in a rush.

"I see." Her account was not unreasonable, but he knew that she was lying. Although quick-witted, she lacked the ability to mask her emotions.

She shot him a swift glance from the corners of her eyes,

seeking reassurance that she had bamboozled him. But as ever, his facial expression revealed nothing of his thoughts.

He had decided immediately that she posed no threat to the Finlay household, save the likelihood that she would one day prove an embarrassment to her hostess. It was his own curiosity about her that continued to hold him in the room. She wasn't of an age to be engaged in schoolgirl follies, but for the life of him he could not imagine what the devil she'd been up to. And he'd bet a pony she wasn't going to tell him.

His silence must have unnerved her. She spun on her heels and flounced to the door.

"I wouldn't do that if I were you," he advised softly.

"*You* wouldn't be here in the first place, sir. *You* are wise enough to keep yourself out of trouble, which I am not." With a resigned exhalation, she turned and held out her wrists. "Go ahead, Lord Kendal. Clamp on the manacles and haul me before the magistrate. I have nothing more to say to you."

He tapped his forefinger on his chin. "How is it you know my name?"

"I—" She nibbled at her lower lip. "Lord Finlay must have spoken it while I was under the desk."

When they were in private together, Finlay invariably called him James. Kendal reviewed their conversation. Admittedly, he had been distracted by the figure under the desk, so perhaps his title *had* been mentioned. But he doubted it.

The wonder of it was that he could not be sure. One of his chief skills was the ability to remember in vivid detail every word of a discussion, as well as the subtle gestures and the facial expressions that indicated what was *not* being said. He resented her for vaporizing his legendary presence of mind.

Would she, if he made her an offer, consent to be his mistress?

Her hand was on the door latch when he regathered his wits. "Tell me your name," he said.

He watched her draw in a slow breath. Then she gave him a graceful, rather old-fashioned curtsy. "Celia Greer, my lord. *Lady* Greer."

The name meant nothing to him. And she wasn't accustomed to using the title, he could tell.

"I do wish you would make up your mind," she said plaintively. "What are you going to do with me?"

Not what he wanted to do, he thought, his imagination taking flight. Not just yet. "Run along, Lady Greer. Your secrets, those few you have chosen to reveal, are perfectly safe."

Her radiant smile all but knocked him to his knees.

"Oh, thank you!" she exclaimed, practically bouncing with relief. "You are exceedingly kind, sir. Is it too much to ask that you wipe every trace of this encounter from your memory?"

"That would be impossible, I'm afraid. But I shall pretend I have forgot. Will that do?"

"I suppose it must." She dipped another curtsy, but her smile no longer reached her eyes.

He could barely make out her words as she turned again to the door.

"After tonight," she murmured, "it cannot matter."

Bemused, he watched her crack open the door, check the passageway in both directions, and dart away.

For a long time he stood in place, staring blankly at the door. She seemed to have taken all the air in the room with her. He had difficulty drawing a breath, and his lungs were not the only sectors of his anatomy mounting a rebellion. He hoped to hell she hadn't noticed.

Who the devil *was* she?

With effort, he took himself to the desk and collapsed onto the chair. He was tired, that was all. The long trip from Paris had worn him to flinders, and then he'd drunk too much wine at dinner and endured too many poetic rhapsodies from that absurd Russian.

Besides, he was not free to pursue the singularly enticing Lady Greer. For one thing, he would be on a boat to Boulogne by tomorrow afternoon. And for another, he could scarcely seduce a lady, one who might well have a husband salted away, while she was under the protection of the Finlays.

Nor did he wish to, he told himself firmly, pleased that his brain had begun to function again. Only once before had he experienced such an instant, overwhelming attraction to a woman, with the same bewildering loss of self-control. On that occasion, though, he had followed his benighted impulses and stumbled headlong into disaster.

He had learned his lesson in a hard school. Now he chose his brief liaisons cautiously, with sophisticated women experienced in the sort of dalliance he had come to prefer. For that matter, he was rarely in one place long enough for matters to become complicated. *Good-bye* was implicit from the first kiss, and passion inevitably burned out about the time his duties called him elsewhere.

As they did tonight.

Finlay would understand if he took his leave without ceremony. Kendal made his way to the entrance hall and ordered his carriage brought around. As he drew on his gloves and accepted his hat and walking stick from the butler, he deliberately refused to spare another thought for Lady Greer.

By the time he returned to London, she would be no more than a distant memory.

Chapter 3

Mired in a long line of carriages slowly advancing in the direction of Berkeley Square, Celia and Lady Marjory plied their fans against the sultry June air.

"We have scarcely moved this last fifteen minutes," Lady Marjory complained, wrinkling her nose. "And whatever is that horrible stench?"

"Horse droppings, I believe." Celia stuck her head out the open window and quickly pulled it back again. "Definitely horse droppings. Shall I lower the window glass?"

"It's far too warm for that, I'm afraid. We should have come earlier or later, to avoid the worst of the traffic, but I never expected such a tremendous crush. Sally must be in alt."

"I imagine she was horrified to learn that the Regent planned to carry the foreign dignitaries off to Oxford tonight."

" 'Twas rather the other way 'round, my dear. Long before sending out her invitations, Lady Jersey knew perfectly well what Prinny was up to. As to why she chose the very same evening for her midsummer ball, who can say?"

"Must you spy a conspiracy around every corner?" Celia asked with a laugh. "I wager you think this has something to do with the czar, but I assure you there is no truth whatever to the rumor. Czar Alexander may be an outrageous flirt, but he is not the least bit in love with Lady Jersey."

"Is that what your Russian general tells you?" Marjory shook her head. "You are sadly naive, my dear. Of course there can be no question of love between them, although I'd not rule out the possibility they are more than acquaintances. But I am persuaded they would enjoy tweaking Prinny's nose, and that may well be the purpose of this ball, although I cannot imagine how they mean to accomplish it. Nor can Finlay, who was sufficiently concerned to send me here as an observer instead of taking me along to Oxford."

"I am relieved to hear that," Celia said. "Not the part about Lord Finlay being worried, certainly, but I feared you had chosen to remain in town on my account."

"Not at all. Indeed, you scarcely require my escort any longer, now that cards have begun to arrive for you quite separate from those addressed to Lord and Lady Finlay." Lady Marjory smiled. "You are no longer 'and guest' on the invitation lists, my dear."

It was true, Celia realized with a shiver of pleasure. She had not considered it before, but the beau monde had definitely begun to regard her as something more than the Finlays' houseguest. Well, perhaps a few of them, anyway. In the great crush of the victory celebrations, most people never noticed her at all.

Certainly Lord Kendal did not, although she had spotted him at four routs, two balls, and one musicale since his return to London.

True, he could not be expected to single her out. They were supposed to be perfect strangers, after all, and she was pleased that he continued to honor their agreement with such exactitude. Apparently that required him to move away whenever she came anywhere near him, so in return, she ignored him with equal deliberation.

All the same, she invariably knew his precise location whenever they were in the same room. And she had an alarming tendency to drift in his direction, although he always managed to elude her when she drew close enough for a purely accidental meeting.

Just as well, she thought as the carriage lurched forward and jerked to a halt almost immediately, throwing her back against the padded leather squabs. At this rate, they would reach Lady Jersey's town house sometime next February.

Not that she minded. Since Kendal was surely in Oxford with the Regent and his guests, Lady Jersey's midsummer ball had lost its flavor before she even arrived. Despite the humiliation of their meeting two weeks earlier, she continued to moon over him like a flea-wit, never mind that she would probably melt into the carpet if he actually spoke to her.

How, she wondered fifty times a day, does a woman stop herself from longing for a particular man? Especially when getting her wish would be a sure prescription for disaster?

"Your Russian will be here tonight," Lady Marjory said. "Did he tell you?"

Celia snapped to attention. She was so accustomed to being alone that she often went sliding off into her private dream-world, as Lady Marjory had more than once pointed out to her. "General Chirikov reserved two dances with me," she said, trying not to wince. What with his great size and rollicking ebullience, dancing with Chirikov was akin to wrestling with a bear. "And he is not *my* Russian, thank heavens. The general has a wife and five children. They are practically all he ever talks about."

"When he isn't reciting poetry," Lady Marjory noted dryly.

"I greatly wish he'd stop doing that. But otherwise, he is exceedingly considerate. And gallant, and sweet. I'm very fond of him."

"So am I, actually. Most men are amazingly transparent, but now and again comes along a man who is not what he seems. Half of London assumes Chirikov to be no more than a boorish clown, you think him sweet, and Finlay tells me he is the very devil on a battlefield. The czar consults with him on matters of state. In short, he is that rare creature who cannot be accurately judged on first impressions, which in my experience are generally reliable."

Celia knew Lady Marjory was trying to tell her something in the roundabout way of a practiced diplomat, and it had nothing to do with Chirikov.

Nor could she be speaking of Lord Kendal, because she had no idea Celia Greer had ever met the earl. Nevertheless, like Chirikov, he was assuredly a complex man. All but impenetrable, in her opinion. Even so, she suspected—purely on her untried instincts—that Kendal was not altogether the distant, self-contained gentleman he appeared to be.

Or perhaps she only wanted him to be otherwise. Seething, for example, with a desperate passion for Celia Greer.

Oh mercy! What if—?

She hid her face behind her fan as the unwelcome notion sprang into her head. Had Kendal told Lady Marjory and Lord Finlay about that night in Finlay's study? Possibly he felt obligated to advise them that they harbored a viper in their nest. Well, not precisely a viper, but a houseguest who disguised herself as a servant and hid out in closets and under desks with no credible explanation for her behavior.

"Have I misbehaved in some fashion?" she asked Lady Marjory, preferring to air her dirty laundry if the cat was already out of the bag. Or something of the sort. Heart racing, she could barely order her whirling thoughts, let alone her metaphors.

"Misbehaved?" Lady Marjory looked surprised. "Not to my knowledge. I admit you are something out of the usual, and perhaps a trifle enthusiastic when it is the fashion to appear bored, even should a Congreve rocket happen to whiz by your head. But your natural exuberance has made you exceptionally popular at a time when most fairly ordinary young widows would be overlooked. What with all these princes and ministers and czars swarming about, I mean to say. During a regular Season, you would be ranked as an Incomparable."

Only until she made a goose of herself, Celia thought, which sooner or later she was bound to do.

As for her unfashionable enthusiasm, she could not help herself. To think that the Haut Ton considered ennui a desirable state of mind. How little they knew! Had those jaded aristocrats spent so much as a week at Greer's farm, they'd have quickly learned to appreciate the pleasures of London.

"But since you brought up the subject of behavior," Lady Marjory said with uncharacteristic hesitation, "and while your deportment has been unexceptionable, there is a matter I have wished to address concerning a particular gentleman."

22

A cannonball thudded into Celia's stomach. Kendal *had* told on her, the lizard! "Please do," she said politely.

"The thing is, my dear, I was wondering if your intentions had altered. 'Tis none of my business, of course, but I was certain you told me that you would never, under any circumstances, consider marrying again."

A wave of relief swept down Celia's rigid spine. Kendal was not a lizard after all. Lady Marjory must be referring to someone else, for there could be no question of Celia Greer wedding the Earl of Kendal.

Nor any other man, for that matter, so what on earth was Lady Marjory talking about?

"My determination is fixed," she said brightly. "One marriage was quite sufficient, thank you. I'll not risk another. Why do you ask?"

"Well, my dear, Lord Henley's mother, who possesses all the tact of an avalanche, has been quizzing me regarding your lineage and fortune. I am certain the viscount means to make you an offer."

"Basil Henley? But he's the veriest puppy."

"He is seven-and-twenty," Lady Marjory corrected. "Precisely your own age, never mind that he trails at your heels like a besotted spaniel. Only one of a large pack of spaniels, to be sure, which is probably why you have paid him little notice. It's as well you have not developed a *tendre* for him, because his unfortunate wife, whoever she may be, will join him under his mama's thumb."

Celia shuddered. "Apparently I have misinterpreted Henley's intentions. He has invited me to join a house party at his estate when the victory celebrations are done with, but I shall most certainly refuse."

"That would be best, my dear. And while we are on the subject, there are others among your admirers apt to mistake your natural friendliness for something more particular. I cannot believe you wish to leave a scatter of broken hearts in your wake."

"Emphatically not." Celia was vividly aware that she

understood next to nothing about masculine intentions, beyond the obvious ones. "I have been thoughtless."

"No, indeed. Go on just as you are, but take care not to single out any gentleman who shows the slightest inclination to snap at dangled bait. I refer to those who are hanging out for a wife, of course. Lovers are a different sort of fish altogether."

The carriage made a turn, entering Berkeley Square precisely as the conversation was becoming exceptionally interesting. But if anything, the coach made less progress than ever, practically inching its way along on the rare occasions that it moved at all.

A lover. Celia had come to London fully intending to take a lover, of course. That had been her plan from the first. A vague plan, since she had no idea how to go about it, but she always figured something would turn up. *Someone.*

But then she saw Kendal from her bedchamber window and knew instantly that she had always been looking for him. No other lover could measure up to the one she had dreamed of for all those dreary years.

Whereupon she proceeded to make an absolute buffoon of herself, demolishing any frail chance she might have had to impress him favorably.

"So long as we are discussing unpleasant matters," Lady Marjory said, waving her fan with uncommon energy, "you may as well know that you have become the object of several wagers. At his club, Finlay spotted more than a few references to Lady G in the Betting Book."

"Whatever is *that*? And there must be a hundred Lady G's in London." Celia frowned. "Precisely what are they betting about?"

"The usual sort of thing. Who will offer for you and be refused. Who will offer less than marriage and be accepted. Do not concern yourself, my dear. A lovely young widow of sizable fortune cannot escape White's Betting Book. I simply wished you to be aware of the situation, lest a tidbit of gossip take you by surprise."

Clearly, certain gentlemen had far too much time on their hands, Celia thought in amazement. Wagering about *her*, of all people. As if she had done a single interesting thing in her entire life!

"How very absurd," she said. "And none of them can possibly win. I'm done with marrying, as you know, and have no intention of taking a lover."

"Indeed?" Lady Marjory raised an artfully plucked eyebrow. "It would be perfectly acceptable for you to do so, in case you have wondered. Virtually expected, as a matter of fact."

"I rather expected it, too," Celia confessed in a low voice. "Not an ordinary liaison, though, and certainly not a back-corner affair. Was a time I dreamed of a grand passion, but it was purely fantasy. I daresay that for all my wild imaginings, I shall dwindle to a pattern card of widowly propriety."

Marjory regarded her speculatively. "Is there something you wish to tell me, Celia?"

For a tempting moment Celia yearned to confide the truth. Not merely her overwhelming attraction to a man she could never have, but her deepest, most hopeless, desire. A child. Many children, with a father who loved them nearly as much as he loved her.

Of all her dreams, that was the one she herself would not permit to come true. Down to the marrow in her bones, she was terrified of passing control of her life to another man. Her independence had been hard won, and she intended to preserve it. Not even a proposal of marriage from Lord Kendal could change her mind on that subject.

A slip on the shoulder from Lord Kendal would be another matter altogether, but she wouldn't bet tuppence on the chances of that happening now. On a single night, in an act of singular stupidity, she had met . . . and lost forever . . . the man of her dreams.

Still, this wasn't the first time she'd scraped herself together after a foolish decision or a crippling disappointment. After crying buckets of tears and mentally kicking herself on the backside a few hundred times, she always accepted the inevitable and soldiered on.

Of course, in the past she'd had her improbable fantasies to sustain her. It hurt to bid them farewell, but she would have to make do with something other than a grand passion.

Perhaps she'd take up gardening.

At long last the carriage arrived in front of Lady Jersey's town house. Laughter and music spilled from the open windows as liveried servants, torches in hand, let down the steps and assisted the ladies to the pavement.

Celia took the arm of a freckle-faced young servant, firmly resolved to enjoy herself at the ball. After all, until a year ago her summer evenings were spent holding her nose with one hand and scouring chicken poop from wooden cages with the other.

No question about it, Celia Greer had come up in the world.

Chapter 4

His shoulder propped against a marble pillar in the ball-room, Kendal watched her move gracefully through the line of the cotillion, greeting each new partner with a delighted smile as if she'd been waiting all evening to dance with him. And when the figure separated them, the men invariably cast lingering looks at where she'd gone.

He was as transfixed as all the others. Supple, graceful, and incalculably lovely in a gown of emerald satin, she had captured his attention the moment she entered the room. As she always did.

He thought back to when first he saw her, clad in that crumpled black dress, a coil of lace from her faux house-maid's cap dangling over her ear.

And to the look of recognition in her eyes.

That continued to puzzle him. By her account, she had arrived in London that very day. She could not have seen him before, nor had he ever seen her. He'd an excellent memory for faces, and hers was unforgettable.

With considerable self-restraint, he had contrived to avoid her since his return from Boulogne, reckoning that he would eventually shed this almost pathological fascination with her. But if anything, it had grown to the point of obsession.

The time had come, he decided, for a formal introduction.

Wrenching his gaze to the crowd milling at the edges of the dance floor, he located Lady Marjory and set out in her direction.

"There you are, Kendal!" she said, when he approached her

27

and bowed. "Finlay told me you were assigned here for the evening, to put out fires. Will there be any, do you suppose?"

"I sincerely hope not. But there is little doubt that everyone else in the room wishes otherwise."

"Not I. Indeed, I shall be all too happy when our foreign guests have returned whence they came. A great lot of temperamental whiners they have turned out to be, insufferably tedious when they aren't creating a nuisance for their hosts."

"This from a diplomat's wife, Marjory? You shock me."

"Fustian. Do you know, I should very much enjoy seeing you genuinely shocked, or at the mercy of at least one sincere human emotion. But alas, I'm more likely to hear a pig sing a Mozart aria."

"Far better entertainment than I would provide, to be sure."

"Ah, I believe that was a set-down. And richly deserved. Will you forgive my impertinence if I introduce you to a beautiful woman?"

"There is nothing to forgive," he assured her, although she had scratched too close to home. But Marjory had not known him when an excess of very human passion had tumbled him into hell.

Before risking another such disaster, he'd sing a duet with that pig.

"Ah, there she is." Marjory pointed her fan at a knot of gentlemen clustered near the terrace doors. "Celia, Lady Greer, our houseguest for the last several weeks. I was at school with her mother, although we lost touch many years ago. It was something of a surprise to receive a letter from Celia, but naturally I invited her to stay with us. Has Finlay not spoken of her?"

"In passing. She is a widow, I understand, with a considerable fortune."

"Yes. And as such, she has drawn considerable attention, not all of it from desirable sources. I worried for her at first, but she is quick to learn." Marjory took his arm. "Come. I shall be interested to see what you make of her."

Even more interested to know what had already passed between them, he thought as she led him toward the circle of men. He was surprised to feel his pulse begin to race. Lord

Mumblethorpe, always gracious, moved aside to make room for them, and Kendal found himself standing directly behind Lady Greer.

Standing for a considerable time, as it developed, since her attention was focused on that damnable Russian. Aglitter in medals and shimmering epaulets, Vasily Chirikov was expounding yet another poem in a voice that threatened to shatter every chandelier in the ballroom.

" 'When all at whonce I saw a crowd, a host, off golden daffodeels.' "

Someone ought to stuff a wad of daffodils down his throat, Kendal thought irritably.

Lady Greer had turned slightly, and he saw from her profile that she was enjoying the recital. That dropped her several notches in his estimation. He was invariably polite to the general, but it was his duty to cater to politically important idiots. With no such obligation, she bloody well ought to find some way to be rid of Chirikov.

Especially while the Earl of Kendal stood waiting—with unaccustomed impatience—to be introduced. He looked forward to the expression on her face when she recognized him.

Would she be flustered? Defiant?

And why the devil was he putting her to the test? He could have arranged to meet her privately, after all. Or avoided her altogether, which would certainly have been the wisest course.

" 'And then my heart wiss pleasure feels, And dances wiss ze daffodeels.' "

Chirikov bowed with a flourish, and the small audience applauded politely.

"How very lovely," Lady Greer exclaimed. "To think you know all of Mr. Wordsworth's poems by heart."

"Ah, not all. I haff not time to learn them because of war. And the poems iss not so beautiful as you." Chirikov took her gloved hand and planted a lingering kiss on her wrist.

Kendal felt his own hands curl into fists. With effort, he straightened his fingers and relaxed his posture, which had unaccountably gone rigid. And just in time, because Marjory tapped Lady Greer on the shoulder with her fan.

She spun around, a bright smile on her face.

It stayed in place when she saw him, but he could not mistake the alarm that flickered briefly in her eyes and the slight squaring of her shoulders. She had set herself for a blow.

Maintaining an expression of polite curiosity, he gave her full marks for poise as Marjory made the introduction. When he bowed, she made a graceful curtsy.

And then, for what felt like a month, they simply gazed at each other.

Kendal knew only a few seconds had passed before he rallied his wits and devised a pleasant greeting, but she was a beat ahead of him.

"I am honored to make your acquaintance, sir. Lord Finlay has sung your praises so often that I came to imagine we had met long since."

The gauntlet hit the parquet floor with a clang only he could hear.

Did she imagine he meant to betray her? Insulted, he let the challenge lie where it fell. "It is my loss that we have not," he said smoothly. "If you are not otherwise engaged, shall we repair the omission during the next dance?"

A young officer of the Horse Guards stepped forward, flushing hotly. "Lady Greer has promised this waltz to me, sir."

Good manners required him to cede the field graciously, but Lady Greer's look of gratitude at her rescuer changed his mind. With a meaningful lift of one brow, Kendal dispatched a silent order to the would-be waltzer.

"B-by all means," the youngster stammered, resigned to his fate. "It would be my honor to do you a service, my lord. Perhaps another time, Lady Greer?"

"At the first opportunity," she promised with a smile, reserving her scowl for Kendal as he led her to the circle of dancers. Hand in hand, they began the formal promenade.

"That was bad of me," he admitted into the stiff silence between them. "But you needn't advertise it to all the world."

"I was expecting worse," she replied candidly, adjusting her face. "Shall I look for an ax to drop at the moment of your choosing?"

"Ax?" He turned her gracefully under his lifted arm. "Whatever can you mean, Lady Greer?"

"Oh, do cut line, sir. We both know I am at your mercy. You can ruin me with a single word."

"As if I would do such a thing. Or have I mistaken the situation? Was I not supposed to forget that we ever met?"

"Yes. But in my experience, people rarely do what they are supposed to do. Can you mean to prove an exception?"

"I mean to keep my word, certainly. Did I give it? Our first encounter is somewhat blurred in my memory."

"Because it can be of no significance to Your Loftiness," she fired back with an open grin. "But thank you, sir. You have restored my faith in gentlemanly honor."

At right about the time he was mightily tempted to abandon it, he thought, desire for her flaring as the dance figure drew them into a more intimate embrace. Her hand settled gingerly on his shoulder as he wrapped his fingers around her slender waist and twirled her in dizzying circles.

On the Continent, the waltz had already escaped these formal patterns, freeing couples to dip and turn free of the other dancers. But this was England, always behind the fashion, and far too soon he was forced to let go of all but her hand for another promenade.

"I'll not speak of our first meeting to anyone else," he said. "But shall we two abandon the pretense it never happened?"

"I believe we already have. But where does that leave me in your estimation, sir? Have I sunk below disgrace? Do put me out of my misery before I make futile attempts to redeem myself."

"The last thing I wish," he said honestly, "is to make you miserable. Quite the contrary. Would you prefer that I keep my distance in the future?"

She stumbled, and he tightened his grasp on her hand.

"No, my lord," she murmured. "I do not wish you to keep your distance."

The words put wings on his feet when they came together again in the close embrace of the waltz figure. For a few measures they both seemed to be dancing on air.

"Mercy me," Lady Greer said with a gasp.

Kendal failed to realize that the music had come to a faltering stop until his partner became a deadweight in his arms. She let go of his shoulder then and pointed to the ballroom door. Resplendent in a bottle-green uniform with a high gold collar and gilded epaulets, Czar Alexander was making a grand entrance. Lady Jersey, a cattish smile of triumph on her face, swept over to welcome him.

Everyone in the ballroom understood the significance of this startling event, Kendal better than most. The czar must have left Prinny's party in the early going and traveled neck or nothing from Oxford in time to make his appearance here. It was without question a deliberate, public snub, designed to humiliate the Regent.

This was precisely the fire Finlay had sent Kendal to extinguish, in the unlikely event it flared up. Now it was a conflagration.

And a bloody damned nuisance, in Kendal's opinion. Short of physically removing Lady Jersey from her own ballroom or the Czar of Russia from a London town house, what the devil could he do about it? Like all scandals, this one would soon be replaced with another. Perhaps, in the not too distant future, London would be gabbling about his affair with Lady Greer.

Did he mean there to be one?

Certainly not when he was thinking with his brains. She was undeniably beautiful, and he was most definitely attracted, but an affair with Celia Greer was certain to become unpleasantly complicated.

The czar, with an imperious gesture, signaled the orchestra to resume playing and waved everyone else from the ballroom floor. Then, with the grace of a couple who had practiced together for just this moment, Czar Alexander and Lady Jersey began dancing the waltz as it was meant to be danced.

Kendal glanced over at Lady Greer, who was gazing with horrified fascination at the spectacle. "Oh, how I should love to dance like that," she said in an awed whisper. "Have you ever done so?"

"Many times. And I expect you will have the opportunity

very soon, now that Sally has so flamboyantly launched it into fashion." Seized by an impulse he was certain he'd later regret, he offered her his arm. "Shall we steal a breath of fresh air, Lady Greer? While this carnival is playing in the ballroom, I daresay we'll have the garden to ourselves."

With barely perceptible hesitation, she placed her hand on his arm.

He led her through the French doors onto the terrace, a wide semicircle of polished marble edged with a railing of wrought iron. Just beyond was a parterre with a small formal garden, and beyond that, a scatter of trees and winding gravel paths.

They stood for a few moments by the railing and gazed in silence at the Japanese lanterns hanging from the tree branches, swaying in the soft June breeze and scattering colored light over the walkways. The scent of roses wafted from the garden, and he thought vaguely that he much preferred Celia Greer's sweet honeysuckle fragrance. Somewhere, a fountain played, the music of the water mingling with the waltz that floated from the ballroom.

He felt an odd sensation, as though he were standing on the edge of a high cliff, knowing that one false step would dash him to the jagged rocks below.

Perfect nonsense. It was only two steps down into the rose-bush garden, where the only danger was the possibility of catching his sleeve on a thorn.

Most females of his acquaintance would be chattering away by now, but Lady Greer seemed content to stand quietly, enjoying the music and the view.

Or perhaps she, too, could think of nothing to say.

What would she do if he led her into the far reaches of the garden, into the shadows of that leafy oak, and kissed her?

No, he told himself firmly. *Not yet,* a restless demon inside him amended. *But soon.*

What he needed, and quickly, was a change of subject before his unruly flesh betrayed him. "Forgive me for chewing on an old bone, Lady Greer, but one matter continues to perplex me. When we met in Finlay's study, you used my name. And I am certain he never mentioned it."

33

She sighed. "Is that why you brought me out here? To quiz me about that deplorable night?"

"Not at all, I assure you. Please forget I mentioned it."

"You may as well know, I suppose." She placed her palms on the railing, lifting her gaze to the sky. "As it happens, I had seen you on two previous occasions. That was many years ago, and from a distance, but I recognized you immediately."

"Well, that is a perfectly harmless explanation. Why did you not say so when first I asked?"

Her fingers curled around the railing. "Because at the time, sir, I was suffering the death throes of terminal mortification. My sole thought was to escape that room before expiring at your feet."

"Then I must thank you for clinging to life, Lady Greer. It would have been an awkward business, explaining your corpse to the constable."

She gave him a dimpled grin. "I live only to serve, my lord."

Laughing, he unpried her fingers from the railing and turned her to face him, still holding her hands. "Where did you see me before?"

"Well, the first time was in the town of Kendal, where the Earl of Kendal quite naturally draws one's attention. On the second occasion, you were riding in the countryside near the village of Sedgwick. My husband's farm is not far from there."

"Indeed?" He frowned. "I recall no one by the name of Greer. If you resided so close by to my estate, how is it we never met?"

A shadow passed over her face. "Oh, we rarely went out in Society. Greer preferred a quiet life, you see. For the most part, he was content to remain on the farm with his books and his . . . hobbies."

You were not content, Kendal thought, wondering why this vivacious young woman had married such a stick-in-the-mud. But he could scarcely ask so personal a question, nor was her marriage any of his concern. He damn well wouldn't appreciate questions about his own.

Or perhaps she knew all about it. The scandal was common gossip in Westmoreland, or had been at the time. For a few painful months he'd even imagined that the sheep were baaing the latest *on dits* behind his back when he rode by.

"Is something wrong, my lord?"

He wrenched his thoughts from a past that was better left where it generally resided, somewhere near the pit of his stomach. "Was I frowning? Pardon me. I was searching my memory for Lord Greer, but failed to locate him. Were you married long?"

"Nine years, two months, and three days. His death was unexpected. A heart attack, the doctor said later, and mercifully quick. I was gathering eggs when it happened, and by the time I heard the servants' cries and ran to the house, it was over."

Her hands had tensed as she spoke. He began to rub them between his fingers. In the silence, the slight scratch of his gloves against hers sounded in his ears like distant thunder.

"I'm sorry," he said gently.

She withdrew her hands and brushed them against her skirt. "Mercy. How came we to such a morbid subject? This is a party, after all, and there is never any point to wallowing in the past. Will you be present at the treaty conference in Vienna?"

The lady certainly knew how to slam a door. And just as well, because he had intruded into territory he did not care to visit. Wanting her was not the same as wishing to become personally involved with her, and he felt distinct relief that she shared his distaste for emotional entanglements. Perhaps an affair with Lady Greer was not out of the question, if she, too, meant to keep her distance outside the bedchamber.

Now he need only discover if she shared his interest in joining him *inside* a bedchamber. After he answered her last question, of course. What was it? Something about Vienna.

"I expect so," he said, wrestling to control a few galloping primal urges. "Mind you, I'm not looking forward to yet another trek across the Continent, although this time I'll not be forced to make long detours around Bonaparte's army."

The orchestra had struck up a country dance, and the sounds of laughter and conversation streamed across the terrace. The party was in full swing again, and Kendal knew they wouldn't be alone under the stars for very much longer.

In unspoken, mutual agreement, they descended the stairs and began to walk side by side in the garden.

Should he test the waters now? Make an approach? Draw her into his arms?

They came near the oak tree. If he led her to the other side, where no one could see them from the ballroom or the terrace, and if he kissed her—damn it all. He felt like a fumbling adolescent, suddenly unsure of himself, shy of a rejection that might not even come.

What the devil was the matter with him? He could hear his voice making polite conversation, which meant a part of his brain was still functioning. And he sensed, bone-deep, the subtle feminine invitation in her sideways glances and the feminine tilt of her head in his direction as they walked.

But he kept moving, past the oak tree and all the other trees where they might have shelter, back onto the curving path that led again to the terrace.

If she was disappointed, she gave no sign of it. Pausing at the top of the steps, she turned to him with a smile. "I suppose you wish to discover what the czar is up to now. Lord Finlay will expect a complete report."

"Lady Marjory will tell him what occurred," he said from a dry throat. "But I have meetings at the Foreign Office early tomorrow morning, so I'd best take my leave now. And I'd as soon not run into any of the Russian contingent, most especially General Chirikov, on my way out. Will you mind if I don't return with you to the ballroom?"

"Not in the least," she assured him. "Vasily Chirikov is a lovely gentleman, but he persists in treating me to rather lengthy poetry recitals. You do well to make a stealthy exit, for he is likely to leap at me the moment I step inside."

"Now I feel guilty for leaving you unprotected," he replied. "Shall we face him down together?"

"Make your escape while you can, sir. And thank you for our walk in the garden. It was quite the nicest part of the evening."

"Yes. I daresay we'll meet again, at some party or another. Have I managed to convince you that you have nothing to fear from me?"

She studied him for a moment. "If you refer to our mutual secret, yes. I am most grateful."

He recognized evasion in her reply. Did she fear him on some other count? Seduction, for example?

Before he could summon a response, she curtsied and turned for the ballroom.

As he watched her, appreciating the fluid sway of her hips, he thought to go after her. But the moment she stepped through the doors, men swarmed over her like bees on a bright flower, Chirikov among them.

He was beginning to hate that damnable Russian.

Couples began to wander onto the terrace, so he slipped back into the garden, meaning to make his exit through the rear gate and to the mews, where his carriage had been ordered to wait.

Alarms were clamoring in his head. No doubt about it, Lady Greer was trouble on two long, shapely legs. And should the pressure of his work ease long enough for him to consider a mistress, there were any number of straightforward females ready and willing to warm his bed.

Why complicate his already complicated life with a woman who confused the hell out of him? He didn't understand her at all, and resented the way she had of thumping his otherwise logical mind into mush. Yes, he would do well to keep a distance between them in the future.

How soon, he wondered, could he contrive to see her again?

Chapter 5

Celia was alone in the breakfast room, nibbling toast and reading the newspaper, when Lord Kendal appeared at the door.

Startled, she dropped a wedge of toast onto her lap.

He bowed. "Pardon me for intruding, Lady Greer. I was hoping to speak with Lord Finlay, but the butler informs me that he is not at home. Do you know where he can be found?"

Remembering her manners, Celia rose. "I'm afraid he cannot. Last night, Lady Marjory received word that her sister has been taken ill. They set out immediately for Maidstone. I have their direction, if you require it."

"Not at all." He went to the sideboard and lifted the coffee pot. "May I?"

"To be sure. It is probably tepid by now, though. Shall I ring for—"

"This will do, thank you." He filled a cup, added a large chunk of sugar, and pulled out a chair across the table from her. "Please, finish your breakfast. Is the illness serious?"

"I believe not. But as Lady Esther's husband is from home, Lady Marjory means to stay with her until he returns. I understand that unless he is needed there, Lord Finlay will come directly back to London. We've no idea when to expect him, though."

Stop babbling, Celia! She seized her teacup and took a deep swallow, unable to mistake the glint of amusement in his eyes. Did he *enjoy* making her nervous?

Not that he had done anything remotely nerve-racking or improper, save to appear in the breakfast room at seven o'clock in the morning, for pity's sake, looking just as elegant in a dark blue coat and fawn pantaloons as he always did in formal evening dress.

While she, anticipating a quiet, solitary morning, had slipped on her plainest muslin gown and barely run a brush through her hair.

The silence grew agonizing, at least to her. Lord Kendal, perfectly at ease, seemed content to sip his coffee and gaze at her from a pair of disconcerting blue eyes.

What *did* a man and woman talk about over the breakfast table?

He certainly knew better than she. And he was a diplomat as well. Wasn't it his duty to make conversation? She bit into a square of toast, regretting it instantly as the crunch crackled like thunder in the small room.

Demonically, in her opinion, he waited until her mouth was full before speaking. "You are up and about exceptionally early for a lady of fashion, Lady Greer."

Now certain he was deliberately baiting her, Celia chewed slowly and rallied her delinquent wits. Some of them were firmly fixed on his broad shoulders and the elegant, long-fingered hand curled around his coffee cup. He had propped his elbows on the table, obviously waiting for her to take his hook.

She let him wait another few moments. Then she shrugged. "I am used to rising with the chickens, sir. And for that matter, it is my understanding that gentlemen of fashion rarely crack open their eyes before noon."

His lips curved in an appreciative smile. "Just so. We appear to share a sordid fondness for mornings, although mine are usually given over to tedious meetings with even more tedious bureaucrats. What do you do with your mornings, Lady Greer?"

Feed the chickens, she thought immediately. They were gone now, of course, along with Greer, but most days she still awoke with the same sense of dread.

"Mostly I laze about," she said blithely. "Lord Finlay has

usually joined me by this time, and we discuss the latest *on dits*. More accurately, I discuss. He only grumbles until well through his third cup of coffee."

Kendal laughed. "I know that grumble well. But it appears I'll not be forced to decipher his instructions this particular morning. Even better, I seem to have been granted a brief, unexpected holiday. Shall I use it to laze about, Lady Greer?"

"I highly recommend lazing, sir. Although I cannot quite imagine you doing so."

"Nor can I. It has certainly been a long time since I had the opportunity. But after a conference this morning at Whitehall, and before my departure for Bath tomorrow with Marshal Blücher, there is nothing that requires my immediate attention."

He set his cup carefully on the saucer. "Except, perhaps, the pair of bays I've been neglecting to exercise. Have you plans for the day, or might I coax you to join me for an afternoon excursion?"

Heat lightning flashed through the breakfast room. She felt the charge pass through her body. And through the electrified haze, she saw the source in his eyes.

He meant seduction. She knew it. In his casually voiced question was the promise of everything she had wanted since the first time she saw him.

No. Not everything. Not nearly so much. One afternoon was all he promised, a few hours only. Already he had given warning that he would be off to Bath the very next day.

She respected his honesty and hated him for it. Which did not stop her wanting him, not the least little bit.

Mercifully, or perhaps with deliberate cunning, he gave her time to consider by returning to the sideboard and refilling his coffee cup. She regarded his back, wondering if he felt even a spark of the fire raging inside her.

There was no sign of it. Save for a slight miscalculation as he cut off an oversized chunk from the sugar cone, he appeared perfectly at ease. She, on the other hand, was splintering into a thousand pieces of female desire, all of them barely held together by sheer power of will.

He wasn't any ordinarily attractive male. She had met a few since coming to London, but none had roused her interest in the slightest. Kendal was . . . compelling. She assumed that he obsessed her because she had dreamed about him for so many years, but in her fantasies he was generally wearing armor, with a recently dispatched dragon lying in a heap at his feet.

Seduction at the breakfast table, over the remains of a soft-boiled egg and cold toast, was not what she had pictured. Not at all.

She had aimed herself higher than this. She aspired to a grand passion. Although, to be painfully honest, that was more than she could realistically have expected from a man such as this one. The flesh-and-blood Lord Kendal offered much less than the Lord Kendal of her dreams.

Was it enough?

He glanced at her over his shoulder, not quite meeting her eyes. "Well, Lady Greer? Will you join me for a drive in the country and a picnic lunch alongside the Thames? I promise to have you home in time for your evening engagements."

With a shot of awareness, she understood that the flesh-and-blood Lord Kendal offered far more than her chaste, fantastical dreams. Surely one afternoon of passion was better than none. And he was the one more likely to be disappointed when it was over. What had she to offer him, when it came right down to it?

"I would be delighted," she said from a constricted throat, surprised to see his shoulders relax. Only fractionally, and solely to a degree that anyone not concentrating so intently on him would have missed, but she was sure of it.

He had wanted her to say yes.

That was all the incentive she required to dive headlong into her very first, and probably only, affair.

She examined her fingernails. Celia Greer was not the stuff of which notorious widows were made, she knew. Cutting a dash in Society was fun, and she meant to do so for years to come. But this once, her heart held firmly in check, she would take a lover.

When she looked up again, he was standing at the door.

"I shall be occupied at Whitehall for an hour or two," he said. "Can you be ready to depart at, say, ten o'clock?"

"Certainly." Once again, unspoken understanding hovered between them. Without words, they had agreed to far more than a picnic luncheon.

She ought to have followed him to the main door, she realized after he was gone, and bade him a formal farewell Instead, she waited until certain he had left the house before charging upstairs to ring for her maid.

The next several hours spun by in a frenzy. Although she had bathed before going to bed, she bathed again and washed her hair. She ordered a fire built so she could dry it, never mind the warm June morning. Then she tried on every gown in her closet suitable for a drive in the country, taking into account what would surely happen afterward.

Modest or enticing? Buttons in the back, or should she provide easier access to her person? Spencer or no spencer? Which reticule? Which fan? Which bonnet?

At precisely three minutes before ten, she studied herself in the mirror and told herself she looked as well as possible, if she discounted the stunned glaze in her eyes.

The jonquil muslin dress, with a cream-colored sash tied in a bow at the back of her waist, was nicely balanced between seductive and innocent. It left her arms bare under skimpy puffed sleeves, but the bodice was cut high enough to require a bit of effort on a lover's part to reach what lay underneath.

Accessible, but not flagrant. *Yes,* with a hint of *no*.

They could both change their minds well up to the point of no return, after all. But would she know when they had reached that point? Or had it already passed?

When she heard the door knocker, a surge of panic knifed through her veins. Mercy me, she thought. Can I do this?

In a last-minute rush to protect herself, she wrapped a Norwich shawl around her goose-bumpy arms and descended the stairs with what she hoped was impressive poise.

Lord Kendal, now wearing a russet driving coat and buff-colored trousers, greeted her with a smile and led her out to the curricle. Two enormous and apparently ill-tempered horses wrestled with the street urchin clinging tenaciously to their reins.

Celia eyed them doubtfully. "They look a trifle . . . impatient, my lord."

"I'll let them run it off when we reach the countryside." He handed her onto the bench. "Or would you prefer otherwise?"

"Indeed no," she replied at once. "I should like it above all things."

"Well, perhaps not *all*," he said, climbing up beside her and taking the reins.

Oh my. Did he mean what she thought he meant?

A sophisticated woman would have trilled a clever riposte, Celia supposed, but she couldn't think of a single one. Heat burning in her cheeks, she watched him guide the restive bays onto the busy street with impressive ease.

She had never before ridden in a curricle, and was surprised how little room there was for driver and passenger on the narrow padded bench. He wasn't touching her, not quite, but her wind-ruffled skirt had begun to dally with his thigh.

He slid her a glance. "Do you ride, Lady Greer?"

Thank heavens, an innocuous topic of conversation! "Not since coming to London," she replied, "and precious little before that. When I have located a suitable town house to lease, I will straightaway buy a horse of my own. I have always wanted one."

"Your husband kept no stable?" He deftly steered around a lumbering coal wagon. "Wherever I am sent, for however brief a time, I immediately secure a good riding horse and a pair like this one for driving. Mind you, I have sometimes bought and sold nags without ever having the opportunity to put them to use."

He spoke of horses for a while, and then of several eccentric characters he'd met on his travels, surprising her with his sly sense of humor. And allowing her time to relax in his company, she was certain, grateful that she had no more to do than enjoy his anecdotes.

And look at him.

Surreptitiously, to be sure, for she had no wish to be caught gaping like a hayseed. She began with his hands, strong and graceful in their tan kidskin gloves as he gently wielded the reins. He was going to touch her with those hands, touch her in places that began to burn just from imagining it.

Her gaze wandered to the well-shaped thigh beside hers, so close she felt it press warmly against her whenever the curricle made a turn. His breeches fit so snugly they might as well have been painted on.

Not yet out of London, and already she was tumbling in a maelstrom of decidedly erotic fantasies!

She wondered if he knew, and reckoned that he did.

He gave no obvious sign of it, though, continuing to speak lightly of his experiences with only the occasional glance in her direction.

But what did she expect, after all? For Lord Kendal, this assignation was one of many, not in the least earth-shattering. Perhaps not even of much interest to him, beyond the masculine pleasure he would enjoy for a few hours. Or minutes. She had no idea how long it would take, once he got started.

Ignorance was most assuredly *not* bliss, she decided. Sometimes, and especially now, ignorance was purely disconcerting. At the least, she ought to muster up a little intelligible conversation instead of sitting beside him like a lump.

But in fact, she realized of a sudden, he, too, had gone mute. They had left the city behind without her noticing it and were traveling along a narrow road lined with hedgerows. To her right, she caught an occasional glimpse of sunlight flashing off water whenever the road curled near the Thames.

Away from the smells and noise of London, she became acutely aware of subtle odors and sounds. The clopping of hooves on the hard-packed dirt road. Birdsong. The rustle of her skirts in the breeze. The faint scent of a citrony cologne, clean and masculine, and the heavier odor of rich leather from his boots and gloves.

She stole a glance at his face, half-shadowed by the brim of his hat under the bright noonday sun. He looked, she thought, remarkably at peace.

Perhaps a quiet afternoon in the country was a treat for him. While she longed for excitement and adventure, Lord Kendal probably relished his rare opportunities to escape them.

She wished he were not quite so tranquil while she was practically smoldering a bare half inch away. Even her inventive imagination could not picture the elegant Lord Kendal smoldering, but he might at least stir up a dollop of enthusiasm.

They came around a sweeping curve and the road straightened for as far as she could see.

Lord Kendal looked over at her. "Shall I let them out?"

One of the bays whinnied, as if in approval.

Laughing, Celia took hold of the panel next to her hip. "Tallyho!"

And then, with the barest flick of Kendal's wrist, they were off.

Eight hooves dug into the ground until the bays found their stride and began to run in perfect unison. The curricle seemed airborne, wheels turning without the slightest bounce. Hedgerows whizzed past in a blur of green.

Exhilarated, she lifted her head to the wind. The horses could not go fast enough for her. Never before had she felt so truly alive. The thrill of speed and danger. Abandon. Freedom!

Her bonnet flew off, catching the wind like a sail a few inches behind her head. The ribbons tied under her chin began to choke her, and she clawed at them with both fingers, lurching from side to side now that she'd let go her grip on the panel.

Noticing her distress, Kendal reined in the bays.

Celia's bonnet settled against her back like a deflated balloon, but the ribbons had got tangled in the fringe of her shawl.

"Permit me," he said, gently pushing her fingers away. His leather gloves grazed her neck and chin as he unknotted the ribbon and detached the fringe. "There."

He set the bonnet on her lap, his gaze never leaving her face. "How lovely you are, Celia Greer." One finger brushed slowly, intimately, down her cheek. "I tried to resist you, you know. It would have been best."

"Not for me," she whispered, spellbound by his sapphire-blue eyes. Who *are* you? she wondered at the edges of her besotted mind. She wanted to *know* him, heaven help her. She wanted him to know her, too, and not turn away when he did.

Then she forgot all the things she wanted, because he lifted her chin with the back of a gentle hand and kissed her.

It was the barest kiss, light and tantalizing and far too brief, but it promised everything she dared to expect. She leaned into him, shamelessly begging for another, starved for affection and beyond pretending otherwise. Her hands curled around his neck.

"Sweet heavens," he murmured, drawing her closer. This time he lingered, touching her eyelids and cheekbones with his lips, licking the corner of her mouth, sliding his tongue across her lips and back again.

She mumbled a protest as he deliberately set her away. When his hands left her shoulders, she felt startlingly naked without the feel of him.

"I think we should go on," he said, chucking the bays into a trot. "More slowly, perhaps. The side road leading to the inn where we'll have . . . luncheon"—his voice cracked—"is easy to miss."

They arrived on the narrow track minutes later, long silent minutes, and he steered the curricle into the turn like a man who had made this same turn many times before.

Had he brought other women here? she wondered, a knife of jealousy digging between her ribs as the inn came into view.

It was a large half-timbered building two stories high, set in a wide field ringed with oaks and willows. She saw a graystone stable to one side and a vegetable garden at the other. Flowers bloomed around the whitewashed inn walls, hyacinths and tea roses and snapdragons. Three brown-and-white-spotted cows grazed placidly in a paddock beside the stable.

Just beyond the buildings and gardens, a sweep of lush green grass led down to the bank of the Thames, flowing narrow and gentle though this fairyland.

Or so it seemed to her. Surely magic had created this beautiful place. The inn must be centuries old, the trees older than that, and the river timeless.

Here, in this place, she would make love with the man who had haunted her empty nights and brightened her days with hope.

Chapter 6

Kendal wondered if she had been expecting him to sweep her directly into a bedchamber.

He certainly wanted to.

But it was not in his nature to behave impulsively, or had not been until he met Lady Greer. It had been nothing short of reckless to bring her to the White Swan, and he could scarcely credit that he'd done so. Before taking any further missteps, he needed to cool down. Considerably.

While Lady Greer waited by the door, he greeted Mrs. Belcher and ordered a light meal to be served alfresco. He also reserved, only for the afternoon, a bedchamber. *The* bedchamber.

Mrs. Belcher blinked.

Her husband popped out of the taproom just then, with the jovial welcome accorded all his customers and more than one curious glance at the young woman silhouetted in the doorway.

Kendal felt a shot of acute regret. Of all the places he might have taken her, why choose an inn where he had been a frequent guest? It was all of a piece, he supposed, with his perplexing behavior of that morning, when Carver informed him that the Finlays were not at home. The natural thing, the expected thing, would have been to leave his card and move on to his next errand. But he could not resist a falsely casual inquiry after Lady Greer, and when informed she was alone in the breakfast room, he heard himself announce that he would pay his regards in person.

So now, willy-nilly, here they were. Ostensibly for a picnic lunch, and perhaps only that. It wasn't too late for either to have a change of mind about unspoken intentions.

He was reasonably certain she had resolved to have him, though. Either that, or she was the most unconsciously seductive female he had ever met. It was his own decision hanging in the balance, his reluctance to take so intoxicating a drink as Lady Greer warring against his undeniable inclination to drink his fill.

Ignoring Mrs. Belcher's pursed lips and disapproving glare, he instructed John Belcher to ice his best bottle of champagne and see to the horses. Then, with unaccustomed impatience racing up and down his spine, he returned to Lady Greer.

She appeared remarkably poised, as though an afternoon tryst was nothing at all out of the ordinary. And perhaps it was not, he thought with an unpleasant jolt. Yes, she was newly come to London, but who could say what she'd been up to in the country? Every male instinct in his overheated body assured him that she was a woman of extraordinary passion.

Men flocked to her in droves, that was certain. He knew, because he had spent far too much time watching her at balls and routs and musicales when he was supposed to be attending to foreign dignitaries.

"My lord?" she said softly.

He realized that he had been standing in front of her like a fencepost for several minutes. Lady Greer had a way of sending his wits and most of his practiced charm to the far side of the moon.

"Mrs. Belcher will escort you upstairs and provide whatever you need," he said in a strained voice. "I expect you'll wish to refresh yourself before lunch."

"L-lunch?"

"We'll take it alongside the river, unless you prefer to remain indoors. And we are in luck, because this morning she baked her famous almond-custard tarts." He smiled. "Join me outside when you are ready."

Looking a bit stunned, she curtsied and followed Mrs. Belcher up the stairs.

Yes, she had definitely expected *him* to be leading her up those stairs. Rarely had he met a woman so transparently eager for a toss between the sheets. He thought for a moment of granting her wish immediately, but reminded himself that he meant to retain absolute control of whatever happened, or did not happen, between them.

Her urgency was both flattering and unsettling. Also powerfully arousing, which is why he made his way outside instead of following her to the bedchamber. Lady Greer had much to learn about the delights of anticipation, and it would be his pleasure to teach her.

Two geese honked a greeting as he crossed the sweeping lawn and made an arc around a sprawl of snoozing ducks, their bills neatly tucked under iridescent wings. When he stopped at river's edge, a trio of hopeful swans cruised by, eyeing his fingers for a possible handout.

Nothing had changed since his last visit more than three years before. He supposed little had changed here since the sixteenth century, when the White Swan was built as a summer residence for a duke's mistress. Her large, elegantly furnished chamber had been Kendal's haven whenever he contrived to escape the city and his duties.

At this moment and in that very room, the lady he meant to bed this afternoon, a lady who might well become his own mistress for so long as he remained in London, was splashing water on her face or brushing her wind-tangled curls. He wondered what she thought of the enormous bed atop its pedestal, and the colorfully explicit frescoes on the ceiling and walls.

The ducks jumped up, squawking as two freckled young Belchers tramped by with a small wooden table and a pair of chairs. Kendal directed them to the shade of a nearby sycamore tree, and a maid soon arrived to lay out the table with linens, silverware, glasses of cool water, and champagne flutes. She was followed by servants carrying platters of sliced ham and roast beef, a salmon pie, potato pudding, a tureen of lobster bisque, fresh-baked saffron rolls, cucumber salad, almond tarts, and a bowl of ripe peaches.

He had just snatched one of Mrs. Belcher's irresistible tarts when Celia Greer materialized at his side.

"What's this, my lord?" she demanded cheekily. "Dessert before grace?"

He returned the tart to its platter and settled her on a chair. "As you observed, I've a lamentable fondness for sweets. Were the Valliants prone to gaining weight, which by sheer good fortune we are not, I'd be round as an ascent balloon by now."

"The Prince Regent should be as fortunate," she said, unfolding her napkin. "Is it treasonous to remark that he looks nothing whatever like any prince I ever imagined?"

"In my experience, few princes measure up to expectations. Royal blood pumps through perfectly ordinary bodies, I'm afraid, a great many of them equipped with bulbous noses, sagging bellies, and warts."

He sat across from her, dismissing the servants with a wave of his hand. "Shall we forget the czars and archdukes and princes who have been cluttering England and making a nuisance of themselves? I wish to hear about Celia, Lady Greer, who is of far more interest than any royal I ever met."

"To the contrary, sir. The story of my life would bore you senseless."

"Nevertheless, I wish to hear it. And since I am paying for lunch, you are obliged to indulge me."

"Am I?" She raised a brow. "But as I didn't think to bring any money, I suppose you must have your way. No doubt you are accustomed to getting it."

"I have that reputation," he acknowledged.

"Very well then, but I'll take no responsibility if you fall asleep with your chin in the soup bowl. Until a month ago, you see, I had never ventured beyond the backwaters of Lancashire, where nothing of interest ever happens. Or if it does, it never happened to me."

She went quiet then, requiring a bit of encouragement to continue, but he knew better than to provide it. The best way to draw information from those reluctant to give it was to create a silence that ached to be filled. Soon enough, she would tell him what he wanted to know.

He applied himself to his soup and waited.

She put down her spoon only a minute or so after he had expected her to. "Very clever, my lord. What means do you use to extricate information should the silent treatment fail? Thumbscrews? The rack?"

He choked on a sprig of parsley. Lady Greer was not to be underestimated. And how many times since meeting her had he told himself that very thing? "I cannot think what you mean," he said after taking a long drink of water.

"Rubbish! I won't pretend to be up on all your tricks, sir, but I do wish you will stop trying to play them on me. Had I any secrets to withhold, you may be assured I've sufficient wit to keep them to myself."

"Thumbscrews notwithstanding."

"Precisely."

Laughing, he leaned back on his chair. "Very well, Lady Greer. Tell me as much or as little as you wish. But I admit to inordinate curiosity about the doings of a Lancashire lass. Keep me entertained, and I promise not to trot out any more of my devious ploys."

"Oh, you will," she replied sagely. "I suspect you cannot help yourself. Nevertheless, I shall provide you a brief sketch of my decidedly uninteresting life, urging you to stop me when you've heard enough."

"Agreed. Now, do cease these absurd protests and tell me your story."

Annoyance flaring in her eyes, she defiantly finished her soup.

He regarded her with admiration. The strong-willed bays that brought them here could take a lesson in obstinacy from Celia Greer.

When she'd let him wait a minute longer than he had forced her to wait, back when he had foolishly thought to manipulate her, she flashed him a grin of satisfaction. Take that, she might as well have said aloud.

He absorbed the blow with a grin of his own. "Touché," he acknowledged, relishing the surprising battle of wits with an opponent more than capable of matching him. This afternoon was not turning out as he had expected, but so far he was glad of it. When the time came, however, he would take up her reins and bring her into check.

"Well then," she said as if delivering a report on the wheat harvest, "I am an only child. My father was grievously disappointed to be saddled with a daughter instead of an heir, but Mama died of a fever before she could repair her mistake. When I was ten and seven, I married Lord Greer and moved to his farm."

She forked a slice of ham onto her plate.

"Did you love him?"

She looked astonished at the question, nearly as astonished as he felt for having asked it. He had never meant to say such a thing, and for a tense moment he was sure she would tell him to go to the devil.

But she only shrugged. "It was an arranged marriage, with my willing consent. Greer was a good deal older, of course, in his late fifties when we wed and rather set in his ways. I adapted to them, sometimes with ill grace, and we rubbed along as well as could be expected."

In those stark words, he sensed years of heartbreak. But why the devil had she given *willing consent* to a man old enough to be her grandfather?

She cast him a shrewd smile. "You are wondering, of course, why I agreed to the marriage. But the reasons were more or less the usual ones in such cases. Father had accumulated a great many debts and planned to escape his creditors by emigrating to Canada. I didn't want to go with him. But there were few alternatives for a young woman with only a patched-together education and no money at all. Then Greer stepped in, providing funds for Father's voyage and a bit extra to help him make a new start. He also gave me a home. It was a good bargain for everyone concerned."

Sickened, Kendal dished cucumber slices onto his plate and pushed them around with his fork. For the cost of passage across the Atlantic, her father had sold her like a cord of firewood.

But perhaps he mistook the situation. After all, Lord Featherstoke had wed a young bride under similar circumstances, and from all accounts, they remained a devoted couple until his death. Lady Featherstoke still mourned her spouse, and was in no hurry to replace him with another.

Besides, he knew very well that marrying for love was no guarantee of happiness.

"So there you have it," she said with impressive nonchalance. "Greer's heart failed him a little more than a year ago, and I was left with a tidy fortune and the right to call myself a lady, although by birth I merely border on respectable. Mama was the daughter of an obscure baronet and father the third son of a country squire. You needn't spread that information around, by the way. I am trying to cut a dash in Society."

"So you have," he assured her, more fascinated by Celia Greer with every word she spoke. He sensed courage in this slender, sometimes naive young woman. A will of iron.

Also an aching vulnerability, which he was by no means willing to address. Restrained admiration was one thing, concern for her personal feelings quite another. Caring about her meant . . . well, caring. Never a good idea, that.

Happily, John Belcher loped across the lawn just then, carrying a silver bucket filled with ice chips and a bottle of champagne. "Not properly chilled yet, m'lord, but I thought you might be wantin' a sip of the bubbly."

"Thank you, John. Put another on ice, if you will, for later."

After uncorking the bottle, his gaze fixed all the while on Lady Greer, Belcher slowly took himself off.

She gazed after him with a wistful expression. "He disapproves of me. Although that is, I suppose, to be expected."

Kendal made haste to reassure her. "Like most men, John Belcher enjoys looking at beautiful women. You must accustom yourself to admiring glances, Lady Greer, for they will follow you wherever you go."

"They have never done so before. But then, I've hardly ever gone anywhere." She split a crusty roll and dipped her knife into the pot of butter. "London has been my target, though, since I was in leading strings. When Greer died, it was all I could do to keep from jumping on the first mailcoach south. But there was the year of mourning to observe, and I was by no means ready to launch myself into Society. Well, I was certainly *ready*, but I'd have sunk like a stone."

"Unimaginable."

Her brows arched. "Have you forgot detaching me from the underside of Lord Finlay's desk? And that, sir, was after two extremely proper ladies had spent a grueling year polishing me up."

"Ah, but diamonds are generally to be found in dark places," he reminded her, pleased to see her small frown vanish after so slight a compliment. For a woman of such extraordinary beauty, she was remarkably unaware of her charms. "Tell me about the grueling year."

"You are a glutton for tedium, it seems. But very well. When Greer was in the ground, I took myself off to Giggleswick. Do you know it?"

He would certainly have remembered such an unusual name, but it rang no bells. "Should I?"

"Well, it's not so very distant from your estate, perhaps thirty or forty miles. But it's true that little Giggleswick is quite overshadowed by Settle, which lies directly across the River Ribble. I grew up in Settle, and was acquainted from an early age with Miss Wigglesworth and her sister—"

"Wigglesworth?"

"A common name in that area, actually. There are several Wigglesworths in Giggleswick, although none are held in such high esteem as my mentors." Her lips curved. "Wilberta and Wilfreda."

He spilled the champagne he had been pouring into her glass. "Wilberta and Wilfreda Wigglesworth of Giggleswick? You are humbugging me, Lady Greer."

"I assure you, sir, that the Wigglesworth ladies are quite real. They are, as a matter of fact, my closest friends, and have always set the style in Giggleswick society. They had a London Season, you see."

"Indeed? I do not recollect meeting them. But perhaps I was out of the country at the time."

"Perhaps. It was half a century ago."

Kendal found himself laughing again—he who so rarely laughed aloud that he scarcely recognized the unfamiliar sound.

"You may well find this amusing, my lord, but they were the

most fashionable ladies of my acquaintance. And since I had made up my mind to learn how to go on in the beau monde, I applied to them for instruction."

"Aside from your penchant for skulking under desks, Lady Greer, I am persuaded you did not learn your manners from a pair of elderly Giggleswick spinsters."

"Not altogether, it's true. I read a great many books about proper deportment, most of them woefully out of date. You'll be impressed to hear that I can, if necessary, glide smoothly through narrow doors wearing wide panniers, and enter a sedan chair without knocking a speck of powder from my towering hair arrangement."

"Remarkable. I should like to see it."

"Perhaps one day, at a costume ball, I shall have the opportunity to demonstrate. Wilfreda's specialties were somewhat obscure, I admit, but Wilberta provided a good deal of practical advice." She took a sip of champagne. "Indeed, by the time I set out for London, I thought myself a paragon of savoir faire. But then I met Lady Finlay and came smack up against the distinction between a veneer of sophistication and the real thing. It was a considerable comedown, I can tell you."

"If it matters, I find your manners enchanting. Far more charming than the languid world-weariness in fashion these days."

Color washed over her cheeks. "Thank you, sir, even if you said so only to be kind. I know it is a flaw I must overcome, but compliments never fail to turn me to pudding."

They had wandered into personal territory again, he understood by the alarms sounding in his head. How was it he wanted to know everything about her, and not know at the same time? "I am curious to hear more about the redoubtable Wigglesworth ladies," he said, steering the conversation to safer ground.

For some minutes, with unfailing good humor, she described their valiant efforts to transform a country bumpkin into a woman of the world. Now and again he interjected a question, or ventured a comment when she paused for a drink of champagne or a bite of almond tart, which she pronounced delectable. But for the most part, he simply watched her, vibrating like a tuning fork in response to her guileless femininity. She was pure music, he thought, graceful and airy, each line and curve of her body playing on his senses like a Mozart sonata.

The curl of her fingers around the stem of her glass mesmerized him. The dance of her lips and the flash of small white teeth as she spoke sent him spinning in circles. And her eyes, gleaming like polished mahogany in the sunlight, held all the mysteries of the universe.

Not in any London ballroom, not in the glittering courts of Europe, had he ever encountered such a woman as this. The spell she cast stole every shred of reason from his carefully disciplined mind. She disordered him. She took him apart, with no promise he'd ever be whole again.

And, he was certain, she had absolutely no idea the effect she had on men. On him. Artless and genuine in a world of artifice and fakery, the world where he felt comfortable, she was altogether terrifying.

Especially when she smiled at him the way she was smiling now, one brow lifted inquiringly.

Had she asked him a question?

He didn't care.

With trembling fingers, he selected a ripe peach from the fruit bowl, removed the fuzzy peel with a small, sharp knife, and cut the fruit into wedges. He was aware of her watching his hands, and of the shuddering silence that had fallen between them.

Lifting a slice of peach between his thumb and forefinger, he brought it to her lips.

After a moment, eyes wide, she nibbled delicately. When she was done he fed her another, and then a third, their gazes locked in a fevered embrace. A bead of juice hovered at the corner of her mouth. He dabbed it with his finger and slowly stroked it across her lips. Her tongue, small and pink, followed his finger.

Never losing his gaze, she found a wedge of peach and offered it to him. He bit deeply, savoring the squirt of rich juice in his mouth, the feel of soft, yielding flesh between his teeth.

She discovered a drop of liquid that had fallen to his chin, sluiced it onto her fingertip, and brought it to her mouth.

Oh dear God. He felt himself dissolving into the grass. At the same time, on fire for her, the need to make love with her searing through his body, he erupted from his chair.

His elbow hit a platter, knocking it to the ground. Rounds of saffron bread tumbled across the lawn.

And then all hell broke loose.

Chapter 7

Ducks, geese, and swans charged up the hill, webbed feet at a gallop, feathers flying. In a clamor of honks and squawks, they fell on the scattered bread like marauding Huns. And when the rolls were demolished, the more brazen among them swept onto the chairs and table, bills clacking as they fought over morsels of ham and custard tarts.

Stunned, Kendal looked around for Celia and saw her fleeing in the direction of a copse of oaks, three belligerent swans at her heels. She screamed and dove into the trees, disappearing from his sight.

Caught up in the feeding frenzy, geese and ducks nibbled at his boots and trousers for crumbs. Surrounded, he could scarcely move without tromping on a wild-eyed bird.

"Shoo!" he shouted to no effect. "Dammit, *shoo!*"

Fighting his way to the table, he grabbed the bowl of fruit from under the bills of two rapacious geese and heaved it across the lawn. Some of the birds went chasing after the peaches, clearing his path. He broke free and ran in the direction Celia had gone, following the sound of her shrieks.

When he caught up with her, she was perched on a branch about six feet above the ground, flapping her skirts at the swans to hold them at bay.

"Get them *away* from me," she cried. "Oh please!"

He wrenched a clump of gorse from a thick bush and flailed at the swans, sending them off in regal high dudgeon.

Celia sank onto the branch in a heap, arms wrapped around the tree trunk, tears streaming down her cheeks. "Oh, thank heavens."

Kendal approached her gingerly. "It's safe now, my sweet. I promise."

Scared brown eyes searched the undergrowth for lurking swans. "Are you sure they're gone?"

"Absolutely. I'll wring the neck of the next bird that comes within a hundred yards." He held out his arms. "Can you jump down if I swear to catch you?"

"Y-yes." Slowly, she loosed her death grip on the tree and sat upright. Then, with a small sigh, she slid into his embrace.

He held her closely, feeling her heart pound against his chest as she clung to him. "They were only looking for food," he murmured. "They wouldn't have hurt you."

"Little *you* know," she said with a return of spirit, letting go of him and backing away. "I'd sooner take on Napoleon's army than any one of those monstrous beasts. They are too stupid to know the difference between food and people. And when they are hungry, they are *mean*."

"But now they are gone, Celia." He smiled. "Since we have battled an army of fowl together, may I be permitted to call you that? Feel free to smack me for the impertinence, if you are of a mind to strike out at someone. Or some*thing*."

"When you address me as Lady Greer," she replied with an answering smile, "I always hear 'Celia.' So yes, please let us not stand on ceremony. Mercy me. After my disgraceful cowardice, I wonder you have not flown off with the birds." Her smile sloped into a self-mocking grin. "I behaved like the veriest goose."

Lord, what a woman! he thought, laughing appreciatively. Were it possible for him to fall in love again, he would surely be head over heels for her.

As it was, he wondered if it would be the better for the both of them if he eased her politely back to London and left her alone to find her own wings. An empty-hearted man, a man such as he, would only anchor her to ground.

But as she gazed up at him from those hungry, heart-wrenching eyes, he lost all will to resist her. She wanted him, in an unfathomable way that was part lust and in larger part something beyond his comprehension.

"Let me show you something," he said, offering her his arm.

She took it immediately, leaning into his body as he led her onto the narrow path beside the river.

His private hideaway, where he used to spend long afternoons with a book and his own thoughts, lay only a few hundred yards from the White Swan. There was nothing special about it, he thought as they came into the clearing. Just a gnarled outcropping of roots against an ancient oak tree where he liked to sit in the shade, and yellow irises springing up in small bouquets, and the soft sound of water rippling over smooth pebbles. Dragonflies hovered in the air, as always. Bees swept past his ears. Small purple flowers huddled among the mosses.

This was as close to home as he ever came, this place of silence and quiet reflection. He glanced over at Celia, expecting to see disappointment on her face.

Her lips slightly open, she looked around her with a dazed expression. "How unutterably lovely," she whispered, letting go his arm to roam to river's edge, and to the boulder where he had sometimes stood to cast a line for trout, and then to the great oak tree. With a swish of muslin skirts, she sank onto the exact spot he had always favored.

Sunlight dappled her face through the leaves as she lifted her chin to the sky. "I could stay here forever," she said. "It sings of peace."

She had found words for what he felt every time he came here. What little peace he had ever found, he found in this place. But the very fact that she recognized that he was bringing her *here* sent shivers down his spine. The intimacy of their shared joy frightened him even more than the unwelcome emotions battering at his heart.

He knelt across from her, sitting back on his heels, determined to quash the maelstrom raging inside him. "Not to rouse unpleasant memories," he said, meaning to do exactly that, "but how is it a few impetuous birds sent you, quite literally, into the boughs?"

She took a deep breath and let it out again. "If you must

know," she said, flushing hotly, "I have a profound aversion to large p-poultry."

He bit back a laugh. "I had noticed. My youngest brother was once attacked by an ill-tempered stray he tried to befriend, and after that he could never abide dogs. Had you a similar experience when you were a child?"

"Much later. Greer kept chickens, you see. Hundreds of them, for scientific research. The farm and nearly all his time were given over to experiments with crossbreeding, and he produced scores of articles and pamphlets on the subject. It was his dream to be admitted to the Royal Society of London for Improving Natural Knowledge."

"Was he?"

"I'm afraid not, although he was highly regarded by those who shared his preoccupation. You may be certain that I was not among them." Her head tipped to one side. "I can tell you this much about chickens, sir. They are stupid, they stink, and they peck."

When she held out her hands, palms down, he leaned forward to see. A scatter of tiny white scars, nearly imperceptible, stretched from the tips of her fingers to several inches above her wrists. "Good God," he swore softly. How could Greer have permitted his wife anywhere near those brutally sharp beaks?

She must have been reading his mind. "Sometimes I was called on to feed them," she said, folding her hands in her lap. "Greer didn't trust the servants to provide adequate care, and he was so besotted with his pets that he never minded when they pecked him, which, of course, they did with enthusiasm. But it did not do for anyone to criticize their natural chickenly behavior, so I dared not protest when they took after me. You may be sure I kept as clear of them as possible, although it wasn't always. Possible, that is."

Her voice faded at the end, but she managed a gallant shrug.

He profoundly wished it weren't too late to grind Lord Greer into bite-sized morsels for his damnable chickens. "I well understand why you detest them," he said.

"And all their relations," she affirmed. "With the exception of songbirds, so long as they mind their manners and stay in their trees."

He silently applauded her attempt to lighten the conversation, but he wasn't quite ready to dismiss the subject. "Speaking of trees, however did you make the leap up to that branch where I found you?"

"I've no idea. Propelled there by sheer panic, I suppose. I wasn't even aware of where I was until you charged to my rescue." She smiled. "Did I ever thank you?"

"Since it was my fault the swans attacked in the first place, I can only be grateful you suffered no harm. But tell me, what became of Lord Greer's chickens after his death?"

"I didn't slaughter them, if that's what you are implying. But neither did I feel an obligation to honor his memory by providing them a home. Letters went out to his friends, announcing that the chickens would be given to anyone willing to carry them off."

She chuckled. "That, I can tell you, was a mistake of the first order. But I never expected such a response. Scores of gentlemen swooped in like locusts on the appointed day and promptly began to squabble over the prize specimens. Fistfights broke out in the barns, the chickens were squawking up a storm, and for once I was almost in sympathy with them. It was quite a scene, I promise you. But by nightfall every last one was gone, and good riddance to the lot!"

He stood. "You never fail to astonish me," he said, holding out his hands. She took hold of them and let him draw her to her feet. Then, gently, he brushed his lips across her scarred wrists, one by one. "I admire your courage, Celia Greer. It is unparalleled among the females of my acquaintance. And most of the men, for that matter, excepting those who fought on the Peninsula."

"You *admire* me?" she said with a gulp. "Truly? I thought you would be revolted to learn I had been living in a barnyard. Well, practically. And I'd never have told you, I vow, if not for those dratted swans."

"Then I must remember to thank them for loosing your tongue. You should not be ashamed of what you could not help, Celia."

"Oh, I'm not," she assured him. "But that doesn't mean I wish everyone and his brother to know of it."

"We diplomats are proficient at keeping secrets, my dear. Yours are perfectly safe with me."

She nodded, and as she did, her eyes went round as dinner plates. "Mercy me!" Snatching her hands away, she began to brush them frantically at her skirts.

Had she only just noticed the dirt and bits of tree bark? he wondered. Clambering up that oak had soiled her pretty yellow gown from bodice to ruffled hem, not to mention the jagged tear along her right hip.

"Oh, no," she wailed. "What have I done?"

"It's of no importance," he said dismissively. "Dresses are easily replaced."

"But I look like I've been dragged backward through a hedgerow!"

Her feminine outrage at not looking her best had been amusing, until he saw a tear gathering at the corner of her eye. It began to dawn on him that she was genuinely distressed. And since he had already decided that she was not in the least vain on her own account, it must be because she had wished to make a favorable impression on him.

She had certainly done so, in more ways than he was ready to admit. Scooping a handful of dirt from the ground, he smeared it over his driving coat and doeskin breeches as she watched in wide-eyed horror. "There. Now we are a matched set."

"I cannot believe you did that," she said in an awed voice. "Whatever were you thinking?"

"Very much what I've been thinking since the first time I saw you," he confessed. "And if you haven't guessed what that is, will you let me show you?"

When he opened his arms, she immediately flung herself into his embrace, welcoming his kiss with blazing fervor. Her small hands clutched at his waist, as if uncertain where to put themselves, and with a tiny gasp of surprise she opened her lips at his whispered instruction.

Had she not been married so many years, he thought at the edges of his disorderd mind, he might have taken her for an innocent. But no innocent would crave, as she so clearly did, everything he was ready to give her. None would kiss him back with such unbridled sensuality. Greer must have been a poor bedmate indeed for his enthusiastic young wife, so little had he taught her.

And then he forgot Greer, and everything else, captivated by the feel of her lithe body pressed against his. She tasted of peaches and champagne. Her earnest passion ignited him like dry tinder, and it was all he could do to stop himself from carrying her to the ground and making love to her on the riverbank.

But she deserved better than a wild tumble on the hard dirt, and he wanted more than the explosive culmination of his own urgent need to have her. Satin sheets and a long, slow afternoon of pleasure, he resolved, gently setting her at arm's distance.

A dazed look on her face, she regarded him uncertainly. "Have I done something wrong?" she asked. "Was I too f-forward?"

"Never that. You are perfect. Beyond perfect. It was I who nearly spoiled everything." He was breathing so heavily he could hardly speak. "Shall we go where we can be more comfortable, sweetness? Or am I rushing my fences with you?"

She scuffed the toe of her half boot in the dirt. "I'm not certain what you mean. That is, I have no experience in these matters. None whatever. Tell me what I am supposed to do."

"Tell me what you want to do, Celia. Tell me what you want."

"S-surely you know. I want *you*."

Alone in the bedchamber, Celia hurriedly scrubbed her face and hands and used a tortoiseshell brush she found on the dressing table to untangle her hair. Then, dampening the ends of a towel, she tried to blot the worst of the grime from her dress. Since there was nothing to be done about the long tear in the skirt, she resolved to forget it was there.

It occurred to her that she might be expected to remove the dress altogether.

Had Kendal left her alone to strip off her clothes? Was she supposed to be waiting for him naked? On the bed? *In* the bed? Oh mercy.

She wandered over to the formidable Elizabethan tester bed atop its high pedestal, the posts and headboard ornately carved from dark mahogany, the crimson velvet canopy and counterpane fringed with gold. Lascivious, she thought. And downright intimidating.

How many other women had he brought to this room, made love to in this bed?

Well, that did not bear thinking of.

She wished he would hurry up. In his company, thinking was impossible. But as the minutes passed there was nothing else to do. And the more she thought, the more nervous she became.

She would disappoint him, of course. But perhaps he wouldn't mind too much. She'd already warned him what to expect, after all.

Ought she to close the curtains? Sunlight flooded the room, and she had the impression lovemaking was generally done in the dark. One by one, she pulled the heavy velvet curtains over the windows until the room was in total blackness. Not good. How would they even find each other? Selecting the window farthest from the bed, she adjusted the curtains until a wide shaft of light fell across the lush carpet. That was better.

Her clothes, she had decided, would stay where they were for now. Possibly he wished to remove them himself. Was she expected to perform that service for him, too?

This was all so mysterious. So *complicated*!

So very delicious.

Her toes curled inside her half boots. Today, her dream of a grand passion was coming true. She could scarcely believe her good fortune. The very man she had longed for all these years would soon take her in his arms and teach her what it was to be a woman.

Hugging herself, she whirled around in a little dance of joy.

And heard applause coming from the direction of the door.

Stumbling to a halt, she saw Kendal framed in the light from the passageway, watching her. He was smiling.

Mortified, Celia swept him a profound curtsy.

He had removed his coat, she saw, and untied his neckcloth. It hung in two swaths of white linen over his tan waistcoat. There were damp spots on his breeches where he had scoured the mud away. She thought he must surely be the handsomest man God ever created.

Still smiling, he stepped inside and closed the door. "You prefer the room to be dark, I take it."

"N-no. I thought perhaps it was supposed to be. Shall I open the curtains again?"

"I've a better idea." Draping his coat over the back of a chair, he went to the hearth and used the tinderbox to ignite a taper. There were a great many candles in the room, set in ornate silver braces on the side tables, and he lit them one by one until the room was bathed in a warm, honeyed light. Finally he crossed to the window and shut out the last bit of sunshine.

The bedchamber felt smaller now, Celia thought. More . . . intimate. Candlelight flickered over his face, highlighting his cheekbones and the strong line of his jaw. He looked overwhelmingly masculine. Infinitely desirable. Heat pooled in her breasts and at the base of her stomach.

He held out his arms, his hands open. "Come, Celia."

Oh, *yes*. Ceiling and walls and floor vanished. She floated into his embrace and anchored herself there, his confidence wrapping securely around her, banishing the last of her fears.

"You have bewitched me," he said softly, grazing the pad of his thumb down her cheek. "Will you cast a spell for both of us now, Celia? Will you give me all your magic?"

"I will give you all I am," she whispered. "Please kiss me."

Gently at first, and then with deep, demanding passion, he promised with his kisses everything that was to follow. She felt his hand at her waist, and felt it move down, sliding over her hip, drawing her closer. Mindless, boneless, she melted into his body, glad of his strength. Needing it. Needing *him*.

She heard him groan low in his throat when her hands began to skate over his back, up to his wide shoulders, along the hard muscles of his arms, shaping him as he shaped her.

Then he swept her into his arms and carried her to the bed. Lowering her onto the soft velvet, he lifted himself over her, his legs pressed to the sides of her legs, his weight resting on one elbow as he buried his face against her throat. She slipped her fingers through his hair, loving its softness.

Whatever she had imagined and hoped for from the lovers in her fantasies, he was so much more. Warm and powerfully male, he transformed illusion into hard flesh and warm blood.

His hands were at her back, undoing the buttons of her dress. And suddenly, vagrant misgivings skittered around in her head like gnats. She found herself wondering about his boots. And hers, although they would be more easily removed. She became two people, one lost in his kisses and murmured words, the other worrying about boots and chemises and breeches.

About bleeding all over this expensive red velvet counterpane.

There would be bleeding, she was reasonably sure. She'd read about it in a book.

His fingers tickling over her breasts scattered her capricious thoughts, but when he knelt to unbutton his waistcoat, they came rushing back again.

How long did this take? She wished it to last forever, which was impossible, and although it had scarcely begun, she began to dread the moment when it would be over. And would it hurt? She didn't care, but she wanted to know.

He must have sensed the questions turning somersaults in her head. Bending down, he brushed light, reassuring kisses on her cheek. "What's wrong, sweetness? Where have you gone?"

"I'm here," she said as he nibbled at her earlobe. "But . . . no. Never mind. I just—"

"Just what? Tell me, Celia. How can I please you?"

"Oh, you do. Wonderfully. But I was wanting to ask you the same question, you see." Once she began to speak, the flood-gates opened. "And what about our boots? I'm afraid I'll ruin this bedspread. And I was wondering what is to happen next, and what after that."

He gazed at her in astonishment. "But there is nothing what-ever to worry about. The boots will come off when we are ready. We are in no hurry, my sweet. And if it concerns you, I'll take care not to . . . that is, you need not fear any . . . conse-quences. As for the rest, you know what happens next."

"No," she said. "Not exactly."

His eyes clouded. "I don't understand."

"But I told you. I've never done this before."

Smiling, he flicked a tendril of hair from her forehead. "Yes, I remember. It's all right, you know. Indeed, you honor me. And dear heavens, how I want you. It's not too late, if you have changed your mind, but please tell me you haven't."

She raised a fingertip to his lips. "I want you so much I am dying for wanting you. But do you really hear what I am saying? *I have never done this before.* None of it. Not ever."

He froze, staring at her blankly.

She saw the moment when comprehension dawned. And then, with an oath, he flung himself off the bed.

"You're a virgin?" He jabbed a finger in her direction. "A bloody damned *virgin*?"

Sitting up, she wrapped her arms around her waist. "I thought you understood."

"How could I? It's unthinkable. Impossible! You were *married*!"

"Even s-so, it's the truth. I couldn't help it, I promise you." His fury washed over her in hot waves. "All I had to give you was myself. You said you wanted me. Why does this matter?"

"It . . . I . . . of *course* it matters. Do you think I'd have

69

brought you here if I had the slightest clue what you were about? What you *are*?"

Before she could summon a reply, he had stormed to the door and slammed it behind him.

Chapter 8

Kendal, relieved to find the passageway empty, looked around for somewhere to be inconspicuous until his body and his temper calmed. But there were no cubbyholes where he could take refuge, and he dared not open any of the other bed-chamber doors. Someone might be inside, doing what he had meant to do with Celia.

Retreating to the far end of the passageway, he stared at the nubby plaster and forced himself to breathe in a steady rhythm.

Anger. He'd not felt it like this—gut-wrenching and hot— since . . . no! He would not, he *must* not dredge up what he'd long since put behind him. What happened then had nothing to do with what was happening now.

He pressed his palms against the cool stone of the wall, pushing hard, expending the tension in his taut muscles.

How had he given Celia Greer the power to do this to him? From the first he'd sensed that she was trouble, but he had refused to heed the alarms that sounded each time he saw her. Or she had a way of silencing them, with her enticing smile and the purely female way she moved, graceful and seductive, alto-gether irresistible to any man with blood in his veins.

Worse, she was interesting. Unusual. She intrigued him. She slid inside him, into his thoughts, and he'd let her stay. He had enjoyed thinking about her, imagining how she would feel against his body. How she would taste and—

Hellfire! Whatever she was, she was not for him. His only problem now was how to return her to London, because damned if he'd drive her there himself. Another two hours pressed against her on the narrow bench of his curricle would undo him past recall.

Gradually, the raging anger and steaming lust seeped from his body, leaving him cold. Weary, too, and disillusioned, as if he'd run a long hard race only to lose at the wire.

Giving free rein to emotions did that to a man. He knew that from experience. The mystery was that he'd allowed it to happen to him again. Indeed, he had walked willingly into the trap, not to put too fine a point on it, because he thought himself impervious to the wiles of any scheming female. He had fancied himself a man rigidly in control of his passions, always measuring out his natural desires in careful doses.

Apparently not.

Already he was wildly tempted to go back and finish what he had started, even though he was the one who had put a stop to it. Rightly so, he told himself. Necessarily so. But for safety's sake, he had better take himself away from here— from *her*—with all possible speed.

He did not glance at the door to the bedchamber where he'd left Celia as he walked swiftly past it to the staircase. No doubt she wanted to see him as little as he wished to see her, although he could not leave the inn altogether until he'd made sure she was safely on her way back to London.

After a few words to John Belcher, who quickly dispatched his son to the nearest posthouse for a carriage, Kendal took a bottle of brandy and an empty glass to a table in the corner of the taproom.

The innkeeper, of course, knew very well that something had gone wrong. Even the scullery maid had heard the news by now. One by one, servants popped in and out of the taproom, manufacturing errands in order to steal a look at Lord Kendal in his shirtsleeves. He felt like the featured attraction at a raree show.

What was Celia doing now? he wondered before mentally kicking the thought away. But it bounced back again, and brought with it the knifing awareness that he could not leave her alone in that erotically charged bedchamber for the next hour.

At the least, he should send a maid to explain the arrangements he had made for her return to the city. And while she was in the room, the maid could retrieve his coat. Then he could be on his way without risk of a chance encounter with Celia. The idea was remarkably appealing.

But of course he would do no such thing.

Kendal drained the brandy glass and left the taproom, striding purposefully up the stairs.

There was unfinished business between them. He had stormed away like a tantrumish schoolboy without demanding the truth from her. She owed him an explanation, dammit, for what she had done.

A quick review of his own behavior confirmed that he had been perfectly straightforward, a man of the world doing what men of the world did when lovely widows signaled blatant interest in an affair. His conscience was clear. He had promised nothing, and when it came right down to it, he had never deliberately tried to seduce her. Without question, Celia Greer had been the aggressor. She had pursued him quite shamelessly.

His only fault was succumbing to the surprisingly intense pleasure he felt when she gazed at him with flagrant, flattering desire. And, too, he had sought her out in defiance of his long-standing rule against taking a personal interest in any female, especially one who showed signs of taking a personal interest in him.

Once he began listing his own mistakes, they mounted in alarming increments. But always, he was reasonably certain, he had only himself to answer to for what he'd said and done, and for what he had allowed himself to feel. At no point had he given Celia the slightest indication that he wanted more from her than a tumble between the sheets. One only, come to think of it. He'd made it perfectly clear that his duties would take him to Bath on the morrow, and to Vienna within a few weeks.

He realized that he had been standing in front of the bedchamber door for a considerable time, his land lifted to knock. Exhaling a harsh breath, he rapped lightly.

No response.

He tried again, and thought he heard a faint "Come in."

73

Dear God, what if she was curled up in a knot of feminine misery, weeping her heart out?

Well, what of it? That had been Belinda's favorite trick, until he finally realized she could cry at will. Once she understood that her bouts of weeping would avail her nothing, they stopped cold. Female tears were a weapon, no more than that.

But his hand was shaking as he opened the door, and he dreaded what he would see when he entered the room.

Whatever he had expected went up in smoke.

Celia, wearing her bonnet and gloves, was sitting on the window bench directly across from him. She had opened the heavy curtains, and sunlight poured over her still body through the leaded panes. She gazed at him from unreadable dark eyes, her usually vibrant face expressionless.

She might as well have been carved from ivory, he thought, instinctively watching for the subtle, telltale indications of mood and intention he had learned to recognize. Even the most experienced politician unconsciously revealed, with the set of his muscles or the throbbing of a vein, something of what he was thinking.

Not Celia. She remained, under his intense scrutiny, as remote and indecipherable as he was reputed to be.

He envied her. It was all he could do to keep his knees from buckling.

He resented her, too, for rendering him defensive. Unsure of himself. She didn't appear to notice that he was practically crumbling before her eyes. For a hundred other nameless reasons, he longed to cross the room and seize her by the shoulders and shake her until she raged at him, freeing him to vent his own surging rage on her.

Perversely, she simply looked at him with that steady, unnerving calm, as if nothing of consequence had passed between them. As if he were an insect that just crawled out from the woodwork.

"I have sent for a carriage to convey you to London," he said, hating the sound of his voice as each word clipped out.

"Thank you," she replied with unruffled politesse. "You will

74

wish to be on your way immediately, of course. There is no need to wait here on my account."

"Nevertheless, I shall remain until you are safely on your way."

"As you wish, sir."

The silence that followed her cool pronouncement roared in his ears.

"Have you nothing more to say to me?" he demanded, hands clenched behind his back.

Her head tilted slightly as she considered. "No. I can think of nothing. Except, thank you for paying for our lunch."

"Bloody hell, Celia! You know what I mean."

"Not really. I thought I did, until half an hour ago, but I was wrong." Her eyes clouded. "If you don't mind, I'd rather not try to guess what I am supposed to say or do to please you now. I'd only get it wrong."

"*Wrong* is pretending this is over until you explain why you lied to me."

One delicate brow lifted slightly. "Lied, sir? About what?"

"Not telling the whole truth is a lie," he shot back, knowing he sounded like a self-righteous prig.

She knew it, too, he could tell from the sardonic curl of her lips. "Oh. You are annoyed because I failed to draw you a map that even a blind man could follow. Forgive me. But I was always so conscious of my own inadequacies that it never occurred to me a man of experience would fail to recognize them. When did I give you any indication that I'd the least claim to sexual proficiency?"

"When you told me you had been married for nine years. When I saw you flirting with every randy young buck in London."

"That," she said with a dismissive gesture, "is an exaggeration. Surely I missed one or two young bucks, if only because there were so many of them hovering about."

Teeth gritted, he stomped across the room and wrenched his coat from the chair back where he'd draped it. With a clatter of wood on wood, the chair toppled to the floor.

"Make up your mind, Lord Kendal," she said too sweetly.

75

"Are you enraged because I am a wanton flirt, or because I have never been bedded?"

"In your case, the one does not rule out the other. Assuming you are the innocent you claim to be. I have no proof of that."

"You would have got ample proof, had you stayed the course. Or so I believe." Her voice quavered on the last few words. "I'm not altogether certain how a man knows, but Wilberta Wigglesworth assured me it is perfectly obvious."

He drove his arms into the sleeves of his coat. "You should have told me from the start."

"Were you not listening when I did? More than once I told you that I lacked experience. I cannot recall my exact words, but I promise you that it mortified me to say them."

"I—that is, you gave me the distinct impression you had been faithful to your husband, and that I was the first lover you had taken after his death. That much was clear, I agree."

"Never mind the randy London bucks, then?" she inquired equably.

Although he was standing in the middle of the room, he felt as if she had him pinned against the wall. It didn't help that the enormous pedestaled bed loomed as a stark reminder of the passion that had flared between them. Even now, loathing her and loathing himself even more, he wanted to fling her down on that bed and quench the fire blazing inside him.

"Let us come to the point," he said. "You prevaricated. Lack of experience does not equal absolute—" Unable to say the word, he waved a hand.

"Absolute what? *Virginity?* Pardon me, Lord Kendal, but at what moment during the little time we have spent together should I have addressed the subject? When we waltzed at Lady Jersey's ball? Over breakfast this morning? In your curricle this afternoon? While you sliced a peach and fed it to me beside the river?"

She stood, clutching her torn skirt with both hands. "Enlighten me, sir. Exactly when should I have announced, out of the blue, that I was a virgin? Perhaps when I was up in the tree. 'Oh, by the way, sir, I happen to be a virgin.' Or, better yet, when you were crouching in front of Lord Finlay's desk, loosing my hair from that nail. 'Thank you, sir, and did you know that you have just had the honor of rescuing a virgin?' "

"Enough!" He slapped his hand against his forehead. "Blast it, I had every right to presume you to be . . . what I thought you were. How could any man wed to you for nine years keep his hands off you, for pity's sake? Can you blame me for finding it unimaginable? And if it were true—"

"Oh, it is."

"Then why the devil did you stay with him?"

"What choice did I have? We took vows in a church, before God and witnesses." She came directly up to him, color hectic in her cheeks. "Little you know of it, damn your eyes. Greer understood that I wanted children. He promised to give them to me. And to his credit, he tried. Only after I persisted, it's true, but eventually he came to my bed every Saturday night and made an effort to do his duty. But he could not."

She poked him in the chest with a hard finger. "I don't know why, and all I can bear to remember of those horrid gropings is *nothing*. After a few months we both gave it up with profound relief."

Shame nosed up his spine. He should have deduced the truth, or suspected it when he learned that she had been sold off to an old man. And yet he could not let go the idea she was somehow at fault. "Impotence is clear grounds for annulment," he said. "You could have been rid of Greer with ease."

She looked startled for a moment. Then her eyes went hard. "In the first place, I didn't know that. In the second, however does one prove such a claim? And in the third, I had no money to hire a solicitor. Do not judge me by your lordly standards, sir. When you want something—justice, for instance, or the freedom to go where you will—you have the means to acquire it."

"You were not a prisoner, surely. And I cannot credit that a woman of your intelligence and spirit endured an intolerable marriage for nearly a decade without contriving some means of escape. Or was it the legacy, madam? He was an elderly man when you married him. Did you stay for the money, resolved to hold out until Greer cocked up his toes?"

She regarded him with immeasurable contempt. "You know nothing, sir. *Nothing!*"

"Then tell me what I am failing to understand. I have asked for no more than the truth."

"On the contrary. You have been too busy inventing false-hoods about me to heed a word I have said. I'll not try to defend my actions or my honor to the likes of you, Lord Kendal. But if you genuinely wish to understand what happened here today, the truth is amazingly transparent. You simply failed to get what you wanted. And in my experience, men cannot bear to be thwarted. They invariably lose their tempers and cast about for someone to blame, or to punish. It's all one and the same."

Not invariably, he thought, clenching his fists. He could not recall a single time in his thirty-four years that he had lost his temper in such a fashion, however great the provocation. He could not accept that he had done so today, with her, never mind that it was patently obvious he'd abandoned every shred of hard-won control in the last few minutes. But why? He had to know *why*.

She wasn't finished raking him through the coals. "You expected what you always expect from an affair—a pleasant interlude to be enjoyed at your convenience. Above all things, it must be played by your rules. No surprises. No entangle-ments. No *complications*. Believe it or not, sir, I accepted those terms unconditionally."

"So you say. But you did *not* play by any rules of fairness. You must have known that I would never bed an innocent without accepting—in advance—the inevitable consequences."

"And what are those, pray tell? Do virgins expect you to marry them when the deed is done? Well, rubbish. You were simply afraid that your afternoon of inconsequential pleasure might become—oh, the horror of it!—*personal*. But you'd nothing whatever to worry about. You may be sure that the last thing on earth I want for myself is another marriage to a self-absorbed despot who wouldn't recognize a genuine human feeling if it bashed him on the skull. I wonder now that I ever wanted you, for even the few hours we had agreed to share.

Please do me one kindness, sir. Go away, now, before either of us says anything else we might regret."

Although she was standing within arm's reach, he felt as if he were gazing at her across an enormous chasm, separated by her secrets, and his, and the aftermath of disaster. Unfamiliar emotions hammered at him like a storm in the desert—fascination, respect, desire, anger, an inexplicable longing to begin again with her, an absolute terror of spending one more minute with her—oh damn! He could not absorb it all. Not now.

When the storm had passed, he knew, all this would be consigned to oblivion. He was, if nothing else, a master at forgetting what he could not bear to remember.

"As you wish, Lady Greer." He bowed and turned for the door. But when he reached it, he could not help but look back at her.

Like a long-stemmed rose, straight and proud and impossibly beautiful, she waited with awful dignity for him to be gone.

I'm sorry, he wanted to say. There were a thousand things he wanted to say. But without a word, he raised the latch and left the room.

Chapter 9

It was barely seven of the morning, already promising to be a sunny day, when Thomas Carver arrived with the hired carriage. He nearly overran Celia as he steered the horses into the inn courtyard. Face red, he tossed the reins to a stable boy and jumped to the ground.

"Clumsy of me," he apologized with a bow. "And the landau has seen better times, I'm afraid. It was the best of the lot, though, and the nags have some spirit to them."

"They will do very well indeed," she assured him. "Was there no driver to be had?"

"I didn't like the looks of him, ma'am. A drinker, I warrant from the stink of his breath. I'm no whipster, but better me than a woozy sot."

Smiling, she stepped into the carriage. "I know we've a long journey, Thomas, but I wish to make a stop along the way. We'll be turning off about a mile past Sedgwick."

"Yes, ma'am." He jumped to the driver's bench and steered the pair of roans from the courtyard at a brisk trot.

It was pleasantly cool for late July. Celia had all but suffocated in the postchaise during the long trip north, and wasn't looking forward to another seventy miles round-trip in any vehicle, even an open one like the landau. Removing her bonnet, she sat back on the cracked leather padding and let the dew-damp breeze sift through her hair.

Thank heavens for Thomas, she thought. What would she have done without him these last few days? She might almost feel guilty about stealing him away from the Finlays, except that they could easily replace a footman and she badly needed him. Indeed, Lord Finlay had insisted she take a reliable servant with her, although he'd doubtless expected that servant to come back again.

But when Thomas saw the Lake Country, it was love at first sight. Or so he maintained, although Celia suspected he was merely reluctant to leave her there on her own. And it was only fitting, she supposed, that he be present at the conclusion of her ill-fated adventure, since he had stood her friend at the beginning of it. When she set up her new household, assuming he chose to remain in her service and despite the fact that he was only three-and-twenty, she meant to appoint him butler.

The trouble with long carriage rides, she decided within a few minutes, was that they gave one too much time to think. In the postchaise, her last encounter with Lord Kendal had replayed in her mind again and again, so vividly she might as well have been reliving it.

For the first two days, encased in a protective mantle of icy calm, she analyzed with remarkable detachment everything he had said and done, and dissected her own behavior with equally sharp scrutiny. At the end, with faults and mistakes abounding on both sides, she acknowledged that she'd only herself to blame.

Lord Kendal had always been leagues beyond her reach. It was she who risked a flight to the sun, and like Icarus, she had been tossed unceremoniously back to earth. All the same, heart-bruised, humiliated and scorned, she could not regret having seized her one forlorn chance to have him.

For Kendal, of course, she had been no more than a pleasant diversion. He never pretended otherwise, and could not have known that she'd fixed on him as the center of all her hopes and dreams. Her sole consolation was that he would never know.

She had fled London the very next morning. Fortunately, Lady Marjory was in Maidstone with her sister, and Lord Finlay too preoccupied with matters of state to question the hasty departure of a houseguest. He had accepted her story about a sick friend with distracted sympathy, helped her arrange for a coach and driver, and sent her on her way.

It was bitter irony that she knew no place to go except where she had lived before, even though it lay within a few miles of Kendal's estate and close by a town that bore the same name as his title. But while she was returning with her tail between her legs, she had no intention of hiding out forever. She had enjoyed her few weeks in London and meant to go back, perhaps as early as the next Season. She would lease a house, launch herself into fashion, and host an extravagant ball. If he were very lucky, Lord Kendal might receive a coveted invitation.

With such thoughts, she endured the first part of her journey home.

And then, on the morning of the third day, the shell of ice that had held her together broke apart and she began to weep. Great racking sobs they were, leading Thomas to descend from his place beside the postchaise driver and hesitantly inquire if she was ill. She sent him back again, pleading a summer cold, and faked coughing and sneezing to cover the sounds of her distress and explain her swollen eyes.

She had cried all the way from Warwick to Manchester, where they stopped for the night, and she cried all the next day, too.

The death of a dream must surely be mourned.

But when they drew up at a comfortable inn not far from the town of Kendal, the tears abruptly ceased. Exhausted, she had welcomed the kind attentions of the proprietor and his wife, who settled her in a spacious room overlooking the River Kent and fed her hot soup and mulled wine. For the first time since leaving London, she slept dreamlessly and awoke the next morning with a trace of optimism bubbling in her veins.

She would make a new life for herself, she resolved over a substantial breakfast. She had done it before, and she could do it again. No more schoolgirl fantasies about grand passions and unattainable men, thank you. It was past time she came to terms with the real world.

In company with Thomas, she had made plans for her

immediate future, arranging to stay in residence at the Merry Goosegirl while they were put into action. The previous day she'd employed an agent to find a suitable house for her in the area of Windemere Lake. And today, she was on her way to lay one ghost to rest and seek advice about the other spirit that continued to hover, despite her every effort to banish him, in the vicinity of her heart.

Celia snapped open her parasol and forced herself to concentrate on the road. They were near the turnoff to Greer's farm, a narrow byway on the left side marked only by a weathered plank nailed to a tree.

When she spotted it, she poked Thomas on the shoulder. He drew up immediately.

"I'll walk from here," she said. "Chances are the track is overgrown by now, but follow me as far as you can and find a place in the shade to wait. I won't be gone more than an hour."

Thomas frowned, clearly disliking her plan. He reminded her to don her bonnet against the morning sun and helped her alight, muttering under his breath. She felt his gaze against her back until the rutty road took a sharp curve.

Celia followed its twists and turns for half a mile. Then she veered off, clambering over a stile that led to a hilly pasture spotted with grazing sheep. At the far end, she knew, was a promontory overlooking the farm.

When she reached it, somewhat breathless, she could barely force herself to look down at the prison where she had been all but enslaved for nine years. Since the day after giving Greer's chickens away, when she left to take up residence with the Wigglesworth sisters, she had not set foot there. Two of the servants agreed to stay on as caretakers in exchange for an exorbitant bribe, which she was happy to pay. At the time even the effort of disposing of the property had been too much to bear. She'd wanted nothing more to do with it, not ever.

Dropping cross-legged onto the thick grass, she gazed at the lovely valley nestled in a fold of hills. Directly below her, the farm spread out in a careless disarray of Lakeland-stone buildings. The house itself was squat and ugly, redeemed only by a flourishing vegetable garden at the back. Wisps of smoke wafted from the kitchen chimney, indicating—to her surprise—that the caretakers were still in residence. She had rather expected them to take the money and flee.

Spreading out from the house like spokes on a wagon wheel were the low buildings that had housed Greer's chickens. Simply looking at them conjured up the sound of their interminable clucking and their pervasive, stomach-turning stench.

She wrapped her arms around her knees, staring with intense loathing at the farm. Kendal could not begin to understand what it had been like. She had scarcely believed it herself, once she discovered what a ghastly mistake she had made.

But when she accepted Greer's offer, she could not imagine a more intolerable existence than the one in her father's house. She despised the ill-tempered brute who had driven her shadowy mother to an early grave, and he despised her in equal measure because she refused to cower under his fist. Any fate, she had thought when he proposed an arranged marriage, would be better than the misery of living with him.

Even her first meeting with Greer, shocking as it had been, failed to deter her. Three times her age, skinny, spindle-legged, and sparse of hair, he was the antithesis of all her girlish dreams. But unlike her father, who always shouted, Lord Greer was soft-spoken. And when she rallied the courage to ask what she might expect from their marriage, he did not slap her for being impertinent. Instead, she had the altogether novel experience of being asked about her own wishes.

That was probably the moment she put aside her revulsion at his appearance and resolved to accept him.

Yes, she would have the running of his household, he had replied. She would, in fact, be wholly responsible for seeing to it that his daily instructions were carried out. And yes, she would be Lady Greer. It sounded so glamorous to her then. *Lady Greer*, not raggedy Celia Stoke, the town bully's daughter.

When she asked about children, though, his lips compressed into a narrow slash of white. His first two wives had been barren, she knew from her father's report, and she had assumed

Greer was sniffing after a young bride in order to get an heir on her. Why else would he marry again?

And dear God, she had wanted children. A lifetime of love was stored near to bursting inside her, waiting to be poured out on them.

With startling reluctance, he professed himself willing to oblige her in the matter of children—so long as she kept them well away from his scientific experiments. At first mention of his vocation, Greer's eyes came alight. He sat straighter on the chair as he boasted of the papers he had published and the remarkable new hybrids he had engineered.

Caught up in his excitement, she imagined herself working side by side with him, engineering hybrids. Whatever they were. She had no idea.

Finally, he pulled a folded sheet of paper from his pocket and read the litany of his own expectations. She was hardly listening by then, lost in a fantasy wherein the fashionable Lady Greer wafted from the nursery, where her precious babes lay sleeping, to her husband's laboratory, where she instantly found the key to his knottiest scientific problem, and on to play hostess to the local gentry at an elegant ball.

She was far too young and inexperienced to sense the rod of iron in that stooped back, or understand the significance of his long list of wifely duties, or recognize his maniacal zeal to be celebrated for his scientific achievements.

He had been a way out, and she had leapt at it. How bad could it be, after all, a marriage of convenience to a kindly old gentleman?

Very bad indeed, she quickly discovered.

Greer didn't, in fact, want a wife at all. He had set out to purchase a household drudge, one who could not up and quit like all the others. Figuring a marriage settlement would be cheaper in the long run, and legally binding on his unfortunate spouse, he struck what was for him a very good deal.

For Celia, it had amounted to indentured servitude.

Leaving the farm without permission was expressly forbidden, and permission was rarely granted. Nor had she time, what with the schedule of duties Greer handed her every morning over breakfast. Her days were spent preparing meals and cleaning up after them, scrubbing floors and laundering sheets. The few servants willing to settle for Greer's cheese-paring wages were lazy and insolent. She soon learned that any attempt on her part to prod them to actual work sent them packing, and a little begrudging help was better than no help at all.

When he put her to feeding the chickens and cleaning cages, she was at the point of despair. By then, knowing her hope of bearing children would never be fulfilled, she had nothing whatever to look forward to. She had wished him dead. She had wished *herself* dead.

A dragonfly hovered near her cheek, the faint whir of its transparent wings recalling her to the present moment.

How long had she been here? Her watch was in her reticule, which she had left in the landau. But no matter. Thomas Carver would simply have to wait for her. She could not leave until every last demon had been exorcised.

She needed to move, though. Rising, she shook out her cramped muscles and began to walk along the top of the hill. Sheep trundled out of her way as she passed, placidly turning their attention to a new patch of grass.

If nothing else, she thought, Greer had taught her the meaning of endurance. However much she longed to pack her few belongings and steal away one moonless night, to do so would have been to cast her integrity in the dust. Better to live with Greer than be unable to live with herself.

On the first anniversary of her disastrous marriage, which went unmarked except in her memory, she made up her mind to stay the course. She'd elected to shackle herself to this awful man, and somehow she must learn to deal with the horrifying consequences.

To begin with, her own attitude required mending. Her constant mood of sullen resentment only fueled her misery, and it was past time she stopped wallowing in self-pity.

In a hundred ways, she could be smarter than she had been.

Now that she had become familiar with Greer's peculiarities, it would not be all that difficult to winkle a few pleasures for herself.

Above all things, she longed for books. Not the ponderous scientific tomes in Greer's library, which he would not permit her to touch in any case, but stories of unfailing heroism and undying love. The next day, she began to scrimp on the meager funds allowed for running the household. Fortunately, Greer never cared what he ate, nor did he take notice of threadbare linens, or tallow candles instead of wax in the rooms he rarely visited.

Within two months she was able to purchase a tattered volume of Shakespeare's plays at a stall in the Kendal market, where she was occasionally permitted to shop for "female items." He even gave her a quarterly allowance—two shillings—although it clearly pained him to part with so vast a sum.

Over the years, book by book, she scraped together a tidy little collection. She also won permission to ride one of the sluggish carriage horses every afternoon for half an hour, and when Greer was particularly pleased with the results of one of his experiments, he could be persuaded to frank her letters. With no one to talk to, she had sought friends by correspondence, writing to people she read about in the newspaper. A handful, Dorothy Wordsworth among them, actually responded.

Always, she performed the tasks Greer assigned her without complaint, giving him no cause to withhold the few privileges she had been granted after she learned when and how to approach him with her requests. So long as it cost him no money or effort, he liked making a show of generosity.

For the most part, though, she lived in a world of her own creation, built from the stories she read voraciously in her tiny bedchamber at night. Come dawn, she transformed herself into Helen of Troy, or Isolde, or Guinevere. While the real Celia cooked and cleaned, Roland defended her honor in mortal combat. Lancelot stole into her bed.

And then, on a sunny Saturday morning in Kendal, she saw

a man emerge from the parish church and cast a radiant smile upon his gloriously beautiful bride.

Something inexplicable struck her to the heart at that moment. Standing there with her basket of turnips, she felt the earth begin to spin wildly under her feet. She'd had to grab hold of a lamppost to keep from flying off the planet, and was still clinging to it long minutes after the wedding party drove off.

From that day nothing was the same. Once seen, he was unforgettable. And while she never consciously intended to draw his image into her fantasies, every one of her heroes began to wear his face.

Worse, she found herself burning for one real experience to make her feel alive. She had gone from child to wife without knowing what it was to be a woman, and was to continue in ignorance for many more long years. But now she had a goal. If ever given the chance, she meant to have for herself a soul-stirring love affair to match the ones she lived in her imagination.

Celia realized that she had come to a stop near an outcropping of limestone. Her Crying Rock. Mercy, this was the last place she had meant to come today.

When even her imagination failed her, when her spirits were at their lowest ebb, she used to climb up here in the middle of the night and sit for hours, tears streaming down her face, trying to pray. She had always believed in a loving God, but sometimes thought He had forgot all about creating her. And when she gazed up at the stars, she could scarcely blame Him. What was she, after all, in the vastness of His universe?

At dawn, feeling more alone than ever, she had stumbled back to the farm and raked the coals of the kitchen fire. Another day, just like the one that preceded it and the one to follow, must be got through as best she could.

But at long last, she reminded herself, a few of her desperate prayers had been answered. A lowly speck of creation ought not be too greedy. She had even been granted a fleeting rendezvous with the man of her dreams, although she suspected that was only because the Lord understood she could not let him go until Kendal had firmly rejected her, in person and without a backward glance. When she could manage it, she would be grateful.

Meantime, she was here to reject Greer and put him behind her once and for all. She had honored every one of her vows, save the one about loving her husband, and had surely earned the right to be free of him.

But he'd not let her go. Even what he had *not* done came back to hurt her. She was still a virgin, and it seemed likely she would always be.

Perhaps, if she'd not seen Lord Kendal her very first night in London, she would have found another man to slake her urgent, unnameable longings. But she did see him. Her brief taste of him had spoiled her for anyone else. And she might have had him, too, if not for her husband's inadequacies.

"Damn you, Greer," she swore aloud. "You have done your worst. From this day forward, I refuse to give you power to hurt me."

A ewe nudged at her skirt, as if concerned for her. She stroked its woolly head, a smile curving her lips. Sheep had little appreciation for melodrama. "I'm all done now," she said, receiving a calm baa in reply as the ewe wandered off.

Celia made her way back to the road where Thomas was waiting, feeling a heavy burden lifting from her shoulders. She would sell the farm as soon as possible, severing the last ties with her former life.

Onward to the future, she told herself. Well, after one last visit to her past, because Lord Kendal was not so easily dispatched as her late, unlamented husband.

But she'd rid herself of him, too, perhaps within a few hours.

Thomas looked distinctly unhappy when she hove into view, skirts stained with grass and her bonnet askew. "I thought you'd gone lost," he said, assisting her into the landau.

"On my own farm? I was merely looking the place over, deciding what repairs to make before putting it up for sale." She located her watch and gasped to see the time. "Mercy me,

Thomas. I never meant to be gone so long. Can you get us all the way to Giggleswick in time for luncheon? The Wigglesworth sisters are expecting me."

Chapter 10

Nestled in the shade of two great chestnut trees, the lovely old graystone house conjured memories of the happiest year of her life. A lump in her throat, Celia took Thomas's hand and stepped from the landau, her gaze roaming from Wilfreda's hand-laced curtains billowing at the open windows to Wilberta's beloved flower garden. The heady scent of roses perfumed the air.

Her foot had scarcely touched ground when the door flew open and Bertie charged out, arms open in welcome. A few paces behind her, leaning heavily on her cane, Freda made her slow way along the gravel path, her wrinkled face wreathed in a smile.

"About time you got here," Bertie scolded, drawing Celia into a breathtaking hug. "We had just decided that we had got our days mixed up, and that you were meant to come tomorrow."

"Your letter said Friday," Freda put in, looking a bit confused. "This *is* Friday, isn't it?"

"Yes indeed," Celia assured her, turning to plant a kiss on her papery cheek. "I am very late, and it's all my fault. Bertie, will you direct Thomas to an establishment where he can see to the horses and have himself a good meal?"

"The Ribble Inn will be best, I think. Do you like salmon, young man?"

While Bertie spoke with Thomas, Celia took Freda's frail arm and assisted her into the house. Other memories flooded back as she stepped into the small foyer. There was the polished staircase she had ascended and descended with a book atop her head until Bertie pronounced her posture satisfactory. *A javelin in your spine, my girl, a javelin!* And there, the long passageway where she had practiced her gliding. *Smoothly. Smoothly. Ladies do not tromp about like common field hands.*

A plump ginger-colored cat ambled from the drawing room and twined around her ankles, purring huskily. She bent to scratch him behind the ears. "Hullo, Mincemeat. Have you missed me?"

"We all have, my dear," Freda said as a pair of identical white cats joined them, tails swishing languidly. "Pudding and Syllabub have been watching out the window all morning for you."

Watching for birds, more like, Celia thought, although they greeted her prettily enough. Stone-deaf and exceedingly spoiled, they wandered off in search of better entertainment the moment she stopped petting them.

Celia placed her reticule on a pier table and untied the ribbons of her bonnet. "I hope you haven't gone to a great deal of trouble, Freda. It was rude of me to descend on such short notice, but I was so longing to see you."

"None of that!" Bertie swept through the door and took the bonnet from her hand. "This is your home. I expect you'll want to freshen up, so take yourself upstairs while I help Mrs. Twill put the finishing touches on our luncheon. She has prepared all your favorites."

A few minutes later Celia joined Freda and Bertie in the small dining room. They had brought out their best china, and the elaborately ornamental silverware was polished to a blinding sheen. One of Freda's embroidered cloths, neatly ironed, graced the small cherrywood table, and the napkins had been folded into the shape of a peacock's tail.

Mrs. Twill bustled in from the kitchen with a tureen of beef barley soup, lingering until Celia had tasted it and rewarded her with a smile. Acknowledged as the finest cook in Giggleswick for the past several decades, Mrs. Twill disdained compliments, considering them redundant.

The visit to Greer's farm had dampened Celia's appetite. She sampled every dish, and there were a great many of them, but was relieved when Mrs. Twill finally retired to her kitchen and she need no longer pretend to eat. Moreover, although they were far too polite to say so, Bertie and Freda were eagerly awaiting an account of her London debut.

Celia put down her fork and began to dish up every snippet of gossip she could recall. Eyes gleaming, the ladies leaned forward in their chairs as she described Marshal Blücher galloping through a mazurka, the wall-eyed Prussian king weighed down with all his medals, and the thousands of common citizens who milled around the Pulteney Hotel day and night in hopes of catching the merest glimpse of Czar Alexander.

She told them about the Ascot races, and the Sunday-afternoon procession in Hyde Park, and the *bal masqué* at Burlington House where she had gone costumed as a shepherdess, only to find scores of shepherdesses in attendance. Fortunately, only one of them had brought an actual sheep, which was soon hustled off to the mews.

She spoke of banquets and balls, routs and musicales, and the scandalous new waltz. Bertie and Freda listened avidly, nodding and smiling, their own forks long since set aside. But as one story followed another, Celia was put in mind of Lord Kendal entertaining her in similar fashion as they drove together to the White Swan. Mercy, would not the man leave her in peace!

"Did you meet the king?" Freda asked in a trembling voice when Celia paused to sip from her water glass.

Bertie shot Celia a meaningful look, and she remembered that Freda had not been informed of the king's madness. It would have overset her to learn of it.

"I believe he remained in residence at Windsor during the victory celebrations," Celia replied. "After all, *someone* had to see to the running of the country, and His Majesty has ever been a dutiful sovereign."

"So he has," Freda affirmed. "So he has. I do wish you had been presented to him, though. He spoke very kindly to me when I made my curtsy not so long ago."

Celia and Bertie exchanged smiles. Freda's recollections of her London Season were gilded by time, wishful thinking, and her own uncertain memory.

After lunch, the ladies withdrew to the parlor for another round of stories. With Mincemeat curled on her lap, purring blissfully, Celia gave a highly censored version of her own minor successes among the beau monde. Above all things, the Wigglesworth sisters longed for assurance that their protégée had made a great splash in society, so she told them what they wanted to hear.

She had become rather adept at skating around the truth, Celia realized with some degree of pride. Not once had she mentioned Lord Kendal, although he had been at the center of every significant moment of her London adventure.

It was not long before Freda's eyes drifted shut and her chin sank onto her lace-edged fichu. Soon a gentle snore vibrated in chorus with Mincemeat's rumbling purr.

Bertie rose. "I have promised the vicar to send a bouquet of roses over to the rectory," she whispered. "Let us continue our visit in the garden."

Freda popped awake with a loud snort. "Visit? But whom are we to visit, Wilberta? I am not properly dressed to pay a call."

"Never mind, my love," Bertie soothed. "It's not until tomorrow. We'll have plenty of time to select our gowns."

Within seconds Freda had dozed off again.

"My sister is not in good health," Bertie confided as they emerged from the garden shed, where they had stopped to procure clippers and a large open-weave basket. "Dr. Ramp has warned me to prepare for a sad day within the year. Poor, gentle Freda. How I shall go on without her, I cannot imagine."

"Surely something can be done," Celia protested. "Another doctor, perhaps, or a change of air . . . ?"

"It is her heart, Celia. And her constitution has always been weak, you know. Our one season all but brought her down, and I never dared permit another. It is a credit to her indomitable spirit that she has gone on so well these many years. She'll wish to die in this house, where she was born, and I shall hold her when she breathes her last. But let us turn the subject before I become weepy."

"Yes, in a moment, but first I must know about your own health."

Bertie selected a lush white rose and snipped the stem. "I'm hale as a draft horse, glory be, and mean to see more of the world before I stick my spoon in the wall. At the very least, I shall bid farewell to Giggleswick when Freda has passed into heaven. Too many memories, you understand. A surfeit of memories never fails to clog one's mind."

How very true, Celia reflected. "Perhaps you'll move into my new house, which would delight me enormously. Mind you, I've not yet decided where to put down roots. What think you of Bowness?"

"You don't mean to return to London?" Bertie frowned. "But you have had your heart set on London since you were a child. Was it such a trying experience, my dear?"

"Mercy me, quite the contrary. I enjoyed myself immensely. Were you not listening for the past two hours?"

"Oh, indeed. But what you failed to say spoke even more pointedly." With a sigh, Bertie placed a rose in the basket. "Forgive me, Celia. I'm an old busybody. One whiff of a secret and I cannot help but snoop it out like a pig nosing for truffles."

Celia brushed her finger over the furry petals of the rose. "You are right, of course. Something did happen, and I wish to tell you about it. But I fear you will be terribly shocked."

"I very much doubt it. Freda is the one pulls out her hartshorn at the slightest hint of scandalbroth. Did you embroil yourself in a scandal, Celia?"

"Not precisely." She dug the toe of her half boot into the gravel. "I threw myself at a gentleman, and he threw me back. It seems I was too small a fish for his supper."

"Mmm."

When Bertie moved to the next rosebush without further comment, Celia stomped after her. This was Kendal's trick, leaving a silence to be filled. "Is that all you have to say? *Mmm?* It was probably the most devastating experience of my entire life."

"More so than accepting Greer?" Bertie lifted a brow. "That *does* shock me. In any event, I cannot help but dislike a man who fails to recognize a diamond when it drops into his hands. Or flings itself there, as you say that you did."

"Oh, it's quite true. Sometimes foolishly, more often shamelessly, I did everything possible to secure his attention. But it was not simply because he is remarkably handsome and uncommonly charming. As it happens, I had seen him before, many years ago. And when I did, something extraordinary happened."

She nibbled at the inside of her lower lip, casting about for words to describe the experience. "It was as if the ground dropped from under my feet, Bertie. Or perhaps I went airborne. And all the while I felt . . . well, as if my whole body, hair to toenails, had gone on fire. The sensation was quite overwhelming."

"Mmm."

Easy for *her* to say, Celia thought dourly. "In any case, by the time I came back to earth, he was gone. And later I realized that my odd flight of fancy was propelled by an explosion of envy. It put me forcibly in mind of my own woeful marriage to Greer, the sight of so splendid a gentleman gazing with unconcealed love at his new bride."

Bertie dropped the clippers and spun around. "Never tell me you have been speaking all this time of a married man! Oh, my. I am severely disappointed in you, Celia. An affair between two individuals free to indulge their passions is one thing, but adultery quite another."

Celia took a step backward, nearly falling over a low hedge. "Mercy, no! The gentleman is a widower now. Some three or four years after the wedding, his wife died of a fever. I read a notice of it in the newspaper."

With a stricken look, Bertie held out her hands. "Oh, my dear, I beg your pardon. It was inexcusable of me to leap to so absurd a conclusion."

Smiling, Celia picked up the clippers. "Clearly I have been a bad influence on you, Wilberta Wigglesworth. Impulsive leaps have always been *my* specialty. And the misunderstanding is purely my fault, for giving you this tale in so disordered a fashion."

When the light had returned to Bertie's eyes, Celia handed her the clippers. "I am terribly confused, you see. I had hoped that speaking of what happened would help me regain some bit of perspective. Not that I ever had the least particle of it before, to be sure. But since this is my day for banishing ghosts, I should like to tell you the rest."

Some of it, anyway, Celia reflected as Bertie nodded and moved on to the next rosebush. She would take to her grave the secret of her romantic fantasies about Lord Kendal, which would only sound ridiculous if spoken aloud.

She watched Mincemeat pad to the shade of a chestnut tree, belly rounded with the leftovers from lunch Mrs. Twill must have served him, and settle down to groom himself. Life was so simple for a lazy house cat—eat, sleep, and be made much of. Mincemeat probably wouldn't recognize a mouse if it bit him on the nose.

"Go on, child," Bertie urged softly.

"I was trying to remember where I'd left off. But no matter. Onward to London, where by sheerest chance, I encountered the gentleman in question the very first day I arrived. It was, I imagined at the time, a sign from heaven." Aware that her cheeks were flaming, Celia was glad that Bertie had gone back to clipping roses. "Pray don't ask me to explain what happened next, but it was the second most mortifying experience of my life. Suffice it to say I made a cake of myself."

"Well, I daresay you did not permit one setback to deter you."

"I'm afraid not. On any number of occasions I spotted him at a social event, but he was careful to keep his distance. And when I pursued him, he always managed to evade me."

Bertie turned to place a handful of roses in the basket. "You finally chased him down, I presume?"

"Not exactly. You recall that Lady Marjory had invited me to stay with her if ever I visited London? Poor thing. I doubt she even remembered knowing my mother at school, and greatly hoped I would never show up. In any event, unaware that the gentleman and I had already met under somewhat unusual circumstances, she presented me to him. Lord Ke— the gentleman, that is, must have felt obliged to ask me to dance. And a few days later he invited me to join him for a drive in the country."

"I see."

"Do you? It came as a great surprise to me. Naturally I leapt at the chance to be with him, and—oh, mercy. How can I explain the rest?" Celia glanced over at Mincemeat, now snoozing blissfully on his back with all four paws in the air. "I w-wanted him," she confessed. "To be precise, I wished—"

"To have him in your bed," Bertie said succinctly. "You needn't be ashamed to say so, at least to me. It is perfectly natural, my dear, and in my opinion, very wise of you. What better way to purge your revolting memories of Lord Greer?"

"Is that what I was trying to do?" Celia's fingers tightened on the straw basket. Bertie knew of Greer's inability to consummate the marriage, of course. Celia had blurted the tale one evening after too many helpings of elderberry wine. "Well, perhaps you are right," she said. "Whatever the reason, I assuredly went to London in search of a glorious love affair. And for a few hours, Bertie, I thought I'd found it. But when he discovered I was not the worldly woman I pretended to be, he threw me off in a flash."

Bertie turned, a militant glint in her eyes. "After making love to you? The cad! Was he resentful to find that he had broached a virgin?"

"He was not to blame, you know. And besides, things had not progressed to the point of . . . broaching when I told him precisely what to expect. Well, I might as well have told him I was a leper. Next I knew, he had charged out of the room.

"I'd no idea what to do, so I sat down and waited for something to happen. It was probably no more than half an hour before he came back again, but it felt like years. And he was frightfully angry. Cold at first, and excessively proper, which is how he tries to present himself, but very soon he was raging at me."

"I trust you raged right back!"

Bertie's shrill cry must have roused Mincemeat, because he trotted up with an expression of catly concern on his pudgy face.

Grateful for a warm body to cuddle, Celia set down the

basket and lifted him into her arms. "For my sins, Bertie, yes. I was the veriest shrew. And that should have been an end to it. He arranged for a carriage to take me back to London, and I've not seen him since. But I cannot seem to put him from my mind. Had all this happened with any other man, I daresay this would score up as only one more example of folly on my part. But you see, it was *him*."

"The gentleman who pulled the ground from beneath your feet. Yes, I do understand. Are you in love with him, Celia?"

Love? Mercy! It did not bear thinking of.

"How would I know?" she asked reasonably. "I am seven-and-twenty, and the only love I experienced in all those years came from you and Freda. Well, and Mincemeat, but he loves anyone who will pet him."

"Don't be missish, child. You understand the question."

"Yes. I just can't think how to answer it. Is it possible to love a man after only a few hours in his company?"

"One can fall in love in the space between heartbeats, my dear."

"Oh."

"I once did, you know." Bertie laughed. "You needn't look so surprised. I was not always a shriveled old prune, and during my London Season, more than one gentleman professed himself head over ears in love with me. They were nothing of the sort, you may be sure, but in those days flirtation was a high art and we all played at it with far more skill than sensibility. There was one gentleman, though, a quiet young man who caught my eye. And at that very moment, I knew I was in love with him."

Enthralled, Celia regarded her closest friend with awe. Bertie Wigglesworth in love! It must have come to nothing, since she had returned home to live as a spinster all these years, but Celia heard no bitterness in her voice. Quite the contrary. Whatever happened between them had left a treasured memory. "May I ask how you could be so certain it was love, Bertie?"

"One simply knows. Mind you, I speak only of love at first sight, which is exceedingly rare. Most poor souls are not so favored, and they must wrestle with their confused emotions until the truth becomes clear to them. But Henry and I knew before a word had passed between us that our hearts were one."

Bertie selected a rose from the basket and brushed the petals against her crinkled cheek. "I am sorry to say that love stories do not invariably draw to a happy conclusion. His family refused to approve the match, and he was never a strong-willed man. It was a difficult time for everyone. I might have persuaded him to settle for love in a cottage, had I persisted, but Lord Henry was accustomed to wealth and privilege. At the end of the day, he would have regretted leaving it all behind."

"He should have done!" Celia declared. Startled at the sudden outburst, Mincemeat sprang from her arms. "You said he *loved* you."

"I am certain that he did. But we do not always love wisely, Celia. And some cannot bring themselves to make great sacrifices, even for what they most want in the world. You must not be sorry on my account. I willingly let him go, after all. And it had become apparent that Freda required me to tend to her, which would have been yet another burden for Henry to accept. He eventually wed the young woman chosen by his parents, and died some ten years ago."

Celia was amazed at how breezily Bertie was able to dismiss her one grand passion. No, more than that. The love of her life. Of course, she'd had fifty years to come to terms with her loss, but still . . .

"Forgive an old woman her reminiscences, my dear. It was not my intention to lower your spirits. Indeed, I cannot think why I began this story, unless it was to demonstrate that love often takes us by surprise, and sometimes requires more of us than we can give. I have never pined for Henry, and while it may appear to have been remarkably dull, I count my life a happy one."

She smiled. "And there, Celia, is the point. However difficult the course, it is always a good thing to love. And should you never complete the race, it remains a good thing to have loved, even for the briefest moment."

With a strangled sound, Celia wrapped her arms around the old woman, crushing the rose between their bodies. A thorn dug into her shoulder, but she scarcely felt it. "Thank you," she murmured. "I will think on what you have said. It will help me understand what is troubling me, I believe, once I have untangled the knots in my head."

Bertie wriggled free, brushing at her skirts. "Is understanding all you are after, child? I would not have expected you to give up on your gentleman so easily. Or have I mistaken the matter? Was he only trifling with your affections?"

Celia took a moment to sort out the questions. "Yes, at this point, understanding is the most I can hope for. He was always beyond my reach, Bertie. I knew that from the start. For all my foolish imaginings and reckless behavior, not once did I mistake his attentions for more than they were. His affections were never involved, nor did he pretend otherwise."

"Mmm."

"Oh, do stop *mmming* at me," Celia said, laughing as she picked up the basket of roses. "There is not the remotest chance that love played any part in the decidedly bizarre little drama we played out together on a summer afternoon."

"And if you are wrong about that?"

"Then you have heard the beginning of yet another love story that cannot possibly come to a happy ending. Be sure I do not mean to go into a decline, Bertie. And be even surer that I will never again go in pursuit of a man who does not want me. Especially *that* one."

"We'll see," Bertie said, taking her arm. "For now, can I persuade you to stay the night? After such a long journey, it would be a pity to leave us so soon."

"Really, I must go back today. At the market tomorrow in Kendal, I plan to buy myself a horse. Thomas is doing his best, of course, but he was not cut out to be a coachman and I require some other means of getting around. What's more, if I am to keep him in my service, I must locate a house and hire on a staff as soon as possible."

"I understand, my dear. Promise that you will visit us again as soon as may be."

"You know that I will, Bertie. And I shall write you every

101

day with word of my progress. Shall we wake Freda so that I can say good-bye, or is it better to let her sleep?"

"Of course you must make your farewell, wretched girl! Then I shall walk you to the Ribble Inn and give strict instructions to that nice young man regarding his duty to look after you. I cannot like the notion of you riding about on your own like a hoyden."

"Widows do not require chaperons these days, you know. Allow me a bit of freedom, Bertie. Surely I have earned it."

"Yes indeed. But you have not proven yourself able to control your wilder impulses, Celia. I greatly fear you will soon dive into trouble again."

"Not I!" Celia protested with a laugh. So long as she steered clear of Lord Kendal, what sort of trouble could she possibly find?

Chapter 11

Celia took another carrot from the bucket and offered it to the mare, laughing as the horse's lips tickled her palm. "Well, Thomas, what think you? Shall I buy her?"

He set down the bucket and passed her a clean white handkerchief. "Seems to like you well enough, she does. But more than that I cannot say, not knowing much about the beasties."

"Nor do I," she said, remembering the sad creatures she had ridden on Greer's farm. Wanting a good horse and knowing how to choose one were quite different matters. Mr. Rollins had practically sung an oratorio in praise of the mare, but since he'd come to the Kendal market to find a buyer, he could not be considered a disinterested party.

Love at first sight led only to folly, she reminded herself. And the white mare's show of affection was more for the carrots than for the strange female who fed them to her. Was Celia Greer so desperate for a friend, even a four-legged one, that she'd overlook any flaw so long as the creature *liked* her?

Mr. Rollins, who had left her alone to make her decision, waddled back across the paddock with an apologetic smile. "Pardon me, milady. I don't mean to rush you. But it happens a gentleman is taken with the mare and wishes to examine her. I told him you had the prior claim, but he is most insistent."

"Don't believe him," said a voice at her ear. "It's a humbug."

Startled, Celia looked up at a handsome, smiling face. A pair of amused sky-blue eyes gazed back at her with open admiration.

"There is no anxious buyer competing for the horse, I

promise you. Only a shill, paid to diddle you into reaching a hasty verdict."

"Oh." She glanced at Mr. Rollins, whose face had gone beet red.

"No insult intended, ma'am. Just business, you understand. I'll take meself off while you decide about the mare."

Celia smiled at the blond gentleman. "Thank you, I think. I had really meant to buy her. Is there some reason I should not?"

"She appears sound enough," he said. "But I'll take a closer look."

To Celia's astonishment, he vaulted gracefully over the fence and began to run his hands over the mare, an intent expression on his mobile face. Seeming to enjoy the attention, the horse made no fuss when he examined her hooves, ears, and mouth.

The man was about her own age, Celia decided, tall and rangy, with a pair of broad shoulders under his white shirt and brown leather waistcoat. She straightaway imagined him standing on the prow of a ship, but of course, she invariably cast every handsome man she saw into one of her absurd fantasies. This one would make an exceptionally fine pirate, she decided. Or perhaps a highwayman.

"You're a seductive wench," he said, "and a bit of a tease."

For the briefest moment Celia thought he was talking to her. But he scratched the mare affectionately behind the ears and moved to the fence, folding his arms across the top rail.

"Were she up to my weight, I'd buy her myself. How much is Rollins asking?"

When Celia told him, he whistled. "Extortion. Offer him half and stand firm."

"But what if he says no?" Now certain the horse was a prime goer, she could not bear to lose her.

"Oh, he'll take the deal. Tell you what. I'll handle the negotiation if you'll watch the brat for a few minutes."

At his gesture, Celia turned and saw a boy standing a few feet away, so immobile that it was no wonder she had failed to notice him. His enormous dark eyes were fixed on the mare with unmistakable adoration.

Knowing little about children, she could not guess his age. Six or seven, perhaps? A cap of black hair was neatly clipped, and he was dressed as formally as any aristocrat she had ever met outside a ballroom. His dark blue jacket was flawlessly tailored, his thin legs were encased in nankeen trousers, and starched shirt points reached nearly to his ears. All this finery for a country market? Poor child. Her heart went out to him.

"Charley, come make your bow to the lady," said the pirate. "I need to see a man about a horse."

Celia heard him leave, his boot heels crunching on the packed dirt in the paddock, but could not wrench her attention from the solemn little boy. He approached her slowly, his posture straight, his arms and small hands rigid as fence posts.

He bowed. "Lord Paxton, ma'am. At your service."

Oh dear. Unsure how to deal with this exceedingly proper young lordling, Celia curtsied. "I am pleased to make your acquaintance, my lord. My name is Cel . . . er, Lady Greer."

"Honored." His face was expressionless, shaped in marble, but his gaze had strayed again to the mare.

Celia studied his coffee-brown eyes, flaming with barely restrained longing under their long, sooty lashes. She had met him before, she thought suddenly. Not this boy, but someone so like him that the marrow in her bones tingled with recognition.

Or perhaps she saw only a reflection of herself, churning with a passion for life that clamored for release.

In any case, she knew this child. Soul-deep, she felt kin to him.

Meantime he was feeling kinship with the horse. "There is one last carrot in this bucket," she said, plucking it from the small pail Mr. Rollins had given her. "Would you care to feed it to the mare?"

His eyes widened. "Oh, yes," he said eagerly. "Will she bite me, do you think?"

The adventure of being chomped by a horse rather appealed to him, she thought. "Well, it's a dangerous business, to be sure. All depends on whether or not she likes the smell of you. Come closer and give her a whiff."

Haltingly at first, and then in a rush, he came directly up to the mare. She obliged by poking at his narrow shoulder with her muzzle.

"I think she likes you," Celia said, giving him the carrot. "Lay this on the palm of your hand and hold it out where she can reach it."

She might as well have offered him the moon. Trembling slightly, he followed her instructions. She could sense him pleading silently with the horse to take the carrot from his hand.

He needn't have worried. After a graceful toss of her head, the mare nibbled at the carrot for a moment and then gobbled it up.

"She did it," the boy cried, jumping with glee. "Did you see?"

"My, yes. And you gave her the carrot in just the right way. Well done."

He beamed with pride. "I never fed a horse before. It was fun."

Celia had to clasp her hands behind her back to keep from hugging him. At this moment she'd have spent half her fortune to buy the horse and the other half to stock up on carrots, merely to see that heartbreaking smile again.

She suspected that young Lord Paxton did not smile very often.

"You, madam, have just bought yourself a horse."

Celia looked up to see the blond gentleman approaching her with an athletic stride. "Did you save me any money?" she asked, grinning. He looked very full of himself.

"A mere four hundred pounds." With careless agility, he leapt over the fence and swept her a theatrical bow. "I begin to think I am in the wrong business. Clearly I have a native talent for horse trading."

"You have certainly convinced *me*," she replied. Until recently, four hundred pounds had been as far beyond her reach as the Milky Way. The fact that such a sum now made scarcely a ripple in her fortune did not alter her appreciation in the slightest. She had spent most of her life scrimping and saving, and had hesitated that very morning to buy herself a three-penny packet of spicy gingerbread. It had seemed too great a luxury, spending such a vast sum for a few moments of self-indulgence. She bought it anyway, gave half to Thomas, and felt guilty as she ate her share.

She realized that the gentleman was regarding her curiously. Or perhaps expectantly. Ought she to offer him a reward? Although his son was rigged out in fine broadcloth and impeccable linens, his own shirt had seen a few too many washings and his boots were scuffed and well-worn. Most odd. Perhaps she had mistaken the situation. For all she knew, he was a servant, or possibly the boy's tutor.

"Most assuredly I owe you a commission, sir, for striking such a bargain. Tell me what is fair in these circumstances."

He rubbed his forehead in a dramatic fashion. "Ah, I have it! Glasses of lemonade all around, and you pay the shot. Agreed?"

"Certainly. What more?"

He cast her a rueful smile. "Fact is, you could meet me ninety-nine times of a hundred and I'd jump at the chance to fill my pockets. But this is definitely your lucky day all 'round, because I happen to be solvent, with a bit to spare."

"He's going to buy me a pony," Lord Paxton piped up.

The man ruffled the child's hair affectionately. "I haven't forgot, brat. But we won't settle for just any pony. You want a real goer. Now, do you recall where we saw that booth with the lemonade?"

Remembering his manners, Lord Paxton bowed. "It's near to where we saw the puppies."

"Lead the way, then. And don't run off."

As if he would, Celia thought, watching the boy steer a path through the crowded marketplace with frightening dignity.

"Scary, isn't it?" the man said, as if reading her mind. He held out his arm. "My name is Kit, by the way."

It was impossible to stand on ceremony with him. "Celia," she said, resting her hand on his forearm. "And yes, he is astonishingly poised."

"Poor chap. Between his tutor, who was spawned in the Middle Ages, and the Nanny from Hades, he doesn't have a chance. Well, you can see for yourself. They are turning him into a machine."

"If you disapprove, why don't you dismiss them both?"

"Would that I could. It's all I can do to keep from strangling them." He inclined his head. "I have nothing to say in the matter, you know. And I'm the last one anyone would listen to. The steward admits me to the house because he must, but with very ill grace. As my lofty brother would put it, I am persona non grata."

"Forgive me." Heat rose to her cheeks. "I didn't mean to pry. I had assumed you were Lord Paxton's father."

"Only his uncle, I'm afraid. Widely known as the Black Sheep. Usually worse, truth be told, but some words are not fit for a lady's ears."

There was nothing remotely sheeplike about him. But her first instincts must have been on target, for he was most assuredly a rogue and wholly unrepentant about it. She liked him enormously.

He led her through the tangled crowd, following Lord Paxton's stiff back. "I am about to let him down, and cannot think how to break the news. There are no ponies to be had. Well, only a pair of demoralized nags hired out to give rides to the children at a penny a pop. The mare you bought is the only decent piece of horseflesh at the market."

"That is surely not your fault."

"Oh, but it is. I raised his hopes, you see, and now I cannot fulfill them. Thing is, I should have known better. The Kendal market is no place to look for horses, and I don't expect I can interest him in a sheep."

Despite his light tone, Celia could tell he was truly distressed. "If you explain the circumstances, I'm certain he'll understand."

"Oh, aye. He's well trained to swallow misfortune without choking, poor lad. If disappointments were golden guineas, Charley would be rich as Croesus."

The boy had come to a stop in front of a stall selling lemonade and cheese pies. He waited like a sentry, arms straight at his sides, regarding their approach with stern indifference.

"Lady Greer? Did you wish me to see to the horse?"

"Mercy!" Letting go of Kit's arm, she spun around. "Thomas, I'd forgot all about you. And I expect Mr. Rollins wishes me to make an accounting. I'll need to acquire a bank draft, and—"

"I told Rollins you would settle with him next week," Kit interjected. "It wouldn't do to pay up before you've put the mare through her paces. You can take her with you today, of course."

"He'll let me take the horse without paying? But he's never seen me before. How does he know I won't simply make off with her?"

"I've given my word," Kit said gently. "Not that it carries much weight, to be sure, but Rollins knows he can dun my brother if you fail to honor your debt. The family has a bit of influence in these parts, my own reputation notwithstanding."

Flustered, Celia introduced Thomas Carver and realized too late that servants were not supposed to be presented to gentlemen, even gentlemen of the black-sheep persuasion. But Kit, smiling broadly, shook Thomas's hand as though they were meeting on level ground.

Thomas, his face a startling shade of purple, stepped back and bowed. "I am Lady Greer's footman, sir."

"My butler," she corrected immediately. "Not that I have a house yet, but when I do, he will be in charge of it."

Since that news came as a complete surprise to Thomas, his mouth dropped open.

"Unless you decide to return to London," she added quickly, "but I hope you will not."

"N-no, my lady. I'll be proud to serve you in whatever position you choose to place me."

"Well then, that's settled," Kit said briskly. "What say we toast your promotion with some lemonade? And after that, I suggest you claim the horse from Mr. Rollins and transfer her to—" He turned to Celia. "Since you have no house, where are you staying?"

Thomas had regathered his poise. "Thank you, sir. I'll see to

109

the horse now, and wait for her ladyship where we left the carriage." With a bow, he took himself off.

"An impressive young man," Kit observed. "And probably the youngest butler in England."

"He's been a godsend," Celia said simply. "Without him, I don't know what I'd have done these last few days."

Kit wagged a finger at her. "You've been holding out on me, *Lady* Celia Greer. And that name is familiar, for some reason. Have you family in Westmoreland?"

"My late husband had a farm not far from here. But he was somewhat reclusive, so we rarely went into Society." To deflect any more questions about her identity, she waggled her own finger at Kit. "Speaking of holding out, I expect you are actually Lord Something-or-Other."

"Dear me no!" he protested. "Merely a younger son, of no distinction whatever. But had we been formally introduced, not that I ever go where formalities are observed, you would have met the Honorable—and I use the term loosely—Christopher Valliant."

Celia's knees turned to butter. Oh mercy!

"I gather you have heard something of my sorry reputation," he said, his face drained of color. "That is unfortunate. I had hoped we could be friends."

"Y-yes. Certainly." She waved her hands. "I mean, of course we can be friends. I should like that above all things. And I've heard nothing about you at all. Well, nothing to the point. You may have been mentioned to me in passing."

His head tilted. "Then what has overset you, Lady Greer?"

"Oh, do call me Celia. And I'm not in the least overset." A bouncer of the first order, she thought, struggling to reclaim her wits. "You simply took me by surprise. The thing is, I believe I am acquainted with your brother."

"Indeed? I presume you mean James—Lord Kendal—since Alex has not been in England for several years. Actually, neither has James, come to think of it. Last I heard, he was in Prussia."

"He returned to London for the victory celebrations, or so I believe. In all that crush, there was little opportunity to speak

110

with anyone for more than a few minutes, but I recall meeting him on one or two occasions. He was exceedingly . . . polite."

"He would be," Kit said dryly.

Realizing that she was wringing her hands, Celia lowered them to her sides. Lord Paxton—Charley—was Kendal's son! She had not known he had a child. Heaven knew he had never spoken of the boy. And while she used to scour the newspapers for any mention of Lord Kendal, Greer generally took the papers off to line his chicken cages before she got her hands on them.

That sweet, starched, highly proper young boy was Kendal's son. Oh my. She turned back to the lemonade stand, heart in her throat, to look at him.

He wasn't there.

Kit realized he was gone at about the same moment. "Lucifer," he swore under his breath. "Where's the brat got off to?"

Celia clutched at his sleeve. "He said something about puppies—"

"Right! Good girl. They were—damn. I can't remember." Taking her hand, Kit led her around the lemonade stall, past a cart filled with turnips and cabbages, and by a small tent spangled with moons and stars. "Fortune-teller," he said. "We came in from this direction." He turned, orienting himself, and tugged her back to where they started.

Just beyond the lemonade seller and a flower booth, Celia saw a high-wheeled wagon heaped with hay. Underneath, on a mound of straw, Lord Paxton sat cross-legged inside a small makeshift pen with a dozen black-and-white puppies swarming over him, yipping for attention.

"Thank God," Kit murmured, squeezing her hand.

When he started to move closer, Celia held him back. Together, they watched Charley giggle happily as puppies clambered over his small body and lapped at his face.

"Kit," she said softly, "a puppy isn't exactly a pony, but—"

"Ah. A supremely good idea, and bless you for thinking of it. Truth be told, I'm not exactly partial to dogs, not even little ones. There haven't been any at Candale since I was a boy." He winced. "It seems that is about to change."

Celia remembered that Kendal had mentioned a younger brother being spooked by a dog. "Shall I help him select one to take home? Are you certain the puppy will be welcome there?"

"Nanny Yallop will have a fit, and Tommy the Tutor will draft letters of protest to Kendal, which will never be read, if I know my brother. Other than that, no problems to speak of."

"I was referring to *you*, Kit. If you hate dogs—"

"Don't hate 'em! They just scare me senseless. But I'll get over it. Besides, I'm rarely in residence at Candale. The mutt will have to find something else to chew on. Do me a favor, though, and extricate Charley from the herd. Tell him he may choose one, and one only, for his special pet. And while you're at it, mention that the pup will require his full attention for a week or two. That will give me time to chase down a pony."

The Valliant men, Celia thought with some amusement, were expert at shifting responsibility when it suited them. Nodding, she went to join Charley inside the puppy pen.

A rotund woman sat on a three-legged stool in the shade of the hay wagon, Mama Dog sprawled at her feet, both observing the scene with mild interest. "You want a puppy, ma'am? Only half a crown. They be weaned and healthy."

"Thank you," Celia replied, sinking next to Charley on the straw. Immediately, five or six puppies swarmed into her lap. "What think you, Lord Paxton? Kit says you can choose a pup to take home with you, but only if you really, really want one."

His eyes shone. "Oh, I do. Really, *really*. Cross my heart."

It took him a long time to make his decision. While they waited Kit brought lemonade for everyone, including the woman who owned the dogs, and stood at a careful distance with his shoulder propped against the wagon as Charley fell in love with one puppy after another.

"Them's sheep collies," the woman said. "Got any sheep?"

"A few thousand," Kit replied, tossing her a coin. "If you have any dogs left at next Saturday's market, the estate manager may want to have a look at them."

"This one!" Charley finally proclaimed, lifting a wriggling

ball of fur in his hands. Scrambling from the pen, he held the pup to Kit. "Is it a boy or a girl?"

Kit examined the dog's backside. "Boy. He'll need a name, so start thinking about it while I speak with Lady Greer."

Brushing straw from her skirts, Celia emerged from under the wagon. "You may wish to keep your distance, Kit. Charley and I will be smelling of more than hay and fur until we have our baths. But wasn't it wonderful to see him so happy?"

"More than I can find words for," he said. "The puppy was only part of it, you know. Half the time he was looking at you. Will you come visit him at Candale, Celia? It's all I can do to pry him from his tutor's clutches, and a guest will give me an excuse to take him from the schoolroom." He gave her a pleading, slightly lopsided smile. "Please?"

Suspecting that Kit Valliant generally got what he wanted sooner or later, Celia swallowed her objections. Lord Kendal would not be pleased to know she was running tame on his estate, but then, he had not even bothered to tell his family that he was back in England. More than likely he would never know she had become acquainted with his brother and his son.

"I would love to pay a call on Lord Paxton," she said. "For the time being, I am in residence at the Merry Goosegirl. Send word there when it is convenient for me to come."

"You'll not escape so easily, Celia. Charley and I will walk you to where your butler is waiting, and on the way we'll settle on a time for your visit tomorrow afternoon. Unless you care to join us for church services in the morning? We could have breakfast after and plan a day in the country. Even Charley is not expected to ply his books on Sunday."

Deeper and deeper, Celia thought. Ever deeper into trouble. "What hour are services?"

Kit planted a kiss on her cheek. "I adore you! Ten o'clock, St. Peter's, and we'll meet you in the vestibule."

The very church where she had first seen Lord Kendal. Oh mercy! But while she was there, perhaps she could persuade the Lord, the true Lord, to extricate her gently from her latest folly.

She absolutely must not become entangled with the Valliant

family. Above all things, she could not let this sweet little boy get caught up in a disaster of her making. Tomorrow she would pray for help in detaching herself from her new friends without causing pain. And until it was accomplished, she hoped Lord Kendal would keep himself far, far away.

Chapter 12

Three days in Bath playing nursemaid to Marshall Blücher, bluffly charming as he was, had done nothing to improve Kendal's dark mood. He arrived at his town house in St. James's Square well after dark, looking forward to a few hours with a brandy bottle, only to find an urgent message from Lord Finlay.

Matters of importance, were they? Kendal scribbled a reply and dispatched it with a footman. If Finlay wanted to speak with him, he could damn well come here to do it.

Kendal had been traveling half the day. He refused to climb into another coach, even for the short trip to Curzon Street, and his reasons had absolutely nothing to do with Lady Greer.

True, he'd been glad of the Bath assignment, which allowed him to escape London—and her—for a few days. But now that he was back, they were bound to meet sooner or later. Not tonight, though, at Finlay's house. She might be out for the evening, but then again, she might not.

Reminding himself not to think about her, which was proving surprisingly difficult for a man accustomed to ordering his thoughts, he washed up, changed into shirt, trousers, and a brocade robe, and waited for Finlay in the library. The sooner this was done with, the sooner he could find out if an excess of brandy would permit him to sleep. Nothing else seemed to work.

When the butler showed him in, Finlay went straight to the sideboard and poured himself a hefty drink. "I'm in a foul mood, James. You'd better have a devilish good excuse for dragging me here."

"None to speak of." Kendal held out his own glass for a refill. "And if you recall, it was you who called this midnight meeting. I merely changed the location."

"Well, no matter. Marjory wasn't sorry to get me out of the house, I can tell you. I've been snapping at everybody today."

"She is returned from Maidstone, then? I trust her sister has recovered."

"Yes, yes. Dicey for a time, and Marjory is worn to a nub, but that particular crisis has passed." Finlay dropped onto a wingback chair with a groan. "Needless to say, there are any number of others queued up to take its place. Heard anything about the Gaverton affair?"

"Gaverton? Good Lord, what's he to do with the Foreign Office?"

"Not a thing. You've met the man. A mushroom with more money than wits, but that can be a dangerous combination. Last night, he hosted a supper party at the Clarendon. Called it a 'salute to the generals,' can you believe! No one of any importance turned up, but Gaverton managed to assemble a few second-rate peacocks, mostly Austrian and Prussian. Every last one of them thinks he won the war single-handedly, of course."

"Let them squabble," Kendal said indifferently. "They've been doing so since the crossing from Boulogne. What of it?"

"This is secondhand information, mind you, but it comes from several reliable sources. There was the usual drinking and boasting, with everyone mad at everyone else. Safe enough, what with the hostility spread around fairly evenly. Then Chirikov jumped on the table, demanded they put peace in their hearts or some such thing, and started spouting poetry."

"Idiot."

"I rather like the man, actually. Good-hearted, if a trifle obsessed. In any case, he centered the fire. They all started insulting him instead of each other. Except for the other two Russian generals, who felt obligated to defend their countryman."

"Brawling schoolboys and a few bloody noses." Kendal sipped his brandy. "This is scarcely an international crisis, William."

"Not yet. But I hear rumblings. At least one Austrian and two Prussians are threatening to call Chirikov out, and I don't need to tell you the consequences if an allied general is shot down on Hounslow Heath. You will see to it that doesn't happen."

"Am I to throw myself in front of the bullet?"

"Almost as bad," Finlay said with a weary smile. "Obviously, Chirikov has to be got out of London. But he refuses to go, because it would appear he was running away."

"So it would. If you expect me to convince him otherwise—"

"I've already tried. Even Wellington tried. York offered to draw him off to Oatlands Park, but still he refused to budge. There was only one man in England worth leaving the city for, said he."

"Some damnable poet, right? I already told you, I don't know any poets."

"Nevertheless, the one he wants to meet lives in your neighborhood. Some chap named Wordsworth. I mean for you to escort Chirikov to the Lakes, nose out his pet poet, and introduce the pair of them."

"The devil I will!" Kendal set down his glass with a thump.

"You leave day after next," Finlay said, brushing a spray of brandy from his sleeve. "I'd rather it were immediately, but Chirikov is going to a mill in Crawley tomorrow. At least he'll be out of London."

Kendal retrieved his glass and turned it in his hand, watching the amber liquid swirl around. There hadn't been a guest at Candale since he could remember. For that matter, he hadn't set foot on his own estate for nearly two years. Nor did he want to go there now, not since old sins and black-shadowed memories began chasing one another through his sleepless nights. Perhaps after the Vienna Congress he would make one of his obligatory visits, but not now.

"No," he said flatly. "It's out of the question."

"I sympathize, James. Really I do. But I've already told Chirikov that you'll be happy to oblige. On the bright side, he's agreed to settle for Coleridge or Southey if you can't unearth that Wordsworth fellow. From what Chirikov says, the Lakes are practically swarming with poets."

"Not that I ever noticed. Shall I put an advertisement in the local newsrags? 'Poets seeking idolators should apply at Candale'?"

"Frankly, I don't give a rat's arse if Chirikov meets up with a rhyming scribbler. I just mean you to herd him north and keep him there for at least a week. Preston will take him off your hands after that. He's organizing a shooting party in Scotland."

He can start by shooting me, Kendal thought. After a week in company with Chirikov, any previously sane man would welcome a bullet in the head. "You will owe me, Finlay," he said in a dark voice. "And don't think I'll fail to collect."

"Fine. Whatever you say. Just get that damnable Russian out of my hair. I'll make arrangements for the journey, of course, and send word of the departure place and time. All you have to do is show up."

"On no account will I spend four days in a carriage with Chirikov. Tell him I've gone on ahead to sniff him out a poet. Tell him what you will. I leave tomorrow, traveling alone."

"I figured you'd say that," Finlay said with a cat-in-the-creampot smile. "He's bringing along a few of his cronies, and I expect they'll drink their way from one pub house to the next. You'll have plenty of time to prepare the house and devise a week of entertainment. One word of advice, James. Provide some women, or know where they can be found."

Kendal erupted to his feet. "I'm not a bloody procurer, Finlay, and damned if I'll turn Candale into a brothel."

"Nobody expects you to. Forget the women. I daresay one of your servants will be able to direct them to the local establishments. Just be prepared for trouble. Some of these chaps are not quite civilized, if you know what I mean." Finlay emptied his glass and stood. "I'll send over a packet of reports regarding the Congress for you to study on the journey. Any questions?"

Is Lady Greer in good spirits? Kendal nearly asked. But of course, he could not inquire about a houseguest with whom he supposedly had only the merest acquaintance. "None that I can think of at the moment," he said, reaching for the bellpull. "Pardon me if I don't show you out."

From the door, Finlay looked back at him. "Whatever is troubling you, James, put it aside for now. Until the treaty is negotiated and signed, none of us can afford to be distracted by matters of a personal nature."

"Go to the devil," Kendal advised him with a chilling smile.

Four days later, on a sunny afternoon, Kendal's coach drew up at the Candale gatehouse.

Wiping his hands on a towel, Angus Macafee hurried out to lift the bar, a look of apology on his face. "Welcome home, m'lord. But we wasn't expectin' you. Should I send word ahead to the house?"

"That won't be necessary, Angus. Your wife and family are well, I presume?"

"Got another bairn since last time we saw you," he said proudly. "A sweet lassie."

"My congratulations." Kendal smiled. "I suppose that means I'll have to adjust your wages again."

"Mr. Spence already did that, and I thank ye heartily. He's in Keswick, by the way. Due back tomorrow, I think. Mr. Christopher is to home, though. Been here nearly a month this time."

Nodding, Kendal signaled the driver to proceed down the tree-lined road to the main house.

So his scapegrace brother was at Candale. He was glad of it, although he'd intended to spend the rest of the day closeted with his estate manager. Apparently business would have to wait until tomorrow, and just as well. Sleep continued to elude him, and after the long trip he was in no mood to arrange a house party for a horde of raging Cossacks.

When the coach drew up at the stable, Kendal found it an effort to wrench himself from the squabs and step outside. It seemed he'd been traveling for a lifetime. Now he had to rouse himself to greet the unfailingly energetic Kit and the household staff, which would be at sixes and sevens to make him welcome when all he longed for was a good night's rest.

And there was Paxton, of course. A knotted rope twisted around his throat. No way to escape an awkward, stilted meeting with the boy, although he might be able to put it off until the morning.

Ostlers rushed to unhitch the horses, and he saw a stable boy scurry toward the house to alert the other servants that Lord Kendal had arrived. Stamping his boots on the ground to loose his taut muscles, he noticed a fine-boned white mare tethered just inside the stable, nibbling oats from a trough. She wore a sidesaddle.

Kit must have invited one of his female friends for a visit, Kendal thought, displeased. Kit was rarely without a woman, if he could possibly help it. He had all the charm in the family, and no sense of responsibility whatever. Really, he ought not bring his ladybirds to Candale with Paxton in residence. Kendal knew he would have to speak to him on the subject.

But that could wait, too. Everything could wait.

He aimed himself toward the house, hoping to enter without ceremony, but was distracted by shouts of laughter coming from behind the stable. What the devil? He took a few more steps before turning back, certain Kit was up to something disreputable. As usual. He might as well find out what all the commotion was about and let his brother know he had come home.

The last word tasted bitter on his tongue, even though he had not said it aloud. Candale had not been *home* to him for a great many years.

The sun was directly in his eyes as he rounded the corner of the stable. Lifting his hand to his forehead, he could barely make out what was going on inside the grassy paddock. He saw Kit first of all, leaning against the railing with his arms folded over his chest, his overlong blond hair gleaming in the sunlight.

A surge of affection swept over him at the sight of his handsome, loose-limbed youngest brother, dressed carelessly as always in leather breeches and a full-sleeved white shirt, his collar open and his waistcoat unbuttoned. Kit the Rogue. Kendal despaired of him. And rather too often he envied him. Kit was the only Valliant brother who knew how to be happy.

There were at least a dozen children in the paddock, dashing about and shrieking like banshees. He recognized two of Angus Macafee's brood, and reckoned from the filthy homespun clothing worn by the others that they were all offspring of servants or tenant farmers.

All but one.

Paxton must have spent the last hour rolling around in the mud. His pants were torn, his shirt filthy, and his dark hair wildly tousled. Kendal hardly recognized him. This was Kit's doing, he thought angrily. At this time of day Paxton ought to be at his studies. And under no circumstances should he be romping in a horse paddock with a pack of commoners.

Shading his eyes with both hands, Kendal looked closer. A figure, a slender female figure if he was not mistaken, was at the center of their game. A wide blindfold concealed most of her face, and a floppy straw bonnet hid her hair. Nevertheless, she was strikingly familiar. One of the housemaids, he supposed, or perhaps the girl Kit was currently favoring with his attentions. The one who belonged to that elegant mare.

She wore an apple-green dress, smudged with dirt, and her supple body made it impossible to look away from her. Arms waving in the air, she wove circles in the paddock, apparently trying to catch hold of the children who darted in and out, making sure to keep just beyond her reach.

"The ogre nearly got you, Betty," Paxton yelled.

"Did not!"

"Did, too!"

The would-be ogre, fingers curled, stomped in the direction of the voices. "I'm hungry!" she growled. "Where is my supper? *Grrrrrr!*"

"You can't eat *me*!" cried a curly-headed boy, flexing his stringy muscles. "I'm too tough."

"Me tough, too," Betty chimed.

Amid a chorus of "me-toos," the ogre stalked the paddock, snarling dramatically. "I fancy tough meat," she warned. "And the first one of you I seize will be swallowed down whole. Feed me. *Feeeeed* me!"

Paxton tiptoed up behind her, silently daring her to catch him. *Wanting* her to catch him, Kendal realized.

And then she did, swooping around and grappling the boy under his arms. "Supper!" she proclaimed, pretending to chomp his neck. Paxton squealed in delight.

"I get to be the ogre now," he declared, when she finally set him down.

"So you do," she said, crouching with her back to the child. "But first you must untie this blindfold."

Paxton fumbled with the knot for a long time, but eventually got it loose. And when the cloth dropped from her face, every muscle in Kendal's body went rigid with shock.

She spotted him at the same moment and went equally still.

For an eternity, or so it seemed to him, they gazed at each other. The children went quiet, too, as if sensing the onset of a storm.

Kit's voice broke the tense silence. "Game's over, ducklings. Take yourselves off now."

Marginally aware of children and onlookers scampering away, Kendal struggled to order his wits. Celia. Here! It was the last thing he expected. The last thing he wanted. Standing now, staring back at him with icy calm, she all but brought him to his knees.

"I take it the two of you are acquainted," Kit said lightly, crossing to Celia and draping an arm over her shoulder. "Hullo, Jimmie. Fancy *you* showing up unannounced. Not your usual style. Shall I take it England has decided it can dispense with your services?"

Kendal restrained himself from vaulting over the fence and decking his brother with a hard right to the jaw. How *dare* he touch her like that? Wrap his arm around her, damn him, as if staking a claim.

Suddenly a madly barking collie pup streaked through the paddock, ducked under the lowest bar of the fence, and attacked his boots with sharp teeth and claws.

"*Stop that!*" Kendal ordered to no effect. It was impossible to tell if the puppy was assaulting a supposed enemy or merely playing, but there was no doubt about his tenacity. Kendal could have kicked him away, of course, but Celia would think him lower than a snake for it. Not that she didn't think so already.

It hadn't taken her long to replace one Valliant brother with another, he thought venomously. Had she set out deliberately to snare Kit in some obscure female plot of retribution? It could not be sheer coincidence that she was here, now, four hundred miles from London, smiling at Kit. . . .

Very well, she wasn't smiling at Kit. She was openly laughing at what the black-and-white mutt was doing to his own beleaguered boots. Having abandoned his efforts to rip the leather to shreds, the pup, one small leg lifted in the air, was pungently marking his territory.

A red haze of fury obscured his vision. And out of it swam a small boy with tangled black hair and dark, scared eyes.

Paxton. Kendal had forgot all about him.

The boy came directly up to him and seized the puppy, raising it protectively to his narrow chest. Immediately the pup began squirming with pleasure and lapping its wet red tongue over the boy's face.

"He's mine, sir," Paxton said in a trembling voice. "His name is Wellington."

"Indeed? Have you taught him no manners, then?"

"Here we go," Kit said with a groan. Uncoiling his arm from Celia's shoulder, he mounted the fence and sauntered over to Kendal. "You sound exactly like Nanny Yallop, Jimmie. And I can think of no worse insult than that. Charley, I suggest you go and clean yourself up. I'll see to Wellington."

Astonished, Kendal saw his dog-loathing brother take the pup from the boy's arms and plant it on his shoulder. Immediately, the dog began chomping on his hair.

After a worried glance at his rag-mannered pet, Paxton sped away.

Celia was walking toward the paddock gate, the blindfold dangling from her hand, never looking in his direction.

Let her go, then, Kendal thought, watching her drape the

123

blindfold over the fence before raising the latch. If he spoke to her now, there was no telling what he would say.

"Go make your bow to Lady Greer," Kit said, an unholy gleam in his eyes. "I'd introduce you, but I'm informed that you have already met. Besides, this spawn of Satan is ripping my hair out. I'll go have him amputated from my scalp and order up some tea while you escort the lady inside."

He was gone before Kendal could stop him. And for that matter, so was Celia. But he caught a glimpse of her skirt as she turned the corner of the stable, and of their own accord, his feet began moving in the same direction.

He followed her to the courtyard, arriving just as a stable boy led the mare outside. Celia's back was to him, and if she was aware he had followed her, she gave no sign of it. He watched her take the reins and stroke the horse's neck.

Go and be damned, he told her silently.

She looked down at the stable boy. "Thank you for taking such excellent care of Aphra, Timothy. I've rarely seen her mane brushed to such advantage. May I beg another service of you? It seems I've left my reticule in the house, which was exceedingly thoughtless, and now I am embarrassed to go in search of it. Will you mind asking one of the house servants to locate it for me?"

"Yes, m'lady. I mean, no, m'lady." Cheeks scarlet, the boy loped off toward the servants' entrance.

Kendal gave quick thought to following him, but before he could move, it was too late.

"Good afternoon, my lord," Celia said, without turning. "Is there some reason you are lurking about?"

Teeth clenched, he aimed himself to a spot about ten feet from where she stood, determined to keep a healthy distance between them. "I had thought to ask you the same question, Lady Greer. Why are you not in London?"

"It occurs to me that my whereabouts are none of your business, sir. But if you must know, I came north to settle my late husband's affairs, primarily the sale of his farm."

"A sudden decision, I apprehend."

"Apprehend what you will. But while you are fabricating unlikely scenarios—a habit of yours, as I recall—you might consider that Lady Marjory had also left London to attend to her sister. In consequence, I had little choice but to remove myself from Lord Finlay's home."

"Never tell me you were concerned about *propriety*."

She came around to face him, her brows arched disdainfully. "The Finlays were preoccupied with family matters. I was more concerned about being a nuisance."

"Understandable. But how is it you have come to be a nuisance at Candale?"

She clicked her tongue. "Are we to have another row, Lord Kendal? Did we not say more than enough when last we met? Really, I see no point to this inquisition."

"Do you not? I arrived home only to find a gaggle of brats racketing about my paddock, with you, of all people, egging them on. It's only natural that I wonder what in blazes you are doing here!"

"On this occasion," she said after a moment's consideration, "playing blindman's buff."

"That is no answer, madam. And I do not welcome your impertinence."

"No more than you welcome *me*, I collect. We are of like mind in one regard, sir. Had I the slightest notion you were on your way home, you may be sure that Candale is the last place on earth I would have been found."

"But here you are," he said incontrovertibly. "In company with my brother, with whom you appear to have struck up a close relationship in a remarkably short time."

Her lips curved. "Yes. We were drawn to each other the moment we met."

She was leading him on, Kendal knew. Deliberately provoking him. And he, saphead that he was, kept rising to the bait. "You must have known I would not approve contact between you and any member of my family after what passed between us."

"Oh, aye. But then I recollected that so very *little* had passed between us. Surely not enough to prohibit friendship with quite

125

the nicest young gentleman I have encountered in recent memory. But lest you imagine otherwise, our meeting was purely coincidental. He came upon me at the Kendal market while I was trying to decide whether or not to buy this mare, and helped me to negotiate with the horse trader."

"A likely story. But you have ever been remarkably inventive."

She gave him a look of mock horror. "Mercy me! Did you fancy I deliberately sought him out because he was your brother? How peculiar. Why would I do such a thing?"

He could think of a score of reasons. To punish the man who had walked out on her, for example. To prove she could seduce at least one of the Valliant brothers. Or just because she was a hot-blooded female in search of a lover, which Kit would have recognized immediately. Kendal could hardly blame him for jumping at what she so freely offered. Lord knew that *he* had jumped.

But none of the reasons that shot to his mind made the least bit of sense. Celia Greer was a complete mystery to him, but there was no mistaking the bright core of integrity at her center. He gazed directly into her eyes and saw it burning there. Burning into him, daring him to go on making an ass of himself.

All the same, knowing he was wholly in the wrong did nothing to quench his unaccountable rage. The rage only *she* was able to stir up in him. That alone was reason enough to want her gone.

She had seemingly lost interest in him. Turning back to her horse, she scratched behind the mare's ears and received a whicker of pleasure in return.

Kendal cast about for something to say. Perversely, he was loath to end this encounter, however unpleasant it had been thus far. He could not bring himself to walk away, nor think of a way to prolong their time together. And for all her disclaimers about the coincidental meeting with Kit, she had said nothing that ruled out an affair between them.

Was his brother the man who finally claimed her virginity?

A knife twisted in his gut. If they were lovers, he would—

What? There was nothing he *could* do.

"Lady Greer," piped the stable boy, darting across the court-yard with a delicate knit reticule in his hand. He presented it to her with a beaming smile.

"Bless you, Timothy," she said, drawing the strings and pulling out a coin. "I am most grateful."

" 'Twaren't nothin', ma'am. Betsy found it under a chair."

"Then she must have a reward, too." Celia extricated another coin. "Give her this, will you, with my thanks."

Unused to being ignored, Kendal was amazed that his own stable boy had failed to take note of his presence. Or perhaps the child had not been in his employment when last he made an appearance on the estate. Most likely there were any number of servants at Candale who had never clapped eyes on the man who paid their wages.

Young Timothy scampered back in the direction of the house, coins clutched tightly in his hand. Clearly he was looking forward to presenting Betsy with her vail.

"He's a lovely boy," Celia said. "His father died last year, leaving seven children and a sickly wife. Timothy was sent out to work to help support the family. Betsy is his sister."

"I see," Kendal said, a lump of guilt rising to his throat. In so short a time Celia Greer knew more about his household than he did. But what matter the woes of a few families when the fate of Europe had been at stake, he told himself. It wasn't as if he had been doing nothing of value all these years.

And why would she so admire Kit, whose sole concerns were wine, women, and adventure?

"If you mean to order me off your property and advise me never to darken the doors of Candale," she said mildly, "pray go on about it. I hope you will not forbid me to see Charley again, although I expect you will. And I shall do as you say, of course. Only, please make yourself clear this time. I so easily misunderstand your intentions, as well you know. What exactly do you want of me, Lord Kendal?"

Infernally, *come to bed with me* was his first thought. His body raised a cheer of approval.

Hoping desperately she wouldn't see what was painfully

obvious to him, he came directly up to her, seized her around the waist, and lifted her onto the saddle. The reins had got tangled in the process, so he helped sort them out, grateful for the slight distraction.

When she was settled, he stepped back, more in control of himself now, although his hands felt on fire from touching her. "You must do as you like," he said tightly. "I trust you will not disrupt Paxton's studies or interfere with the schedule mapped out by his governess and tutor. Otherwise, you are free to come and go at Candale."

For the first time he had startled her. It gave him a perverse delight to see the look of surprise on her face, especially since he had not meant to say what he had just said. It had been his firm intention to tell her it would be better if she stayed away, at least while he was in residence.

Once he was gone again, a week or two from now, it made no difference what she did. Surely in Vienna, where sophisticated and uncomplicated females would be trolling for the sort of casual liaisons he favored, he would be able to exorcise Celia Greer from his thoughts.

"I'll not come here until you have left," she said quietly. "To do so would be difficult for me, if not for you. But likely Kit and I will arrange a few excursions with Charley, if you've no objection. It's summer, after all, and young boys cannot spend all their time with books."

Kendal nodded. "As it happens, I expect guests within a few days, and I'm not altogether certain they will conduct themselves in proper fashion." Lord, how pompous he sounded! He tried again, more simply this time. "If you take Paxton off of an afternoon, I'll be glad of it."

She closed her eyes for a moment, and he saw her hands clutch at the reins. Why had permission to spend time with the child affected her so greatly? She must have wanted it very much, in spite of her apparent indifference to whatever decision he made.

"Thank you, my lord," she said. "Be assured I'll not take undue advantage of your kindness."

He bowed, fairly pleased with himself for having regained the poise that generally went missing whenever he was in her presence.

She nudged the mare into a turn and rode away in no great hurry as he stood frozen, gazing after her with terrible, unthinkable desire. *Look back,* he begged silently. *Look back and tell me you are not so indifferent to me as you seem.*

But she did not.

Chapter 13

His headache had grown worse, but Kendal persisted, determined to make a start at catching up with estate business. He meant to be ready for an accounting when Spence returned from wherever the devil he'd gone. Keswick, was it?

Not that he'd made a sliver of progress since settling at his desk four hours ago. He had given strict instructions that he wasn't to be disturbed, but the butler had brought a supper tray to the study anyway. To his credit, Geeson only placed it on a side table and withdrew as silently as he'd come.

It was still there, the tray. Kendal had no appetite. Nor very much interest in tracing profits and losses from the several enterprises that kept Candale and the Valliant family in funds, although there had been a time when he'd enjoyed managing the estate and expanding the family businesses.

So far, he could tell that his steward oversaw Candale with the parsimony of a born accountant. But it was equally clear that Spence lacked the imagination to increase production and develop new markets. In the final analysis, that meant that the tenant farmers and shepherds had little opportunity to improve their own lots.

Most of their families had been at Candale since before he was born, and few were better off than they'd been when he left to take up his duties with the Foreign Office. He had not precisely neglected them, he told himself. But neither had he done anything of value on their behalf.

On the other hand, what did they expect of him? Until a few months ago England had been at war. Everyone was called on to make sacrifices during the war years, and his own services were required elsewhere. He refused to feel guilty for what could not be helped.

There was more than enough guilt heaped on his head already. He couldn't remember the last time he had gone to bed without a score of unaccomplished tasks weighing on him. A diplomat, even a good one—and he fancied he had some claim to that distinction—never actually completed anything. Nothing of significance, at any rate. He had spent five years catering to swollen egos and smoothing the path for men with the authority to make decisions. When it came right down to it, he'd done little more than chat up important people and winkle information from them.

He was heartily sick of the whole business, but the alternatives were even less appealing. Candale was poisonous to him now, he had no taste for soldiering, and what else was there for him to do? Sometimes he could almost envy Kit, who did whatever he liked with no thought of the consequences.

As if summoned, his brother sauntered into the study without knocking.

"Go away," Kendal grumbled. "I'll deal with you in the morning."

"And I'm glad to see you, too," Kit replied cheerfully. "Have a drink. Looks like you need one. Hell, I'll even pour it for you."

Kendal accepted a glass of claret with murmured thanks and set it on the desk. "Did you come to beg another loan? I promise you, there will be nary a farthing until you provide me a coherent plan for spending it to some useful purpose."

"Shall I tell you I mean to buy a plot of land and a flock of sheep? Will that open your pockets?"

Kendal swallowed a laugh. "You will have to tell me something credible, although I cannot imagine what that could be."

"No more can I. But relax, Jimmie. I've no intention of dunning you, at least this one time. In fact, I wasn't expecting to see you at all. What brought you home of a sudden?"

"Nothing good." Kendal put down the pen he'd been holding and steepled his hands. "My superiors have ordered me to entertain a contingent of Russians who came over for the victory celebrations. There are reasons to spirit General Chirikov out of London, and for my sins, I was elected to do it. How many friends he'll bring along with him and how long they will stay, I've no idea. I set out ahead to alert the staff and arrange for suitable pastimes. Hunting, shooting, that sort of thing."

"Hmm. I may stick around, then. Is it too much to hope these particular Russians are flush in the fob and partial to gaming?"

Kendal released a small sigh. "I will be very glad if you stay, Kit. And no, you may not pick their pockets at cards and dice. But I might be convinced to pay you—straight out, not a loan—for helping me keep them occupied. I don't suppose you happen to know any poets?"

"Good God no!" Kit shuddered. "Exactly what sort of house party is this to be? If you mean to stage amateur theatricals and poetry readings, you can't pay enough to keep me here."

"Understood. But I expect—devil it, Kit, I don't know *what* to expect. Something closer to chaos than musicales, most like." He stood, picked up the glass of wine, and walked over to the open window, welcoming the cool evening breeze against his face. "I won't blame you for fleeing in advance of the Cossack hordes."

"Hordes I can live with. It's opera singers that terrify me. You can count on me, Jimmie, no salary required. Not that I won't remind you of my devoted service at some later time, when my finances are at low tide."

"I never doubted it," Kendal replied easily. "Tomorrow afternoon, if you have no other plans, let's go for a ride and try to figure out what we are to do with a troop of Russian soldiers."

"Agreed. In the meantime, despite the fact that you officially barred the study door even to family, I have come here to talk about Charley."

Damn. Kendal swung around and gave his brother a stern look of dismissal. "Can this not wait, Kit? I presume he is well enough for now."

"He is healthy, if that is what you mean. But I saw Pruneface

Yallop galloping out of here shortly before supper. You must have quizzed her with your usual lack of mercy."

"Rather the other way around," Kendal said with a harsh laugh. "From her report, Lord Paxton is generally well behaved until his Uncle Christopher pays a call, at which point he runs wild as a baboon. You are regarded as an unwholesome influence, I'm afraid."

"God forbid the poor kid be allowed to enjoy himself for a week or two. She's turning him into a mole, James. He's allowed a short walk in the morning and another in the evening, but only if the weather is fine. It's bloody unnatural."

"He should be permitted more exercise, I suppose. When our Russian guests depart, Miss Yallop and I shall discuss a reordering of the boy's daily schedule."

"Bully for you. Will that include five minutes of your own time, or do you mean to avoid him altogether while you are home?"

"Certainly not. But I shall be kept busy with Chirikov and his entourage, and must return to London when they have gone. On this trip, there will be little time to spare for personal matters."

"As opposed to which of your previous trips?"

"Do you mean to read me a lecture, Kit?"

He laughed. "That *would* be a change, considering how many times you have drawn and quartered me for the most trivial of offenses. Actually, I quite like the notion of changing places with you. Best do it right, though." He went to the desk and settled in Kendal's chair, propping his elbows on the desk and steepling his hands.

Kendal could not fail to recognize his own habitual posture whenever there was unpleasant business to be dealt with. "Cut line, infant."

"Don't be impertinent, young man," Kit said, mocking his brother's cool voice. Then he frowned. "You are supposed to be standing before me with your head bowed, Jimmie, looking suitably penitent."

"Ah. I beg your pardon. But am I not playing Mr. Christopher in this farce?" Slouching to the chair in front of the desk, he slumped down, crossed one ankle over his knee, and lounged back, wineglass dangling from his hand. "What *now*?" he drawled sullenly.

Kit shouted with laughter. "Very good, for a stiff-necked diplomat. But if you are going to play me, you require a touch more insouciance, not to mention a devilish gleam in your eyes. Can you be devilish, Jimmie?"

"Not for any sustained period of time." It was true, Kendal noted with some surprise. Already his posture had begun to straighten, his body re-forming itself to its natural shape without instructions from his mind. "If I must hear a litany of my flaws," he said, losing interest in the game, "please get on with it. I have work to do."

"Right. And that's flaw number one. Here am I, the brother you have not seen for what, eighteen months? But you can scarcely wait to shovel me out of the room. Are you not the least bit curious what I've been up to?"

"I'm rather sure I don't want to know," Kendal said dryly.

"Good, because I'm damn well not going to tell you. Not anything you wouldn't like hearing, at any rate. Suffice it to say I have been a model of rectitude."

Kendal felt guilt nibbling at his conscience. "You know I'll always make time for you, Kit. Forgive me. I'm tired from the trip and out of sorts."

"Because of Celia?"

The question took him by surprise. But then, Kit always did know how to set an ambush. "What has Lady Greer to do with anything?" he asked with false disinterest.

"You tell me. Lightning bolts were flying between the pair of you, Jimmie. I expected the grass to go on fire."

"That was your imagination. If I seemed . . . annoyed, it was only because I arrived to see Paxton rolling about in the dirt and chumming with the servants."

Kit's eyes flashed with anger. "You weren't used to be so high in the instep, my lord earl. Pray tell, who *is* the boy to play with if not the servants' children?"

"I have no idea. But overfamiliarity with the staff is not an option. I shall make that clear to everyone concerned, and trust that you will not countermand my orders once I am gone."

"No promises on that score," Kit advised him in a mild voice. "If you wish Charley raised by your own inflexible standards, then you must remain at Candale and see to it yourself."

Kendal took a drink of wine. "I suggest we change the subject now," he said, his voice tinged with warning.

"Fine." Kit waved a long-fingered hand. "I was wanting to get back to Celia anyway. She told me the two of you met in London."

Not to *that* subject, Kendal thought, sweat breaking out on his nape. "And—?"

"Little more, I'm sorry to say. By her account, you were introduced at a ball and met in passing a time or two after that, purely by chance. But as you doubtless know, the lovely Lady Greer gives much away with her expressions and her eyes. She was attempting to conceal a fascinating tale, I am persuaded." Kit waggled his brows. "Perhaps a *scandalous* tale?"

Kendal made sure his own expression revealed nothing at all. "Do you accuse the lady of lying?" he inquired gently.

"Only of being tiresomely discreet. And really, I thought little of it until you clapped eyes on her in the paddock and went whiter than salt. What's more, I doubt you followed her to the stable to inquire about her health."

"I *escorted* Lady Greer to her mount, as any gentleman would do. You, as I recall, preferred to accompany a yapping puppy."

"Damn stupid choice on my part, I agree. Celia—"

"Lady Greer."

"To you, perhaps."

"And what precisely is she to *you*?" The question snapped out of its own accord, carrying in its wake a thunder of regret. Kendal stilled his breath, not wanting to have asked, not wanting an answer.

"Oh. I see," Kit said softly. "You're bloody jealous."

"Spare me!" Kendal erupted from the chair, the glass he'd forgot he was holding dropping from his hand. It rolled to a halt near the desk, leaving a pool of claret on the carpet.

135

For several moments he stood there watching it soak in, his thoughts a red blur.

"It's not so unlikely, the two of us," Kit said diabolically. "I'm only a younger son, but she could do worse."

Kendal roused himself for a wintry reply. "I fail to see how. Unless she has a taste for carrying food and a change of linens to whatever gaol you happen to be favoring with your presence."

"Oh, I don't know as how that would be necessary. For a woman like Celia, I might even consider reforming." Kit stretched broadly. "She is looking for a house to buy, you know. Wants to be on the lake. I mean to teach her to sail."

Kendal began to pace the room, if only to keep himself from throttling his brother. There was no telling if Kit was serious about paying his attentions to Lady Greer, although it seemed unlikely. He'd always been a hell-raiser, sent down from school a score of times and often disappearing for months on one of his unsavory adventures. It was unimaginable, Kit settling into parson's mousetrap.

Or was it? He'd a weak spot for children and might well trade his independence for a passel of brats, so long as he managed to snag a wife with sufficient fortune to support the family. Kit could not be an especially successful smuggler, for he never seemed to have any money.

On the other hand, he never had the least bit of trouble getting any woman he wanted. If he had set his sights on Celia Greer, she might decide to take another husband after all.

Kendal realized that he had come to a stop in front of the hearth, and wondered how long he had stood gazing blankly at the empty fireplace. Kit was ominously silent, which generally indicated that trouble was brewing, but Kendal refused absolutely to address the subject of Lady Greer again tonight. Or any other night.

He turned, forcing an impassive expression to his face. "Do me the kindness, Kit, to take yourself out of my chair."

Ignoring that, Kit fixed him with a cold stare. "Do you know what Charley is doing at this moment?"

Kendal glanced over his shoulder at the mantelpiece clock.

"It's nine o'clock. I expect he is at his studies, or readying himself for bed."

"Which shows how little you know. I doubt he's even had his supper. Right now, and for the past several hours, he has been sitting in his room on pins and needles awaiting your summons."

"Did he expect me to ring a peal over him for that display in the paddock? I assure you, I had no such intention."

"Old Yallop assumes that you will. She has been threatening him with your wrath ever since hauling him upstairs and into a bathtub. What's more, she made sure the footman scrubbed him with a horse brush, lest the smell of grass or dirt from an afternoon of play offend your aristocratic nostrils."

Kendal banished the picture that shot into his mind at hearing those words. Miss Yallop's notion of discipline was unacceptable, but what was done, was done. He would see that nothing of the sort happened again. "I've no intention of speaking with Paxton tonight," he said. "Perhaps you should inform Miss Yallop that he is to be put to bed now."

"The hell I will!" Kit bore down on him like a bull on the charge. "Charley would only lie awake for hours with the sword of Demosthenes hanging over him."

"Damocles. Sword of *Damocles*."

Kit slammed his hand against his own forehead. "You cold-hearted, uncompromising jackass! That's precisely what is needed here—a literary emendation! Meantime a little boy is shivering in his boots, and you won't spare a few minutes to put him out of his misery. Who the devil *are* you, James?"

Damned if he knew. Nobody his own brother wanted to know, that was clear enough.

And what use was he to Paxton? However miserable the boy might be now, he would only feel worse after a few minutes in the company of a man who could scarcely bear to look at him. "I have no idea what you mean, Christopher. Lord Paxton need have no fear of a raking down. You are the one can convince him of that. Tell him that I shall speak with him tomorrow after breakfast and hear an accounting of his studies."

137

Kit raised his chin and his fists. "You'll see him *now*, dammit."

"Are you giving me orders, Kit?"

"I'm trying to help a seven-year-old boy who is terrified of his own father."

"You know better than that, on every count."

Kit stalked to the wall and rammed a fist into the plaster. "Next time it will be your face," he swore in a raw voice. "Was a time I idolized you, James. Almost as much as Charley does. What became of the brother I grew up with?"

"I thought you knew," Kendal replied glacially.

"Yes. But the child is not to blame. Stop punishing him."

"I have never done so. You don't know what you're talking about. Duty keeps me away. And besides, what have I to offer a boy of his age?"

"Nothing, apparently." Kit turned, rubbing at his injured hand. "Not any longer. Was a time you took me on your lap and read me stories, and played at marbles with Alex, and did all you could to hold what remained of our family together. You were little more than a child yourself, James, but I begin to think you were a better man then than you are now."

Kendal had a sudden, vivid memory of Kit a score of years ago, hair pale as flax, thin and bony, although his long legs and wide shoulders promised the height and strength he'd grown into. And Alex, who began small and dark—rather like Paxton, come to think of it—only to develop into the tallest of the Valliant brothers and the most striking in appearance.

It had been left to him, about the time his voice began to change, to see to their welfare. He remembered getting through the days as best he could and then sitting alone in his room at night, shivering at the thought that he was doing it all wrong. The responsibility had very nearly overwhelmed him, and he would have run from it if he could.

He wanted to run now, from Paxton. Kit would say he had been doing just that.

Crossing to his desk, he sat and buried his face in his hands. Distantly, he was aware of Kit at the door speaking to the butler, and knew what he had in mind.

Well, let it be. Might as well get it over with, but Lord, what a hellish day. Raising his head, he sifted through the file of reports he'd been examining, unable to remember why he'd brought them out in the first place.

A few minutes later, hearing a light rap on the door, he planted his elbows on the desk and steepled his hands.

Kit snorted.

Blast it, a man had to do *something* with his hands. With a sharp look at his brother, Kendal left them where they were.

Paxton, impeccably dressed, his newly washed hair shining, took two steps into the room. "You wished to see me, sir?"

"Yes." Kendal made an effort to gentle his voice. "You needn't keep such a distance. Move closer, where I can see you."

The boy took a few more steps, his gaze fixed on the carpet, only to come to an abrupt halt. He looked up at Kendal with wide, pleading eyes. "I didn't do it, sir. Cross my heart."

"Do wha—? Oh. The wine stain. No, I did that." He cleared his throat. "How are you getting on, Paxton?"

"Very well, sir." He glanced once more at the carpet, as if unable to credit that Lord Kendal had made such a mess.

"Your lessons are progressing on schedule?" Kendal persisted when the boy failed to say anything more.

His face brightened. "Mr. Symington says I will likely take honors at Harrow, sir." The light dimmed. "He says I am to be sent away at Michaelmas."

"Do you not wish to go?"

"Mr. Symington says there will be lots of other boys there. I expect I shall like that."

Kendal doubted it. In his experience, the heirs of wealthy peers were invariably singled out by the senior boys for special torments. "Well, perhaps you needn't be enrolled until the spring. I'll discuss the matter with your tutor. In the meantime Miss Yallop has brought a few matters to my attention. Most can be taken up at a later date, but she insists that the dog be dealt with immediately. Is it true he spends the night in your bedchamber?"

"No, sir. Well, not *all* night." He slid a glance at Kit, who was leaning against the mantelpiece with his arms folded over his chest. "He is there when I go to sleep, but he is gone when Nanny Yallop comes to wake me up."

"And how does that come about, do you suppose?"

Paxton flushed. "I cannot say, sir."

"There is also the problem of where he chooses to do his business. Your dressing-room floor, I believe."

"Only a few times," Paxton said quickly. "Sir. And I always clean it up right away."

"Even so, Miss Yallop objects most strenuously to what she describes as a 'lingering stench.' Until the puppy has learned to control himself, he will do better in the barn. Don't you agree?"

Paxton shot another look at Kit, who nodded encouragement. "But, sir, I'm the one who lives in my room, and I don't mind the lingering stench. Besides, how can Wellington be trained to control himself if he's always in the barn?"

Good question. Kendal rubbed the bridge of his nose, thinking an international treaty would be easier to negotiate than this absurd civil war between nanny and mutt. "I take it that your uncle has a hand in all this, most particularly the mystery of how the dog disappears into the night?"

Lips white, Paxton shook his head. "Wellington is my responsibility, sir."

"I see." Kendal had fully meant to banish the dog from the house, but that no longer seemed a good idea. There was no real harm done, except to Miss Yallop's sensibilities, and she had far too many sensibilities. Besides, he was not of a mood to play the villain tonight. And a villain is what he would be, should he snatch Paxton's puppy away within hours of arriving home. "Kit, ring for the butler again, will you?"

Paxton stood like a condemned felon waiting for the noose to drop around his neck.

Kendal wanted to reassure him, but had no idea how to speak with a child. Especially this one. "Young man," he said in a severe voice, "I expect you to make every effort to instill a bit of discipline into your puppy, and to keep him out of Miss Yallop's sight whenever possible. Do you understand?"

"N-no, sir." His eyes lit with hope. "Does that mean I can keep him in my room at bedtime?"

"For the time being. We'll have to see how well he adjusts, but I'll not evict him until he has been given a chance to prove himself. Tomorrow, I shall inform Miss Yallop that the dog is permitted to remain in the house, subject to your own discretion, and that you will not abuse the privilege."

"Oh, I won't, sir. Except, I don't know exactly what my discreption is."

"Just use your head, child. None of us wants Miss Yallop plaguing us, right? Give her no reason to do so."

"I'll try, sir. But sometimes," he added candidly, "I think she doesn't need a reason for plaguing."

Kit barked a laugh.

"Your lordship?" the butler said from the door.

Relieved to put this awkward encounter to an end, Kendal stood. "Geeson, please inform Miss Yallop that she may retire for the night, and ask her to attend me here at nine o'clock tomorrow morning. I'll expect Mr. Symington at nine-thirty. Also, send one of the maids to help Lord Paxton ready himself for bed. Have you had your supper, Paxton?"

"Yes, sir."

"The tray was returned to the kitchen untouched," Geeson informed him blandly.

"Indeed?" Kendal almost laughed. The butler, who had known him since he was in short pants, was always properly deferential when he spoke out of turn. "In that case, instruct the maid to bring up a glass of milk and a plate of biscuits. And a bone, if one is to be had."

"Very good, your lordship."

When he was gone, Kendal turned back to Lord Paxton, who was regarding him with openmouthed astonishment.

Why was that? he wondered. He had never been unkind to the boy. True, he had seen him no more than a handful of times in the last several years, but the household staff had been ordered to treat Paxton with all the respect due to the Kendal heir. He would reaffirm that order before returning to London, in case a few of the servants had become lax in their duties.

He reminded himself to have Geeson arrange for the floor of Paxton's dressing room to be scoured every morning. That should mollify Miss Yallop, who would be seeking new employment once Paxton was dispatched to Harrow. He would make sure to bring up the subject of references when he spoke with her tomorrow, if only to keep her quiet about the dog.

What else? He was too tired to order his thoughts. "Kit, why don't you take Paxton upstairs, in case Miss Yallop has misunderstood Geeson's instructions."

"Oh, she's skulking around, I have no doubt." Pulling himself from the wall, Kit held out his hand. "Come along, Charley. We'll face her down together."

Instead of hurrying over to his uncle, as Kendal had expected, Paxton took the last few steps to the edge of the desk and bowed. "Thank you, sir," he said. "I promise that Wellington will behave himself. And I'll use my discreption, too. Cross my heart."

"Very well, Paxton. We'll speak again tomorrow at ten o'clock. Good night."

"Good night, sir." With another bow, he crossed to where Kit was standing and took his hand.

Kendal didn't dare to look at his brother again. He'd had enough disapproval for one day, thank you very much. "Don't come back, Kit," he said. "I've work to do."

Kit closed the door behind him without a word, which spoke louder than anything he'd said all evening. Settling back on the chair with a groan, Kendal mauled his hair with a shaking hand. Damn! In this house, he never seemed to put a foot right, or say what he ought, or do what was best. Was a time he had loved Candale, but now he could scarcely abide a single hour here, let alone the ten or more days he'd be forced to play host to a Russian maniac.

And there was Paxton, who deserved better than he could give him. And Kit, who seemed to have appointed himself unofficial conscience to his brother, which was rather a stretch for a man generally one step ahead of the constables.

And Celia Greer. The very last person he ever wanted to see again right here on his doorstep, and nothing he could do about it. Not since she gave him the opportunity to forbid her to set foot on the estate, which he ought to have done, but didn't. He could hardly withdraw permission now.

Still, she had appeared no more pleased to see him than he was to see her. With any luck, she'd keep well out of his way.

He was counting on it.

But devil take it, how could he purge her forever from his thoughts? She haunted his days. She drifted through his dreams, on the rare occasions he had been able to sleep since—

No! He would *not* gnaw on old wounds tonight. With deliberation, he reached for the ledger of household accounts and set to work.

Chapter 14

Three days later General Vasily Chirikov charged onto the Candale estate with four junior officers in tow. He seemed to have been expecting that Mr. Wordsworth would be there to greet him, but allowed that there was no way the time of his own arrival could have been anticipated. Tomorrow would do well enough.

It was going to be, Kendal reflected dismally, a very long week.

He had traced the poet's direction and sent a letter, but his courteous request met with a firm no. Mr. Wordsworth could not spare the time for a meeting, not even with a gentleman come all the way from Russia to see him. He conveyed his good wishes to Lord Kendal and General Chirikov.

Kendal tried again, this time by sending his agent to deliver a note. But the birdlike woman who answered the door refused to admit him, promising to give the letter to her brother. There was no reply.

So much for Wordsworth, and Kendal had yet to scratch up a substitute. He'd been informed that writers were thick on the Lake Country ground, but they all seemed to have scarpered— Southey to London, De Quincey to Scotland, and Coleridge to the devil knew where.

Only Mr. Tittleton, who claimed to be the true author of *Paradise Lost*, was available to grant an audience. Kendal rather thought Tittleton and Chirikov deserved each other, but reluctantly declined the offer.

Poetless, he set himself to distract Chirikov and entertain his pack of hard-drinking subordinates with hunting parties and fishing parties and dinner parties. But there was nothing of interest to shoot, they complained. No tigers. No bears. As for fishing—*pah!* A sport for little boys.

The dinner parties were disasters of the first order. The young officers, who spoke no English, drank deep and chewed with their mouths open, occasionally bursting into raucous song. The neighborhood gentry, shocked to their toes, sat petrified until the last cover was removed. Then, with mumbled excuses, they fled.

Meanwhile Chirikov moped.

The men took target practice on the sheep, trying to lop off their ears. Kendal put a stop to it, so they turned to shooting at the chimney pots.

Chirikov sulked.

A lieutenant tried to force himself on a kitchen maid, who clobbered him with a rolling pin. Kit plucked a terrified tweeny from the grip of a sodden major and gave him a bloody nose.

After four days Kendal had had enough. Ruthlessly, he offered the ambitious Lord Lonsdale a chance to be the envy of his cronies. Would he care to host a contigent of the Russian delegation for a week of shooting on his estate? Beginning the very next day?

Lonsdale, heaven bless him, accepted immediately.

Next, Kendal convinced the officers that there was better hunting farther north, where Lonsdale resided. Perhaps even a bear or two.

Chirikov was roused from his brown study long enough to wave agreement to Kendal's plan, although he himself refused to budge from Candale. He meant to stay until he shook hands with William Wordsworth or the arrival of Judgment Day, whichever came first.

On this particular morning, Kendal was tramping up Crosby Fell in the company of his brother, trailing Chirikov at a considerable distance. For all his size, the man could climb like a goat. Earlier, the Russian general had set out on a pilgrimage in search of daffodils. A *host* of daffodils, to be precise, just like the one in Mr. Wordsworth's poem.

Kendal hadn't the heart to tell him there wasn't a daffodil to be found in late July, any more than he'd been able to confess that Wordsworth had twice refused invitations to meet his most devoted acolyte.

"You know, I quite like the fellow," Kit said as he clambered over an outcropping of stone. "He's a trifle queer in the attic, of course, but a great gun when he forgets all that rhyming twaddle."

"Don't mention guns to me," Kendal said, following his brother over the rocks. "And when does he *ever* forget?"

"Oh, I've managed to pry him from the house for a few neck-or-nothing rides while you were doing whatever it is you do. He takes Charley up with him and they race across the countryside, shrieking like Mongols."

Paxton *shrieking*, for pity's sake? Riding out with that great Russian bear when he should be at his lessons? Kendal suspected that Lady Greer made up a fourth during those riding expeditions, although she doubtless arranged to meet with the others somewhere beyond the boundaries of Candale.

They had not, he noted with a sting of resentment, invited *him* to come along.

Naturally, he would have refused. Nevertheless . . .

He dug his whitethorn walking stick into the ground. Kit was taking unholy pleasure from watching him twist in the wind, but the scoundrel had also been damnably useful of late. Yesterday he removed Chirikov from Kendal's hair for an entire afternoon of fishing at Derwent Water.

And they hadn't fished alone.

Lady Greer had found the best worms and baited her own hooks, Paxton informed him when the small party—all but Lady Greer, of course—returned to Candale with their catch. The boy had snagged a tiny, paper-thin fish all by himself, and shyly presented it to his father.

Standing there, fish held by its tiny tail fin between his thumb and forefinger, Paxton looked so earnest that Kendal could not help but accept it with feigned delight, promising to have it cooked up for his supper.

For once, Kit had shot him a look of approval.

Kendal wondered what had become of that fishlet. It made

one bite for a kitchen cat, he supposed, wrenching his thoughts to more urgent matters. "I've run out of poets, Kit. What makes Chirikov imagine the countryside is littered with them?"

"You only need the one," Kit pointed out. "He wants that Wordsworth chap."

"Who has already turned me down. Twice."

"Indeed? Did you offer to pay him? Writers are notoriously poor, you know. Or perhaps you ought to haul your aristocrat arse to Rydal and ask him in person. Your letters can be more than a little off-putting, Jimmie. The handful you've sent me these last five years certainly were."

"I daresay. But considering that half were addressed to whatever prison you were currently patronizing, with a bank draft enclosed to secure your bail, I can scarcely be blamed for—"

"Right." Kit lifted his arms in surrender. "I forgot that part. But even your Christmas letters—and I was always at Candale for Christmas—sounded like a cross between a sermon and a government dispatch. When I read them to Charley, I had to make up the words. God knows I couldn't use the ones you actually wrote. 'Convey my regards to Paxton,' of all things. 'Buy him something and charge it to the estate.' "

"I take your point, Christopher. Thank you."

"Oh, you're welcome, Lord Kendal. Always happy to oblige. And you needn't glower. Indeed, were I you, I'd be flattering a younger brother who happens to be in a position to do me—meaning you, that is—an enormous favor." He grinned. "But then, what do I know? You're the diplomat in the family."

"What favor?" There was only one service he required at the moment, as Kit very well knew. "Never tell me *you* can produce Wordsworth?"

"Hardly. I haven't read a poxy poem since school days. But I know someone who can serve him up on a platter, should that someone rouse herself. She won't do it on your behalf, I am convinced, but it's just possible that I can persuade her."

Her was Celia Greer, naturally. Kendal dropped onto a convenient boulder, swearing under his breath.

"Are we stopping?" Kit sank cross-legged to the ground.

"Past time. These new boots are rubbing blisters. What say we wait here until Chirikov comes back down?"

"Fine. And you can explain to me why Lady Greer has failed to come forward before now. Why the devil didn't she tell me she was acquainted with Wordsworth?"

"The fact that you have not seen her since the day you came home might have something to do with it," Kit observed mildly.

"Yes. Very well. But she's seen Chirikov, and she knows he is enamored of that bloody poet. Has she refused to introduce them merely to spite me?"

"My, my, *someone* has a lofty opinion of his own significance. In fact, Jimmie, when our little group sets out on an expedition, poetry is a forbidden subject of conversation. That's supposedly for Charley's sake, but primarily for my own. Yesterday, though, and I don't remember how it came up, Celia happened to mention the Wordsworth connection to me."

"And you can persuade her to use that connection?"

"I believe so. Your problem is convincing me to exert myself. Bribing me, to be more accurate, and this is one favor that won't come cheap. How often do I get you in my power, Jimmie? This once? Can't blame a fellow for taking advantage."

"No. But I can fling you off this mountain, and I bloody well will if you don't stop gloating. Name your price and be done with it."

"That impertinence will cost you an extra fifty pounds," Kit advised him. "But here's the primary deal. Saturday is Charley's birthday, which I expect you had wholly forgot. He wants to go fishing again, so we've planned a picnic on Windemere Lake just across from Belle Isle. You know the place. We used to go there when we were lads. You will be on hand for the picnic and on good behavior, which means pretending you are delighted to be there and going along with the fun." Kit's face hardened. "What's more, Charley wants a pony. But I've been unable to find one fine enough for him, so you will make sure he has the best pony to be had north of Birmingham. Agreed?"

Kendal turned his back and folded his arms, gazing out over

the fells. "If you couldn't do it, how the devil do you expect *me* to locate a plaguey pony?"

"The Foreign Office lets you negotiate the future of England, Jimmie. Surely you can unearth one small horse for a little boy."

It always came back to Paxton. Hellfire! Why wouldn't Kit leave this alone? It was none of his damn business, for one thing. And he, more than anyone else, ought to understand why—

"I'll try to rustle up a pony," he said tightly. "But will Lady Greer keep her end of the bargain, once you inform her what that is?" He never questioned that Kit could convince her to try. From the time he learned to babble his first words, Kit could talk the birds out of trees.

"Fact is," Kit admitted with a shrug, "she doesn't even know Wordsworth. But she's been writing back and forth with his sister, and I'm counting on her to convince said sister that her brother ought to meet my brother. Who will bring his resident Russian along to tea, naturally. It's not such a long shot as you are thinking, by the by."

"At the moment it sounds as if I'd have a better chance of flying to the moon."

"Well, that's because you've always underestimated me, Jimmie. And I expect you have no idea what Celia is capable of. Miracles, I'm hoping, and I'm not referring to recruiting the poetry fellow. But never mind that. Have we a deal?"

"Just deliver the poet, Kit. I don't care how you do it. I'll be at the picnic, and I'll find a damned pony. Good enough?"

"Not nearly," Kit replied. "But it's a start."

Chapter 15

From the parlor window, Celia watched the Earl of Kendal's crested carriage pull into the courtyard of the Merry Goosegirl. It had barely come to a halt when the door flew open and Vasily Chirikov sprang out.

Despite her jittery nerves, Celia could not help but laugh. The general meant to greet his idol in style, and he looked splendid indeed in a dark green coat edged in red and trimmed with yellow buttons, braid, and epaulets. His sash was white, striped with gold and tied with fringed knots. The entire left side of his chest dripped with medals, and an enormous sword was slung from his belt in a brass-studded scabbard.

She hoped the Wordsworth household was prepared for an invasion.

Lord Kendal waited for the steps to be lowered before alighting with his customary grace, looking austerely elegant in dove-gray pantaloons, a charcoal-gray coat, and pristine white linen. The silver knob atop his black walking stick shone under the bright noonday sun.

Celia adjusted her bonnet, pulled on her gloves, and went outside to meet them.

"Lady Greer!" Chirikov boomed, sweeping his black cocked hat from his head and thundering in her direction.

Next she knew, Celia was enveloped in a pair of tree-trunk arms, with her nose buried in medals and a sword hilt plowing into her stomach.

"You haff saved me!" he proclaimed. "I vill build a church in St. Petersburg to honor you."

"Unless you also mean to bury the lady there," Kendal said pointedly, "it might be well to permit her to breathe."

Chirikov let go so abruptly that Celia was thrown off balance, and she might have toppled had not Kendal steadied her with a firm hand on her elbow. The touch of his soft kidskin glove against her bare flesh sent lightning zigzagging up and down her arm.

"Thank you," she said, stepping free of his dangerous grasp.

Chirikov was gazing at her with the woebegone expression of an oversized puppy that had committed an indiscretion. "Forgiff me. I am haffing many nerffs today."

She smiled brightly. "Miss Wordsworth assures me that her brother is most eager to make your acquaintance, sir. But I do believe that she will be a trifle taken aback if you greet her wearing such an impressive weapon."

"Hah! Kendal tells me same think. I must leaf it in coach, yes?"

"Decidedly," said the earl, gesturing to the carriage. "Shall we be on our way?"

Chirikov and the stack of books he'd brought along for Wordsworth to sign filled all of one bench, so Celia was forced to sit beside Lord Kendal on the other for the journey to Rydal. She was forcibly reminded of the last time they had traveled side by side, and where they were going, and what had happened there.

If he remembered that day, he gave no sign of it. He was wearing what she thought of as his "diplomat face," ineffably calm, gravely polite. She'd wager *his* heart wasn't jumping about in his chest like a mad March hare.

He inclined his head. "If I may inquire, Lady Greer, how was it you succeeded in bringing about this meeting so expeditiously? Your message this morning was unexpected, though certainly welcome."

She tried to match his cool tone. "I have long intended to pay a call on Miss Wordsworth, and Kit's . . . er, Mr. Valliant's request merely coincided with my own wishes. I am only sorry that she insisted you make one of the party. The afternoon will prove tedious for you, I'm afraid."

"Not at all." He looked over at her, his eyes wintry. "But I regret that you find yourself *sorry* on my account. Does my company offend you, madam?"

Stunned at the question, she shot an embarrassed glance at Chirikov. Fortunately, he was paying them no attention, wholly preoccupied with the volume of poetry spread open on his lap.

"How can you ask such a thing?" she hissed under her breath. "I had thought the situation quite the reverse. And in my message, I told you that I meant to travel on horseback and meet you at Rydal Mount. It was you who insisted on picking me up at the Merry Goosegirl."

"The morning was overcast, and I feared you would be caught in a downpour. But let us not squabble, Lady Greer. Why is it Miss Wordsworth requires my presence at tea, do you suppose?"

He was deliberately setting her on edge, she decided, and then making it her fault when she tumbled over the side. It was a diplomat's trick to gain the upper hand, but she was having none of it.

"I expect it was your purse she invited to tea, my lord. Poets are ever in search of wealthy patrons, and you happen to be the local potentate. Likely she hopes you will commission her brother's next epic, or at the very least, fund a ballad or two."

"God forbid," he said with a grimace. "I'd sooner sponsor a band of pestilential Morris dancers. But tell me, why have you taken rooms at the woefully named Merry Goosegirl? Would not your own home be more comfortable than a country inn?"

She'd sooner sleep under a hedgerow than spend another night at Greer's farm. "The property will be put up for sale when repairs are completed," she explained. "At the moment workers are tearing down most of the outbuildings and reroofing the house, which is naturally creating a great deal of noise and dust. An agent is trying to locate a suitable house for me in Ambleside or Bowness, but meantime I shall remain where I am."

He cast her a sideways glance. "Alone?"

What in blazes was he implying? "For the most part," she said between her teeth. "If you discount the queue of lovers waiting in the passageway outside my bedchamber. I don't admit just anyone, you know."

She was pleased to see his head snap back against the leather squabs as if she'd slapped him.

A tense silence enveloped the compartment for nearly an hour as the coach wound its way through Applethwaite and Ambleside, finally slowing as Rydal came into view.

Up a steep lane from the road, Rydal Mount was set amid several acres of gardens, with a lovely view of Rydal Water and the northern reaches of Lake Windemere. A perfect setting for a poet enamored with the beauties of nature, Celia thought, calmer now.

She had spent most of the last hour devising clever, sophisticated replies to Lord Kendal's provocative questions—far too late, of course. It was a wonder the carriage hadn't ignited from the invisible sparks shooting between them. At one point she had wrenched her gaze from the window long enough to see his hand clutching the knob of his walking stick with enough force to melt the silver.

But he had donned his diplomat face again by the time a footman opened the carriage door, and he handed her onto the gravel walkway with distant courtesy.

She longed to kick him where it would hurt.

Chirikov jumped down, mustache twitching and arms full of books, his sword still swinging from its scabbard. He had forgot to remove it, and Celia hadn't the heart to remind him.

What a dear man, so excited at the prospect of meeting his idol. With blistering willpower, she consigned Lord Kendal to the devil. This was Vasily Chirikov's day, and nothing must be allowed to spoil it.

A short, thin woman with gypsy-brown skin scurried out to greet them, hands fluttering in agitation. "Lady Greer? But of course it is. Who else could it be? I am so delighted to meet you."

"Thank you for inviting us on such short notice," Celia

replied, torn between a polite curtsy and a warm hug. She had exchanged only a few letters with Dorothy Wordsworth, but their correspondence had been precious to her. Most of the people she wrote to during her bleak years with Greer never wrote back, but Dorothy had faithfully replied each time, perhaps as hungry for pen-friends as Celia had been. She'd have written more often to Dorothy, but Greer was never convinced that franking a letter didn't cost him anything. He had even begrudged the price of paper and ink.

Reminding herself yet again that her husband's parsimony had made her a rich widow, Celia introduced Lord Kendal and the crimson-faced General Chirikov. Several books toppled from his arms onto the gravel when he bowed, but Dorothy quickly scooped them up, brightening when she saw her brother's name on the spines.

"You admire William's poetry?" she inquired dubiously, eyes fixed on his sword.

"With all my heart," Chirikov swore. "Bless you, luffly lady, for permitting me come into your beautiful home."

Celia caught Kendal's amused glance and could not help smiling back when he took her arm and led her behind Dorothy and Chirikov into the house.

The poet waited for them beside the mantelpiece in a large drawing room, one wall lined with bookshelves and the others covered with framed portraits. A sofa and a few wooden chairs were set around the fireplace, and a thick Turkey carpet covered the floor.

As for William Wordsworth himself, Celia could not be impressed. Although he stood taller than average, Kendal topped him by a hand and Chirikov, of course, dwarfed everyone. Wordsworth's narrow, slightly droopy shoulders and a Brutus cut designed to conceal his receding hairline, not to mention legs somehow out of proportion to his body, did not help his cause.

But there was clear intelligence in his sharp eyes as he greeted his guests with old-fashioned formality.

Chirikov, suddenly shy, held back, and Celia regarded his

blanched face with concern. He looked, impossibly, on the point of swooning.

Then Kendal, with practiced ease, got them all settled— Wordsworth and Chirikov together on the sofa, Celia perched on a hard chair next to the one holding Dorothy's skinny body, and himself with one arm relaxed on the mantelpiece as he stood, overseeing the lot of them.

Well done, my lord, Celia thought, resenting his aloof appraisal of the scene he had orchestrated. He needn't look as if he'd gone slumming by coming to Rydal Mount. This wasn't exactly Versailles, to be sure, but the general and the poet seemed to be hitting it off well. They were totally absorbed with each other, although Wordsworth seemed to be doing all the talking. His words were indistinguishable from where she sat, and he appeared to have forgot anyone else was in the room.

She looked over at Dorothy, who was squirming on her chair and watching her brother with rapt attention. Celia had hoped to become better acquainted with her pen-friend, but her attempts to begin a conversation met with so little encouragement that she soon abandoned the effort. For half an hour she sat quietly, watching the hands of the ormulu clock on the mantelpiece.

Kendal had grown sufficiently bored to leave his perch and explore the bookcases, which put him from her sight unless she swiveled on her chair to look at him. She refused to give him so much satisfaction. Not that he was likely to notice, of course. She wished she had thought to wander over to the bookcases before he did. When, she wondered, would Dorothy rouse herself to serve tea?

Finally, unable to sit still a moment longer, she reached over and plucked at Dorothy's sleeve. "Will you show me the gardens, please? We had the barest glimpse of them from the carriage."

Dorothy started as if jolted from a trance. "Oh, yes indeed. I have been so very rude. Do forgive me, Lady Greer. William was unsettled all morning, you understand, what with an earl and a general of the Russian Imperial Guard coming to call. But he seems quite comfortable now, so I believe it is safe to go."

As they left the parlor Celia glanced over her shoulder at Lord Kendal. He held open a large, leather-bound book, to all appearances thoroughly absorbed with its contents. Had he looked up, she might have beckoned him to join them in the garden. Or perhaps not. In any event, he did not give her the chance.

Kendal saw her go, her pale lavender skirts clinging deliciously to her rounded hips and long, graceful legs. He might have followed her, had she given him the slightest indication his company would be welcome. But what did he expect? After his inexplicable, stunningly cruel attack in the carriage, she could only be wishing him at Jericho.

What had possessed him to speak in such a way to her? Had Chirikov been paying the least bit of attention to his caustic remarks, the general would have called him out on the spot.

Not that Lady Greer required a champion to defend her. She had rendered him to sausage with chilling ease, leaving him to stew in his own fury while she blithely turned away and proceeded to enjoy the lakeland scenery.

The blame was entirely his, which infuriated him all the more. Each time they met, his reprehensible conduct astounded him. Celia Greer had demolished a lifetime of rigid self-discipline simply by existing, but he could scarcely expect her to disappear from the face of the earth merely to preserve his sanity.

What remained of it. Quite irrationally, he resented her for being what she was. With so small a thing as a toss of her golden curls or the flash of a dimple when she smiled, she snatched away his reason like a cat making off with a mackerel.

Above all, he resented her for wielding such power over him. Naturally, the solution was to avoid her company at any cost. But the cost, he had already discovered, was exceedingly dear. Ever since that afternoon at the White Swan, he had been paying with sleepless nights, aching loins, and suicidal notions of leaping again into the fire.

He had done precisely that by insisting they travel together to Rydal. Oh, he'd justified his folly with the assumption that Chirikov's presence would keep his temper in check, but he suspected the entire Russian army could not do that. Not with Celia Greer in the vicinity.

After today's debacle, he knew better than to tempt fate or his own flagging self-control ever again. He would, he resolved, put miles between them. Whole countries. He would be the first to arrive in Austria for the Congress of Vienna and the last to depart when it was concluded, perhaps on a ship bound for China.

But now, he accepted after several minutes trying to convince himself otherwise, he had no choice but to make his apology to Lady Greer.

Returning the book he'd been holding to the shelf, he glanced over at Wordsworth and Chirikov. The poet was still nattering about some topic of monumental unimportance while his audience of one regarded him with unabashed adulation. They wouldn't notice a herd of woolly mammoths charging through the drawing-room doors, let alone his quiet departure.

Kendal stepped outside, blinking against the bright sunshine, and heard laughter coming from the rear of the house. He followed the sound, pausing in the shadow of an ivy-covered pergola when he saw her.

She was swinging from a tree.

Her skirts flew up, revealing shapely ankles and a generous portion of stockinged legs as she soared, laughing with delight. Beside her on another swing, a young boy was straining to match her dizzying height.

"Harder!" he shrieked to the girl who was pushing him.

"I'm *trying*!" she shouted in reply. "When is it my turn?"

Immediately Lady Greer scraped her half boots on the packed dirt to slow herself and jumped off the wooden bench. "Mercy me!" she exclaimed, staggering in circles as the two children laughed uproariously. "I am quite colly-walloped. You had best take my place, Dora."

"Will you push me, ma'am?" the girl asked, settling in the swing.

"Just to get you started." She glanced in his direction, and Kendal suspected she had been aware of his presence the moment he arrived. "Then you must excuse me while I find my balance again. I am too ancient a creature for such exertion."

When Dora had been propelled to a satisfying height, Lady Greer spoke briefly with Dorothy Wordsworth and another woman seated beside her on the grass. Kendal had not even noticed them. Then she moved in his direction, brushing down her ruffled skirts, a look of polite inquiry on her face.

"Is it time to depart, my lord?"

"Not unless you can figure a way to detach General Chirikov from his poet. They are growing together like vines. Will you walk with me for a few minutes, Lady Greer?" He held out his arm, rather afraid she would refuse to take it.

With transparent reluctance, she placed her hand on his wrist and permitted him to lead her across the lawn, away from the children and the avid eyes of the ladies, who had been watching curiously.

Suddenly unwilling to launch himself directly into troubled waters, he cast about for an innocuous remark. "What exactly does it mean, Lady Greer? To be colly-walloped?"

"What?" She frowned. "Oh, *that*! I have no idea, sir. I just invented the word. How shall we define it?"

The way he was feeling defined colly-walloped fairly well, he would guess. Scatty. Fuzzy-headed. Poleaxed. "Perhaps we should leave it as is, meaning whatever anyone wishes it to mean."

She smiled approval. "Dorothy was wondering if she ought to serve refreshments, but she dislikes interrupting her brother when he is in full cry. He rarely has occasion to discuss poetic theory since Mr. Coleridge took himself off to wherever he's gone, and he seems to be enjoying himself with General Chirikov."

"The salivating worship of an acolyte has its appeal, I suppose."

"And sarcasm does not become you, sir." She removed her hand from his arm. "The general is, to be sure, somewhat extravagant in his devotion to Mr. Wordsworth, but he is by nature a man of excessive emotions. Has he told you how he came to love the poems with such ferocious zeal?"

Chastened, Kendal shook his head.

"Perhaps you won't think him such a fool if I explain. A winter campaign in Russia is all but unendurable, by his account, and in the long, cold nights, his undernourished men froze to death by the score. But Bonaparte was advancing, and Chirikov had been ordered to hold position whatever the hardships. Requiring a distraction to preserve his clarity of mind, he elected to improve his command of English."

She took a deep breath. "Really, you should ask the general to tell you about his experiences in the war. It quite broke my heart to hear of such unimaginable horrors."

"I am astonished that he spoke of them to a lady," Kendal said stiffly.

"You *would* be," she said with a sigh. "But I do not wish to be sheltered from life, even at its worst. In any case, Chirikov's physician offered to tutor him, using the only book written in English that could be found. It was *Lyrical Ballads*, containing poems by Mr. Wordsworth, and the general memorized every one of them. I'll not try to explain how they affected him during those hellish months, or why he found peace of heart by reading them again and again."

She made a graceful gesture. "Indeed, I scarcely understand it myself, being unacquainted with his circumstances or Mr. Wordsworth's verses. But they resonated in his soul, and he promised himself that should he survive the war, he would make a pilgrimage to England and pay honor to the poet who gave him the will to endure."

A wood warbler chirruped overhead, and Kendal realized they had come to a stop under the branches of a silver birch. Celia—he could not think of her as Lady Greer, however hard he tried—gazed up at him with eyes that dared him to ridicule Chirikov.

All he wanted to do was kiss her senseless.

Which only proved that he, not the Russian, was the real fool. He took a backward step, and then another, putting distance between them. Putting her beyond arm's reach, truth be told, because he could not trust his arms to behave themselves. They remembered all too well how it felt to be wrapped around that slender, vibrant body.

Damn his arms, and every other part of him that had gone to battle with his thoroughly honorable intentions. He had set out to clear his conscience with an apology, escort her back to the Green Goose, or whatever that stupid inn was called, and wash his hands of Celia, once and for all.

And he could do it, too. Serenely. With practiced ease. What use were his years of diplomatic service, after all, if he could not rid himself of one troublesome young woman without giving offense?

It helped not to look at her, though. He fixed his gaze at a point beyond her shoulder and shaped his lips into a thin smile. "I have misjudged General Chirikov," he acknowledged graciously. Conceding the obvious was the usual strategy in these situations. "Thank you for clarifying what I failed to recognize."

"Oh, you are most welcome," she said, mocking his stilted tone. "Should you require enlightenment on any other subject, I would be most happy to provide it."

"Thank you yet again. But what I *require* . . . that is, what I wish—" He seized a deep breath. "In point of fact, Lady Greer, I owe you a most profound apology for my disgraceful behavior in the carriage."

Silence.

A minute—or was it an eternity?—went by, and still she failed to respond. It was nothing, she should be saying. Or, better, I was at fault for overreacting to a few perfectly innocuous remarks.

But she only looked at him, head tilted expectantly, her stillness drawing his gaze to her face despite his every effort to hold it away.

"What?" he asked from sheer frustration.

160

"You said that you owed me an apology, sir, and I quite agree. I was waiting to hear it."

When pigs take flight! was his first, admittedly childish thought. No one of his acquaintance actually apologized in so many words. They acknowledged the need to do so and that was the end of it. Groveling was not expected from gentlemen of his class, and it was certainly not in his nature.

"But never mind," she said airily. "I've heard worse from you than I did today, although your lamentable manners never fail to astonish me. Were it not years too late, Lord Kendal, I would certainly advise you to reconsider a career in the diplomatic corps."

The thin slice of his brain that still functioned ordered him to bow and walk away, but he felt his heels dig in. "And I would advise *you*, Lady Greer, to remove your lovely nose from any and all matters concerning my family."

If he thought that his open declaration of war, which he immediately wanted to call back, would deter her, he was dead wrong.

"At last we come to it," she said. "I'm only surprised you waited this long."

"Surely it is obvious that this situation is intolerable for everyone concerned."

Her brows arched. "Not for me, sir. Not for Kit. And certainly not for Charley, who needs all the friends he can get. No, Lord Kendal, *you* are the one thinks it intolerable, which I find incomprehensible given that you are no part of anything we do. Can you explain it to me? Why does it so disturb you that I have spent a few hours in company with the boy?"

"Nearly every day," he gritted. "His lessons are disturbed. His governess complains. Household discipline has suffered."

"Good heavens, just listen to yourself!" She speared him with a look of disdain. "The child cannot be locked up with his books all summer for the convenience of your *servants*. He should be outside, like Tom and Dora Wordsworth, laughing and playing as ordinary children do."

"Lord Paxton," Kendal said icily, "will have responsibilities beyond those of a rustic poet's offspring. As heir to the title, he must prepare himself. And I assure you, one day he will be grateful for the education, self-discipline, and sense of duty his teachers instill in him now."

"I see, my lord. You wish him to become a facsimile of yourself."

"That is highly unlikely, madam. What I do *not* wish is your continued meddling. It disrupts order. And have you considered the effect on Paxton when you lose interest in him and wander off to find yourself a new toy?"

"As you have done?" she fired back, her small hands clenching at her skirts.

"That will be quite enough, young woman." His voice was a file grating on metal. "I'll take no lessons from a presumptuous female, especially one whose own standards of conduct and morality have been deplorable, to say the least."

The blood drained from her face. "You would know," she said softly.

"Indeed." The devil was driving him now. "Are we clear on this matter? Candale is closed to you. That applies from this moment, and continues when I am gone back to London. You will not set foot on the estate."

She nodded.

Fight me, damn you! But she only gazed at him, pale and still, her thoughts unreadable. She had been just so when he returned to the bedchamber at the White Swan after—no. He must not think on that again, not ever again.

He meant to read her a list of instructions, but could no longer remember what they were. He knew only that he must, *must* escape her now. Sketching her a bow, he walked away, ordering his legs not to break into a run.

Her voice floated to him from a vast distance, although he'd gone no more than a few yards. "What of Charley, my lord? I understand that you despise me, but am I forbidden to see him altogether, simply because he is your son?"

He stopped. Turned. Rage and pain distilled inside him,

coming together in a searing knot before erupting in a blast of white heat.

"But that's the thing, you see. He is *not* my son."

Chapter 16

"He *told* you?" Kit's gaze shot up from his sketchbook to fix on her in disbelief.

Celia gazed back helplessly. She had not meant to repeat Kendal's words to anyone, let alone to his brother, and had made it through most of the day with her determination intact. But out the words had come, and she could not call them back.

Nor did she want to. Adult secrets and adult strategies for concealing them were hurting Charley, and *something* must be done to change that. What that something could be, she'd no idea, but surely the place to begin was with the truth. It had not occurred to her that Kit might be hearing it for the first time, and she was relieved to learn that he already knew.

"I'm certain he never meant to say what he did," Celia replied at last. "But I provoked him, and he spoke before he could stop to think."

"Kendal spoke without thinking?" Kit folded his arms across his bent knee. "Now you really do amaze me."

"I seem to have that effect on him, likely because I am forever blurting out the most prodigiously awful things when we are together. This time we were quarreling about Charley, and I said something particularly unconscionable. He fired back, and I cannot say which of us was the most stunned to hear his words. He went white as paper, while I just stood there with my mouth open. Then he turned on his heel and walked away. Chirikov and I waited with the carriage for an hour before giving up on him. I've no idea how he got home again."

"On a job horse," Kit said, his voice bemused. "After midnight, come to think of it. He went directly to his study and locked the door, but that's not so unusual these days. Not since Chirikov moved in, at any rate. And he was gone this morning before I came downstairs. Walking on the fells, according to his valet."

Celia looked down the long sloping hill to a nearly dry riverbed, where Charley and Vasily Chirikov were gathering pebbles to build a fort. Kendal would be furious to know she was here with them. With Charley. But his anger no longer had the power to hurt her, and there was too much at stake to fear his displeasure. She already had *that* in abundance.

Kit had resumed his sketching, his pencil moving swiftly over the large sheet of paper. He sat with his back against a tree trunk, one knee propped to hold the sketchbook and the other leg stretched in front of him. "Hold still," he ordered when she tried to ease a cramp in her leg. "And don't lose that expression."

She froze, annoyed that he could be drawing a stupid picture at this particular moment. Did he fail to understand *why* she had addressed the subject of Kendal and Charley? They should be making plans. Devising solutions. "What expression?" she muttered between clenched teeth.

"You'll see in a minute. And I need to concentrate, so be quiet."

The Valliant men just loved ordering people about, she thought with considerable ire. Even Kit, usually sweet-natured, expected to be obeyed without question.

"There!" he said after what seemed to her like an hour. "Come have a look."

Unwrapping her stiff, crossed legs, she crawled the few yards to where Kit sat and leaned over to see the picture.

"Oh mercy!" It was her face, she supposed, although surely that murderous grimace belonged to someone else. So did the breastplate and the leather lacings crossing over otherwise bare legs, not to mention the notched spear raised for a strike. "Is this how you see me?"

"On occasion, such as now. Beneath the surface of the exceedingly proper Lady Greer, there lurks the fierce spirit of an Amazon warrior."

She whooped with laughter. "The Amazon analogy is dubious at best, but *proper*?"

"My exquisite tact is famous throughout Westmoreland," he said with a grin. "Have a peek at the rest and tell me what you think."

She took the sketchbook and studied the drawings he had made of her. There were seven in all, some only a few telling lines, others shaded with delicate precision. He had caught her laughing, and in a pensive mood, and once looking positively angelic.

"I believe you flatter me," she said. "For the most part, anyway. But this?" She pointed to a sketch of herself reclining on a Grecian couch, one knee lifted in a decidedly wanton pose. "This is not the creature I see in the mirror."

"You don't know how to look. But it's true that you will never see yourself as a man does, and I expect a man in love with you would draw you quite differently. He would keep pictures like this one in his heart."

She'd no idea what to make of that astonishing statement. "I know nothing about art, but you appear to be extremely talented. Have you considered a career as a painter?"

"Actually, I don't paint, not even with watercolors. Sketching is an occasional hobby, no more, and what you imagine to be talent is primarily a gift for observation. James would not credit it, but I am an excellent judge of character, most particularly that which lies beneath the surface."

"I can well believe it." She slanted him an assessing look. "For example, you probably know what I am thinking at this very moment."

"Far too easy," he said, taking back the sketchbook. "You are itching to know if James spoke the truth about Charley."

"Well," she demanded. "Did he?"

Kit leafed through his sketches until he located a page with five small, detailed renderings of Charley's face from different angles.

She studied them and saw, or thought she saw, a clear resemblance to Kendal in the line of the boy's jaw, the lift of his cheekbones, the narrow, aristocratic nose. "To judge by these—"

"Ah, but you mustn't. That's how *I* see Charley, and naturally I seek any possible resemblance to my brother. Or perhaps I put it there, unconsciously. If Charley were standing here now, you'd notice that his face is softer and more round, like that of most boys his age. The face I drew is the one he will grow into. Perhaps. Only perhaps."

"Have you shown these to Lord Kendal?"

"Perish the thought. He already considers me idle and useless, and I'd not have him know that I laze about drawing pictures. Besides, it would not help the situation. When James looks at Charley, he sees only Belinda."

"Her loss must grieve him terribly," Celia murmured, never having considered that possibility. It made cruel sense, she supposed, to avoid a child who brought the pain of losing his wife to mind simply by existing. "I once saw them together, you know. On their wedding day."

"Yes? I don't recall meeting you."

"Mercy, I wasn't an invited guest. But I happened to be in Kendal for the Saturday market, and when the bells began to peal, I dashed to the church along with everyone else. The bride and groom had just emerged from the vestibule, and I remember a flower seller rushing up the steps to shower them with daisies. Lord Kendal plucked one midair and presented it to his new wife. Then she kissed him, and the crowd cheered."

"Did you applaud as well?" he asked wryly.

"Oh, indeed. He was elegant and handsome, and she was the most beautiful creature imaginable, and they looked so happy they could fly."

"I expect they were happy, that particular morning." He leaned back against the tree, folding his arms behind his head. "And I fear you have a romantic heart, Lady Greer."

"I did. At the time." She picked up a fallen leaf and began to tear it into small pieces. "Well, perhaps I understand the situation a bit better now, although I cannot approve. Thank you for explaining."

Kit's brows shot up. "I've explained nothing. You have leapt to conclusions, is all, and shot past the target by leagues. Kendal neither misses his wife nor mourns her, except in the way civilized people mourn any untimely death. If he lost anything, it was only the romantic dream you thought you were witness to outside that church. Nothing could have been further from the truth, I assure you."

"Oh." Her heart began to turn somersaults in her chest. She wasn't at all sure she wanted to hear the explanation, but wild horses could not have dragged her away now.

He had closed his eyes. The warm July breeze ruffled his hair, burnished to gold by the sunlight streaming through the leaves and branches overhead.

"James would cut out my liver with a spoon if he knew I had spoken to you of these matters," he said after what seemed an eternity. "Tell me why I should give you the rest of it."

"There is no reason. Unless you think my knowing will somehow be of help to Charley."

"Precisely." He opened one eye. "I can't imagine how it could, but at this point there is nothing I wouldn't try. When I'm gone again on my travels, he will need a friend."

"He has that already, for all the use I can be. Lord Kendal has forbidden me to come onto his estate, but he neglected to specify that I was never to spend time with Charley outside of Candale. I'm sure that's what he meant, though."

"Do you always do what you are told, Celia?"

"I'm here, aren't I?"

His lips curved. "Well, so you are. And I believe we are of one mind where Charley is concerned. But where to begin? The thing is, these roots grow deep. What has James told you of himself?"

"Nothing to the point. Certainly nothing remotely personal. We are the barest of acquaintances, Kit."

"If you say so. And I suppose he wouldn't confide this particular story, even to a lover."

Celia's cheeks went on fire, but she managed a careless gesture. "In my case that cannot apply. And if you have ever thought so, think again."

"Right. Well, Chirikov will soon be clamoring for us to

bring out the picnic lunch, so I'll talk fast and make this brief. The Valliant family was storybook happy, or that is my recollection, until Mama and Papa went to visit our estate in the Highlands. They planned to be gone a month, and we had no idea anything was wrong until a messenger arrived with the shattering news. He gave it to the new Earl of Kendal, leaving James to tell the rest of us."

A barely perceptible shudder passed through Kit's lanky frame. "They were caught in a snowstorm on Rannock Moor, and all of them, the earl and countess, drivers and servants, even the horses, froze to death. They weren't discovered until a week later."

"I'm so sorry," Celia murmured into the silence that followed. "How terrible."

"Yes, especially for James. We were all devastated, of course, but he was the one saddled with responsibility for the estates, not to mention a pair of rambunctious brothers. I was five at the time, Alex nine, and James had just turned twelve. He grew up overnight, it seemed. That's what I most remember, actually—how he changed beyond recognition. Before, he was in and out of trouble with the rest of us, devising the cleverest of our pranks and taking all the blame when we got caught. Always laughing, too. He almost never laughs now, not from the heart. Have you noticed?"

She nodded, unable to speak past the lump in her throat. But he must have changed again, because she clearly remembered him smiling and laughing on his wedding day.

"He became a right proper earl," Kit went on reflectively, "starting the very moment he came into the title. He'd always been a tenacious chap, and immediately set about learning everything he needed to know, from accounting and investments to estate management and crop rotation. Alex was sent to Harrow and I was handed over to a tutor, so we rarely saw him. But never mind all that. I'll cut directly to Belinda, if you will be kind enough to fish some lemonade from that basket. My mouth is dry as sandpaper."

With shaking hands, Celia found the bucket containing a large jar of lemonade. All the ice in the bucket had long since melted, but the lemonade was still fairly cool. She filled two glasses and gave one to Kit, who smiled encouragingly.

"It's a hard story, I know," he said. "But don't be distressed, or I'll not be able to finish it."

"I'm well accustomed to hard stories," she assured him, her own sorry experiences fading to nothing in comparison. All this time she'd assumed that the wealthy, handsome, oh-so-clever Lord Kendal had enjoyed a charmed life from birth. How little we understand of others, she thought, feeling selfish and shallow of heart.

"I guessed that," Kit said softly. "One day, perhaps you will confide your own story to me." He drained his glass and held it out for a refill. "But for now, James is on the block, and Belinda is getting ready to lop off his head."

"They were in love," she said, stubbornly clinging to the illusion of how a happy marriage ought to be. They had created that illusion for her, Lord Kendal and his bride, on a long-ago Saturday morning. "I could not have mistaken that."

"*He* was in love," Kit corrected gently. "Belinda's father invited himself and his daughter to Candale, hoping to arrange a marriage, and James fell head over heels for her. Well, so did we all, I suppose. She was beautiful, high-spirited, and seemed to dote on him. So they wed, although it cost James a pretty penny in settlements, and everyone expected them to live happily ever after."

He tilted his head, frowning slightly. "In point of fact, Belinda was much like you—on the surface. She had a gift for making people feel important, for one thing, and a natural, sunny exuberance that lit up a room the moment she stepped inside. Unfortunately, she was also a—pardon the word, but it's the only one that applies—a slut."

"G-good heavens."

"Oh, she behaved herself for the first year or so. But James had a great many responsibilities and could not always dance attendance on her. She grew bored, and turned her attentions elsewhere. To Alex, I suspect, although he's never admitted to it. He came home from Cambridge for the Christmas holidays, and shortly after Twelfth Night, without explanation, he bought a commission in the army and left the country."

"Surely you are wrong. She cannot have seduced her husband's own brother, for pity's sake."

"She tried to seduce *me*," Kit said flatly. "Not until years later, though, which is why I didn't twig to what she was about in the early days. I imagine several of the footmen could have told a merry tale, or maybe not. She was careful, and possibly faithful, early on. Even Belinda realized that her excesses would not be tolerated until she provided the Earl of Kendal an heir."

Celia took a swallow of tasteless lemonade, her stomach roiling. She could sense what was coming next, and knew it would be unbearable.

"For the smartest man I've ever known," Kit said, "James was blind to what everyone else could see. When Belinda announced her pregnancy, he was in alt. And when Charley was born, he was altogether besotted with the child. Disappointed that Belinda refused to nurse the babe, I recall, and surprised when she virtually ignored both husband and son thereafter, but the proud papa made up for her lack of attention. He even rigged up a sling and carried Charley on his back when he rode out to visit the tenant farmers."

"I don't understand," Celia interrupted. "From what you are saying, he never questioned that Charley was his son. *His*. Not some other man's."

"True. Which is why we can assume that he was sleeping with Belinda when Charley was conceived. What we don't know is who else she had taken to bed, or to the hay in the barn, or to the other places where she entertained her lovers. There were plenty of lovers, we all became aware in the year after Charley was born. That was when she crept into my own bed, and scared the devil out of me, I promise you. It was all I could do to pry her loose."

Celia shook her head in disbelief. How could any woman want another man when she was loved by Lord Kendal? It was beyond her comprehension, beyond even her own vivid

171

imagination. She wrapped her arms around her waist, afraid she was about to vomit lemonade onto the lush grass.

"Hard to credit, is it not?" Kit asked sympathetically. "I've had years to get used to all this, but I'll never understand. Belinda had a sickness of some kind, an insatiable appetite for men—a variety of men—and from then on she gave it full rein. Even James could not fail to see what she made excruciatingly obvious. It was about then he signed on with the Foreign Office and began to travel. Belinda was furious, of course. She had wanted to cut a dash in London, but he wouldn't take her along. Lord, he could scarcely bear the sight of her. He disappeared for months at a time, while she tumbled every man that would have her."

"And Charley?" How could Kendal leave him behind?

"Charley got lost in the wash, I'm afraid. I fled Candale, too, fairly sure I'd wring Belinda's neck if I stayed around. We all let Charley down, one way or another, although Kendal made the trip from London to see him fairly regularly. Until Charley's third birthday, anyway. That was when everything fell apart."

Kit swiped his sleeve over his forehead. "Here's where it gets really ugly, Celia. Are you certain you wish to hear the rest?"

At the moment she wished to kill a dead woman. "Go on."

"Well, so here it is. I came home for the celebration, which went better than I had dared to hope. But when Charley had been packed off to bed, Belinda started drinking heavily. She was in a strange mood, even for her. We were in the salon, the three of us, and it was like being in the room with a lit rocket. But she said nothing when James and I laid out the chessboard, and after a while I forgot she was there. And how much she hated being ignored," Kit added on a harsh breath.

"She must have been working herself up into a fine frenzy," he continued after a moment. "All of a sudden she stalked up to the table and swiped the chess pieces onto the floor. 'I have something to tell you,' she said. Then she went back to the sideboard and poured out three glasses of brandy. When she knocked one onto the carpet, James went over to her. I couldn't hear what he said, but she swore at him. Then she shoved a glass into his hand.

" 'It's nearly midnight,' she said, lifting her own glass. 'I think we ought to drink to Charles on his birthday. And to his father—whoever the devil he is.' "

"Dear God." Celia's nails dug into her thighs. She knew the rest without hearing it.

"At first," Kit said, his voice ominously husky, "I wasn't sure what she meant. But I remember the look in her eyes when she tossed her drink into James's face, and I remember her next words exactly.

" 'Not you,' she said. 'Maybe the stableman, maybe one of Lord Lonsdale's footmen, maybe the butcher in Kendal or the baker in Bowness. But not you, my lord husband. I came to despise you nearly from the first, so very noble and fastidious and self-righteous as you were and are. So insufferably *tedious*. I took precautions whenever you bedded me, sir. And while I cannot name the boy's real father, you may be certain that Charles is not your son.' "

"She was lying," Celia said immediately.

"I have always thought so. He wouldn't give her the glamorous life she wanted, and she set out to punish him in return by taking away what he most valued. But at the end of the day we'll never know if she was speaking the truth. And she may well have been, however much you and I wish to believe otherwise. James never questioned it."

"Then he is a fool." Celia waved a hand dismissively. "I cannot be sorry for him if he chooses to credit the word of that . . . that *bitch*!"

"A milder word than I'd have chosen," Kit said when heat flooded to her cheeks. "And to his face, I've called my brother far worse than fool. But his mind is long since closed on this matter. The Valliant men are obstinate as granite blocks, Celia, and James is the worst of us. Also the best, in every way save this one. I continue to be astonished at the way he treats Charley. Or, to be precise, at the way he refuses to deal with him at all."

Because he was so hurt, she thought. Because he had loved Belinda.

Celia could not find it in herself to make excuses for Lord Kendal, but she understood better than Kit how it felt to awaken from a dream, however misguided, into a nightmare that was all too real. She knew how it was to escape from pain by detaching herself from everything that put her in mind of it. And she had learned, from Kendal himself, the aching vulnerability of daring to love, only to be rejected.

Dear heavens. Until this very moment she'd not even mustered the courage to admit that she had fallen in love with him.

Well, there it was. Irrelevant now, to be sure, but she loved the man.

And she would get over it. What choice did she have? Nothing had changed, except that she had been forced to confront her own feelings precisely when they were of no significance.

"What can we do, Kit?" she asked with a direct gaze into his troubled blue eyes.

"Nothing I know of. If I wasn't fairly sure he could beat the stuffing out of me, I'd try to pound some sense into his thick head. But he'll soon be off again, and Charley will be alone again. I am hoping you will stand his friend and watch out for him. It's more than I've any right to ask, but there is no one else who cares for him."

"You could stay," she pointed out.

"Yes." He winced. "I *should* stay. But I won't. Feel free to despise me for it, and to be honest, I rather loathe myself every time I say good-bye to the boy and set out on one of my adventures. But that's the way I am, Celia—unable to stay put for more than a few weeks. Even Charley senses when my feet get itchy, sometimes before I do. He is far too forgiving, that one. Probably because he has been taught to expect nothing from those who are supposed to love him." With a groan, Kit stood and splayed his arms. "Here I am, trying to palm him off to a stranger. Do me a favor, Celia, and slap me good and hard."

"Better you go on feeling wretched," she ruled sternly. "I'll not give you leave to abandon Charley, nor blame you when you do. He is not your son, after all. Kendal must face up to his responsibilities. Which leads us back to where we started, of course. I'll do what I can for the child, you may be sure, but chances are his lofty lordship will put a stop to it. We are not on the best of terms."

"I know." Kit helped her to her feet. "Perhaps you can mend fences tomorrow at Charley's birthday party. I've invited every family in the neighborhood to a picnic, and James has given his promise to come."

"He'll not be pleased to see me there," she warned.

"Does that matter?"

"Not in the least. But I'll ride over when the party is in full swing and try to keep out of his way. Above all things, we must not spoil the day for Charley."

"Right." Kit pointed down the hill. "Speaking of the devil, here he comes. At least, I think that is Charley under all that dirt."

"I found a frog!" The boy charged directly up to Celia and held out his prize for her inspection. "See?"

She examined the woebegone creature and nodded approval. "A fine frog indeed. He looks to be very agile, I must say. How clever you must have been to capture him."

Charley glanced over his shoulder at General Chirikov, who was lumbering up the steep slope with a wide smile on his mud-streaked face. "Uncle Vasily caught the frog," the boy confessed. "And he said that ladies don't much care for frogs, but I was sure you'd like this one. He doesn't bite or anything. Would you like to keep him?"

Celia gazed into the boy's earnest brown eyes and recognized that he was offering her a treasure. It was all she could do to keep the tears that gathered in her own eyes from streaming down her face. Solemnly, she held out her hands and accepted the gift. "Thank you, Charley. He is quite the finest frog I've ever seen. I'd love to take him home with me. But what about his family? Won't they miss him?"

"No," Charley said very softly. "They won't even know that he's gone."

Dear God. Celia glanced over at Kit and saw her own anguish reflected in his eyes. He looked as helpless as she felt.

In his own way, Charley had just put *himself* into her hands. How could she cast him off? But she could no more take Charley with her than she could the frog, which had begun to wriggle for escape.

Seizing a deep breath, she lifted her hands to her face and planted a kiss on the damp froggy forehead. Then she brought the wide mouth to her ear and pretended to be listening.

"Mercy me," she said. "I don't speak frog language very well, but I am almost certain he is telling me he wants to go home."

Charley's eyes widened. "He can talk? Really? Can I hear him?"

Rather sure she'd backed herself into a corner, Celia looked to Kit for help.

"Frogs only speak to females," he said. "Or so I am told." He gave Celia a best-I-could-come-up-with shrug.

She returned her attention to the frog. "I can't actually hear him, Charley. It's more a matter of feeling in my heart what he is trying to say. He is very pleased to have met you, by the way, and thinks it was exceedingly kind of you to give him to me. But he's rather sweet on a young lady frog he's been courting, and wants to marry her and raise some tadpoles."

"Oh." Charley's face went red. "I didn't know that."

Nor did he understand all that business about courtship and tadpoles, Celia thought. It was certain, though, that the last thing he wanted was to hurt this frog. "I think we should take him back to the river, Charley, and set him free. I'll miss him, of course, but perhaps you and I can come back and visit someday."

"Promise?" Charley said eagerly. "Cross your heart?"

Knowing it meant a commitment to this love-starved child, she waved the frog in a vaguely crosslike gesture over her breasts. "I promise. Now show me where you found him. And let's hurry, before General Chirikov eats all our lunch by himself."

Chirikov, his mouth full of ham sandwich, waved as they set out down the hill. "Iss good to let frog go," he called.

"I like Uncle Vasily," Charley confided when they reached the Winster River, barely a stream at this time of year. "He showed me how to build a fort. But it was mostest fun when we threw rocks and broke it down."

Men! They set out so young to be warriors. With relief, since she had not the least bit of fondness for slimy creatures—even ones given to her with love—she crouched beside the muddy riverbank and opened her hands. Without a backward look, the frog sprang away and disappeared under a clump of ferns.

Trying not to be too obvious about it, she washed her hands in the muddy water and rubbed them against her skirt. Charley was gazing somewhat forlornly at the spot where the frog had vanished.

"He'll be happier where he belongs," she said reassuringly.

"But how will we find him when we come back? We don't even know his name."

Eyes burning, Celia drew the boy into a tight hug. He was so warm against her, his small hands clutching at her back, his soft hair tickling at her chin as he buried his face against her neck. I love you, Charley, she told him silently, somewhat like a frog trying to speak feelings without words.

"His name is Ribbit," she whispered. "I'm pretty sure that's what he said."

Charley lifted his head to smile at her. "Iss good!"

Chapter 17

Celia arrived at Charley's birthday picnic just when the fishing was getting under way.

Kit immediately appointed her official hook baiter, but there were few takers for her services. The children liked the wriggly worms far better than the few tiny fish they managed to pull from the lake, and after a time they set aside their poles in favor of worm races.

There were at least three dozen children of varying ages at the picnic, and half as many adults, mostly parents. Servants had been recruited from Candale to set up the canopies and tables, serve the food, and mind the horses and carriages. When he set himself to business, Celia thought, Kit knew how to get things done.

After the fishing, she joined a game of tossing coins into jars and garnered a third-place ribbon. Charley, with the focused intensity of a marksman, took first place and gallantly presented her with the winning penny. It was in her pocket now, and she knew that she would keep it always.

A light breeze ruffled her hair as she relaxed under a tree, watching Charley play Puss in the Corner with the two Wordsworth children and a pair of lively twins. Smaller than the others and unable to outrun them, Charley had been "Puss" for rather a long time.

A few boys were shying pebbles across the placid surface of Lake Windermere in a game of Dick, Duck, and Drake, while several girls rolled hoops and played at shuttlecock nearby. Kit was rounding up stray children for a three-legged race, but the adults, sedated by a lavish luncheon and the midafternoon sun, were seeking quieter entertainment. Some had set out for walks, others were trying their hand at archery, but most had settled comfortably in the shade to exchange gossip.

Celia was sitting on a blanket with Mary Wordsworth, the poet's wife, who had long since dozed off, and Dorothy Wordsworth, who kept her restless hands busy with her knitting needles. There was no telling what that tangle of green yarn was meant to be, but it was growing rapidly.

Not so rapidly, though, as Celia's barely restrained anger.

The guest Charley most wished for, the one he had watched for whenever a vehicle trundled along the track leading to the lake, was not here. Her heart had squeezed with pain to watch him hide his disappointment and welcome the latest arrivals with his frighteningly impeccable manners.

Even on the child's birthday, even though he had given his word, Kendal had chosen not to come.

She squirmed on the blanket, catching the snoozing Mary Wordsworth with the heel of her slipper and jolting her awake.

"Wh-what is it?" Mary asked in confusion.

Celia patted her hand and stood. "Forgive me, Mary. I seem to be exceptionally restive this afternoon. Perhaps a walk will help me shake off my fidgets."

She had meant to ramble alongside the lake, but the sound of laughter drew her instead to the archery field, where General Chirikov had just sent an arrow several yards wide of the target.

As she approached he slotted another arrow, sighted carefully, and let it fly. This time the misguided missile soared into the boughs of a tree, sending a startled bird off its shady perch with an irate whoop. All this to the great glee of the children, who were watching the general demonstrate his skill, or more accurately, his notable lack of it. He grinned at them after every shot.

Celia watched him launch a quiverful of arrows, and when he finally hit the target at its farthest edge, the onlookers rewarded him with vigorous applause.

179

"I stop now," he said, handing the bow to one of the boys. "Iss good sport. Will you shoot, Lady Greer?"

"Mercy, no. I am far too likely to slay an innocent bystander. Would you care to join me for a walk, sir? It will be much safer, I assure you."

Pronouncing himself honored, the general schooled his long stride to hers as they wandered in a southerly direction along the bank of the lake, sometimes exchanging impressions of the scenery but more often walking in companionable silence. Celia was surprised to hear nary a line of poetry the entire hour, and remarked upon it as they made their way back to the picnic area.

"Ah, I haff not reason say poems more times," Chirikov confided. "Mr. Wordsworth hass tell me many places to go, the whons where he hass writed about. So I go see them, and they iss like the poems, but not like the poems. Because there iss places, and feelinks, and words. Iss same, but different. So I understand iss better keep poems here, because feelinks iss best." He thumped at his chest directly over his heart.

Taking his meaning, she gave him a smile, although she couldn't help but think it as well that he had chosen to internalize his poetic rhapsodies.

"Next," he announced, "I vill learn to shoot weeth bow and arrow so hit eyes of bull every time."

Celia laughed. "And you will be a master of the art in no time, I am sure. But if you don't mind, I shall keep myself well distant during the early practices."

"Ah, but no worry. Tomorrow I go to Scotland for shoot with gun."

"You are leaving, then?" She felt inordinately sorry to hear it. When he had returned to Russia, it was unlikely they would ever meet again.

"I haff much luffed this England," he replied, "but now must go home. Soon, we take ship from Edinburk. I vill miss you, luffly Lady Greer, and you sweet smile and kind heart."

Tears welled in her eyes as she stood on tiptoe to plant a light kiss on his chin. "I shall miss you, too, General, and for the same reasons."

He flushed. "I iss not luffly. But I thank you."

They came within sight of the picnic, and Celia noticed right away how quiet everyone had gone. The children continued to play in small groups, but they were uncommonly subdued, and the adults sat or stood with carefully proper deportment. They might have been in a drawing room, or attending a funeral.

She looked around for Charley and saw immediately why everyone's high spirits had suddenly muted. Lord Kendal, wearing a russet coat and wide-brimmed hat, stood rigidly in front of Charley. Kit was behind the boy, one hand resting protectively on his shoulder.

They did not appear to be quarreling, from what Celia could tell at such a distance. Rather, neither Kendal nor Charley seemed to be saying anything at all. Finally, Kit made a gesture toward the canopied picnic tables and they headed in that direction.

A trifle late for luncheon, she thought sourly, the sight of Kendal fanning the coals of her anger. Not only had he arrived hours after everyone else, but apparently without the pony Kit had trusted him to supply.

For Charley's sake, Celia decided to make a quiet departure while her temper was still in check. Of late, Kendal could not be in her company without provoking a row, and her own mood was scarcely peaceable.

"I shall take my leave of you now," she told the general. "Later, will you give my apologies to Charley for not bidding him good-bye? I think he would be disappointed to learn I am leaving early, but I really must be on my way."

Chirikov looked displeased. "You haff someone be with you, Lady Greer? Iss not good for lady to ride alone."

"I've only a short way to go, sir. My butler, Mr. Carver, is waiting for me in Winster and expects me there shortly. I don't wish to worry him by arriving late."

"I take you there!" Chirikov spoke like the general he was.

Celia could not oblige. Alone, she might be able to steal off undetected, but not with this Russian behemoth in tow. "I came on horseback, sir, and you by coach. Besides, the most direct way to Winster is over the hills, and I shall be there in a trice. Good-bye, my friend. It has been a great joy to make your acquaintance."

Before he could raise further objections, she moved quickly away, choosing a circular route that avoided the tent. Kendal was now seated on a folding chair, and Charley was rummaging through one of the picnic baskets.

Reaching the spinney where Aphra was tethered, she unloosed the reins and led the mare to the path that would take them to Winster. Every minute or so she glanced back, but from all she could tell, no one had seen her depart. Soon she reached the top of a low rise and paused to look down at the picnickers.

At two of them, anyway—the tall man and the little boy alone under the blue-and-white canopy. She could barely make them out. Kendal was still seated, and Charley stood beside him, the top of his head even with his father's shoulder.

His *father*, whatever Kendal chose to think.

Were Charley not there to hear it, she would go back and make that perfectly clear.

The next hill was long and steep. She mounted it slowly. Thomas wasn't expecting her until four o'clock, and being sweet on a pert redhead in Winster, he'd not welcome an early end to his afternoon off.

She took another look, a lingering look, from the summit of the hill. At this distance, the picnic party was only a splash of color on the green grass. Just beyond, sunlight glittered from the smooth water of the lake like a scatter of diamonds on blue silk.

So long as she had to wait for half an hour before proceeding to Winster, why not wait here? Glancing around, she saw a small copse of ash trees where Aphra could be sheltered from the late-afternoon sun. When the mare was serenely nibbling grass, Celia went back to her chosen spot and sank cross-legged onto the ground.

She meant to enjoy the silence and the beauty, but within seconds unhappy thoughts began jumping about in her mind like beads of water on a hot skillet.

Almost certainly she had just seen Kendal for the last time before he returned to London. With Chirikov leaving tomorrow, there would be no reason for the earl to remain at Candale.

And so, it was over.

She would have no opportunity to beat sense into his head. He would go, leaving ashes in his wake. And there was nothing, *nothing* she could do.

How could he be so resolutely blind? Sometimes he put her in mind of Greer's chickens. One of the servants used to draw a line in the dirt with his finger and position a chicken with its beak pressed to the line. When he removed his hand, the chicken would hold in place indefinitely, fixed on that line and unable to see anything else.

Kendal had done something of the like. He would not look beyond the path he'd carved for himself out of the devastation of his marriage. He refused to allow for other possibilities, choosing instead a course that promised safety from emotional entanglements. The fact that it was leading him nowhere seemed not to matter.

She understood mistakes, heaven knew. She'd made a great many of them and would make a great many more. What she failed to comprehend was Kendal's persistence in repeating the *same* mistake over and over again.

There really ought to be a limit to any man's obstinacy, a point where he realized it was time to try something else. It wasn't as if he were *happy*, after all.

And still, she believed in him.

She lay back on the grass and closed her eyes, feeling the sunlight sift into her body, the breeze whisper over her bare arms. She believed in him.

She must assuredly love him, to accept what he was doing without losing all faith in the man. He would eventually come around, she was certain. But she feared it would be too late for Charley.

She knew that it was already too late for her.

It is always a good thing to love, though. Bertie was right about that. And she *had* loved. She *did* love. Loving Kendal was the most precious, the most wonderful experience of her life, and she would never permit the loss of him to tarnish what she felt.

Which wasn't to say she would not go on hurting, deeply, for a very long time. Fine resolutions about clinging to the high road were well enough in theory, but empty days and lonely nights had a way of reducing noble aspirations to simple human longings. She never walked into a room without wanting to see him there, smiling at her.

But she would survive. No, survival was an insufficient goal. Sometimes that was the best one could do, she had learned during nine years of marriage to Greer, but it was dreaming of better things that had enabled her to endure. What a fool she would be to deny her dreams now, when she needed them more than ever. Celia opened her eyes and gazed up at the clear blue sky.

She refused to yield. She trusted in heroes. She imagined miracles.

Minutes or hours later, she had no idea, she felt an eerie tingling at her spine. Sitting up, she shaded her forehead with a hand and peered down the long steep slope of the hill.

And saw Kendal. He was no more than a hundred yards away, making his way toward her with a hurried stride.

She scrambled to her feet and waited for him, unable to think beyond the fact that he was here.

But she *must* think, and have all her wits about her. She studied his face as he came closer, trying vainly to read his expression. His own gaze never lifted. He was watching the ground, fixed on it like a damnable chicken.

When he drew within a few feet of where she stood, he halted. She saw him suck in a long breath and expel it before he looked at her, his mouth compressing to a narrow line. Obviously as an afterthought, he sketched a cursory bow.

"How did you know where I was?" she asked, of all the ridiculous things.

He made a vague gesture toward her horse, a white silhouette against the green grass and trees. "Chirikov said you were on your way to Winster, and this is the most direct route. I was not certain I could catch up with you, Lady Greer, but it is imperative that we speak."

"Not about my appearance at Charley's birthday party, I trust. His wishes transcend your own, sir, and—"

"Not about that. I am here to beg a service of you, nothing more." A sheen of sweat glistened on his brow. "The other day, at Wordsworth's house, I spoke out of turn. Unforgivably. It was pure nonsense, of course. I was not myself. I rarely am, in your company, and you have suffered for it. But in this case I went beyond all bounds, and fear that my indiscretion will do harm to Paxton should you repeat what I said."

As if she would do anything to hurt Charley! She might have taken offense, were she in a position to do so. But since she had already blabbed the whole to Kit, there was no use pretending she was above reproach.

"I know what it is you wish me to conceal," she said. "And you may be sure I wouldn't dream of spreading even the most trivial snippet of gossip relating to your family. But the fact is, sir, I have spoken on that particular subject *within* the family, to your brother."

The color in his face leached away. "Damn Kit."

"He is not to blame," she said hurriedly. "It was I who raised the issue, and only because I wanted him to explain what you would not. He understood that nothing we said would go any further."

Kendal looked away from her. "Your curiosity was sated, I take it?"

"To a degree." *Hold your temper, Celia.* "Kit told me only the barest fragments, the bits that might help us figure how to be of help to Charley. He was, and is, our only concern."

"And did you find any revelations in all this exchange of confidences, Lady Greer, beyond the obvious conclusion that I have been an unfit father to a child who is not mine?"

"You cannot know that, sir."

His gaze shot to her face. "I have the word of his mother, and the evidence of what I see. He bears no resemblance to any member of the Valliant family, past or present. You could search in vain through the portrait gallery for eyes the shape and color of his. Believe me, I have done so."

"Would the picture of a distant ancestor reassure you, Lord Kendal, if you found one who sported black eyes?"

"Probably not," he conceded grimly. "In fact, my wife's eyes were dark brown, but that is nothing to the point. She had no reason to lie to me, and nothing to gain by doing so. Quite the contrary. She must have known the consequences to herself if I learned the truth."

"Indeed? Have you not wondered, then, why she told you?"

"A thousand times." He rubbed the back of his neck. "It makes little sense, but little that she said or did made sense to me. In any case, I had become aware of her . . . indiscretions, and she understood that the marriage would continue in name only. Perhaps she had learned that I'd consulted a solicitor regarding a legal separation, although I was hesitant to remove Paxton from his mother at so young an age. But if she knew I was considering it, she might have assumed I would permit her to keep the boy if—"

"If you thought he was not yours." Celia moved closer, where she could better see his face. "I am mostly ignorant of the matter, to be sure, but from Kit I got the distinct impression that Lady Kendal paid precious little attention to her child. Practically none. Have you reason to think she *wanted* to keep Charley?"

"Not for herself," he acknowledged after a moment. "More likely she simply wished to deprive me of him. In her mind, I had failed to be the tolerant, openhanded husband she'd bargained for. This was, I suppose, her way of seeking retribution."

"I daresay. But if that was her purpose, why do you assume she was speaking the truth? Would not a lie have served as well?"

He made a sweeping gesture. "Do you imagine I have not considered that? I confronted her time and again with my suspicions, but her story never changed. Yes, she might have lied to me. She had deceived me in countless other ways, beginning the day we first met, and you will not be surprised to learn she did not come to our marriage bed a virgin. Mind you, I accepted her story about a riding accident. I believed everything she told me. I was in *love* with her, God help me."

Heart pounding, Celia held in place, forbidding herself to reveal how his words affected her. "When you love, you must trust," she said quietly. "But she has been dead for many years, my lord, and I expect you ceased loving her long before that. Why do you continue to trust her?"

"Is that what I'm doing?" He lifted his gaze to the sky. "The thing is, I don't know the truth. Is the boy my son? There will never be an answer. I can *never* know."

"Just so. But what does it matter?"

"How can you ask that?" He slammed a fist into the palm of his other hand. "Of *course* it matters. What man does not wish to be sure that his children are his own?"

"Not a one, I would imagine. Women are fortunate in that regard. We cannot help but know. But your *wishes*, sir, are impossible to satisfy. For every other purpose, you have acknowledged Charley as your own. He bears your name. He will inherit your title and properties. You forbid him only the one thing he truly wants and needs. A father."

"How so, Lady Greer? Unless you, or my reprehensibly indiscreet brother, tells Paxton what I never mean for him to learn, he will have no reason to suspect I am not his father."

"Which will leave him, then, to wonder why his father does not love him." She slipped a hand into her pocket, feeling for the penny Charley had given her. "I'm not at all sure it wouldn't be kinder to tell him flat out why you rarely come home, and pay him no attention when you do."

Kendal's voice was dangerously soft. "The war has taken thousands of men from their homes, madam. I have been in service to my country."

"Hurrah for you. And what excuse will you find, I wonder, when the Vienna Congress is concluded and you have no war, nor the tying up of loose ends after a war, to keep you away? Will you request appointment as ambassador to some

187

court or other? Pitch a tent in the House of Lords? Ship off to India?"

"My plans are none of your concern," he said coldly. "And they will have little effect on Paxton, who will soon be in residence at Harrow."

"Oh, excellent. One way or another, you can easily contrive to see him no more than once or twice a year, if that often. And I expect he will go on thinking that the sun rises and sets at your command. Already he is persuaded that you are the bestest and most important man in all England. He has told me so any number of times, with such pride that it broke my heart to see how terribly much he admires you."

She was beyond control now, she knew. And she could not care. Stalking up to him, she raised her chin and forced him by power of will to meet her eyes. She read denial on his face, in his stiff posture and icy blue gaze, and still—still she believed in him.

"There is nothing Charley would not forgive you," she said. "He thinks you are perfect. Which must mean, since you have no time for him, since you cannot care for him, that *he* must be at fault. So he tries in every way to be what he hopes will please you. What his mean-spirited governess and small-minded tutor tell him you expect of the Kendal heir."

Her hand, the one that had found the coin, was clenched into a fist. She slammed it at Kendal's chest. "They have tried to break his spirit, sir. But for all your neglect and all their efforts, he won't be broken. Charley is in pain every day of his life, but he is stronger than you or I will ever be. He refuses to let go of love. If he must, he'll find it in a puppy or a pony or a frog. He has an infinite capacity for giving and taking love wherever he can."

Kendal's face had gone white. A muscle ticked wildly at his jaw. But he held his ground, his posture rigid. "Are you quite finished, madam?"

"No. But soon, I promise you. Two things more, Lord Kendal. For one, consider this. Could Charley, whoever sired him, be any finer than he is? I know you would like to change his eyes to blue, to match your own, but in what other way would you alter him?"

"How can I answer that?" he replied harshly. "I scarcely know the boy."

"By your own choice. I met him less than a fortnight ago, but it required only a few moments to mark what a splendid child he is. Any man, any man but you, it seems, would be proud to call him son."

She had said enough, Celia knew. Too much, probably. She never knew when to stop. And she had not the slightest indication from Kendal that he really heard, let alone heeded, a single word of her tirade.

He was standing like a granite monolith, expressionless, waiting for her to be done.

In for a penny, she thought, opening her hand to show him the coin. He regarded it incuriously, but she felt the tension in his stiff body when she tossed it in the air and caught it again. For good measure, she tossed it two more times.

When she was sure she had his attention, she closed her fingers around the coin. "For a *second* thing—no, I hadn't forgot—let us play a game together."

"That seems singularly inappropriate under the circumstances."

He sounded a trifle uncomfortable, she thought. Even nervous. "Nevertheless," she said, "this is the fastest way to be rid of me, so I urge you to go along. You needn't say a word, by the way. I will toss the coin, and when it is midair, you will silently choose heads or tails. Agreed?"

His eyes narrowed. "There is some significance to the choice, I presume?"

"Certainly. This is a magical coin, sir. It holds the key to the secret you most wish to decipher. It can tell you, absolutely, whether or not Charley is your son."

"That is ridiculous! And I am in no mood for pointless games."

She tossed the coin back and forth between her hands. "Indulge me. I guarantee you will find an answer. It may not be the one you want, but what have you to lose at this point?"

"Very well, Lady Greer, proceed if you must. But do it quickly."

With a flick of her wrist, she sent the coin to a great height and they both watched it tumble down again, reflecting the sunlight as it spun around. At the last moment she snatched it midair and laid it on the back of one hand, covering it with the other.

"And so, my lord, here is the answer. Have you made your choice?"

"I have," he replied stonily.

"The coin has done so as well. Heads, Charley is your son. Tails, he is not. Heads, you will love the boy as once you did, before your wife poisoned you against him. Tails, you will go on as you have done since then."

He frowned, studying her hands intently. "I fail to take your meaning. You told me to choose before I knew what was signified by the turn of the coin."

"Well, yes. But then, you have been making choices in ignorance all these many years, have you not? When Charley's paternity was placed in doubt, you chose tails. You elected not to love him. Now we shall find out if you were right all along. Or crushingly wrong."

She held out her hands, the one still atop the other. "Shall I show you the coin, sir?"

"I—" He closed his eyes, his face pale as death. "No. I don't want to see it."

"I thought you would not. The truth about Charley, whatever it may be, is never so devastating as facing the truth about yourself. And that, you know, is the message this coin has already given you."

Stepping forward, she took one of his hands and pressed the coin against his palm, closing his stiff fingers around it. "Keep this, Lord Kendal. Charley gave it me, but it belongs to you. One day, you may recognize its value."

She left him then, before the tears in her eyes broke free. Striding swiftly to where she'd tethered Aphra, she took the reins, mounted, and headed in the direction of Winster, her heart pounding madly in her chest. Only once, when she was far enough away that he could not see the tears scalding her face, she risked a look back.

His hand was still fisted around the coin. He had not moved.

Chapter 18

Churning beneath the smooth surface of Kendal's mind, beating against his focused calm, the beasts prowled relentlessly.

Rage. Guilt. Fear. Uncertainty. Dread.

They were strong. Ferocious. They would break free, he knew. But he could hold them back for now.

The coin burned in his hand. He stopped on the crest of a hill directly above the picnic site and unclenched his fist. The penny, ordinary and worn, lay flat against his palm.

It showed heads.

But there was nothing to that. If the coin held secrets and truths, he was not prepared to decipher them. The beasts would tear him apart soon enough.

They must not have the boy, though. Paxton—Charley—asked little enough of him, which was as well, since he'd little to give. But what he could find in himself, he would scrape up and offer to his son.

There. He had said it, if only to himself. His son.

He neither believed it nor disbelieved it, but the facts regarding the child's conception, whatever they were, had no relevance now. He knew his duty.

What he didn't know was how to be a father. He had done a poor enough job when the role was cast upon him twenty years before, although Alex and Kit had managed to survive his bungling without notable scars. He would simply have to learn. And to be sure, he could scarcely do worse by Charley in the future than he'd done in the past.

Releasing a painful breath, he slipped the coin into his pocket and started down the hill.

Before he had taken more than a few steps, his gaze fixed on the ground, a shout from near the lake snapped him to a halt. Looking down, he saw people running to the shoreline.

Chirikov pulled off his boots and plowed into the water, swimming rapidly.

Kit was pushing a rowboat into the lake. Two men helped him shove off, and a third man joined him in the boat. Kit grabbed the oars and began to row.

Kendal looked beyond them, in the direction they were headed. To Belle Isle, he thought at first. He saw the pale backs of several boys who were swimming toward the island, almost upon it, and other boys crawling onto land.

Then, at a point some distance behind them, he made out a small disturbance in the water. One of the boys must be in trouble.

He broke into a run.

The crowd parted for him as he came up to the edge of the lake. He heard a voice say, "It's Paxton, milord," but somehow he had already known that.

From this far away it was impossible to tell precisely what was happening. The boat was still moving through the water. About fifty yards ahead of it Chirikov waved a hand. Kendal saw Kit point with an oar. Chirikov swam a short way to his left and dove.

He was underwater a vast time. The boat had nearly reached him when he shot up. Almost immediately, he dove a second time.

Blood thundering in his head, Kendal watched helplessly. All around him, children were crying. They were terrified, as was he, although he knew to hold still and maintain his calm. *Oh please dear God.*

When Chirikov came up again, a small figure was barely visible in his arms. Kit steered to where he was treading water and reached out his hands. The moment Kit had Charley in his arms, the other man began rowing frantically for shore.

As the boat drew closer Kendal could see his brother holding Charley facedown across his thighs, pushing at his back, trying to pump water from his lungs. *Oh God.*

It seemed to take forever. Oars dug into the lake. Kendal willed Charley to breathe. Slowly, too slowly, the boat came closer.

Unable to wait, he slogged into the water to meet them, mud sucking at his boots.

Kit, grim-faced, shook his head.

No!

Standing, balancing himself as the boat rocked, Kit put the small, limp form into Kendal's arms. Charley's still face and bare, narrow chest were pale as bone. He felt unutterably cold.

Kendal carried him back to shore, his mind clawing for some way to expel the water and put air into the child. He knew something. He had heard something, a long time ago, when he was on a ship to Naples.

Before the memory took shape, his body knew what it was. Grasping Charley's ankles, he held him upside down and shook him hard. Water dribbled from his mouth and nose, streaming down his closed eyes and forehead.

The boy's leg muscles tensed.

And then he coughed. Water spewed out, and more water.

Kendal put an arm under his chest and brought him parallel to the ground, still facedown. Water and vomit poured from his mouth. Coughing violently, Charley fought to clear his lungs.

Tipping the boy's head downward, Kendal shook him again, not so hard this time. More water came up.

The blue-white flesh was turning pink, he saw as Charley's struggles began to subside. The racking coughs grew less insistent, less frequent.

Then Kendal heard a frail, hoarse sound. "Papa?"

Turning the boy in his arms, Kendal gazed down at his wet face and bloodshot eyes. Charley looked back, dazed, his lashes clumped with water. "Papa?" he said again.

"I'm here, Charley." Bending his head, he brushed a kiss against the child's cold lips. "I'm here."

With a husky sigh, Charley closed his eyes. "Papa."

Panic surging through him, Kendal pressed his ear against

the small chest. But the heartbeat was strong, the skin beginning to warm, and Charley's breath came and went with only a slight rasp. Someone held out a blanket and helped him wrap it around the boy.

Relief was making him dizzy. Through burning eyes, he saw Chirikov clambering up the bank, his face stark with fear. When Kendal nodded at him, he dropped to his hands and knees, panting like a dog, hair and mustaches dripping lake water.

Kit ran up then, his gaze focused on Charley. Gently, he brushed a strand of wet hair from the boy's forehead. "The carriage is ready to go, Jimmie. Take him home. I'll ride for the doctor."

In the passageway outside Charley's room, Kendal and Kit paced, their wet boots making a squishing noise. Servants huddled in the shadows and on the staircase, waiting for word.

The doctor had been inside the room a damnably long time.

He'd arrived shortly after Charley was rubbed down with warm water, dried carefully, and put to bed, Kendal standing watch all the while.

The boy had spoken only once during the carriage ride. "I almost drownded, Papa."

He sounded, Kendal had thought, rather proud of his adventure. But talking made him start coughing again, and he obeyed when Kendal told him to hush. Sometimes dozing, sometimes with his dark eyes fixed on his father's face, he lay swaddled in the blanket on Kendal's lap, wrapped in his arms.

At last the door swung open and Dr. Pritchard emerged, carrying his black leather case. He was smiling.

Kendal swept down on him, backing him up against a long-case clock. "Well?"

"His lungs are clear, as clear as can be expected, his heartbeat is steady and strong, and his color is fine. After a good night's sleep, I've no doubt he will be little the worse for his swim."

"How can you be sure of that? He was underwater a long

195

time. He wasn't breathing when Chirikov brought him up. You didn't see how he was then."

"That is true. But I have practiced medicine in the lake country for twoscore years, my lord, and seen more than my share of drownings and near drownings. Except for a sore throat, and possibly a day or two of sniffles, Paxton will be fine."

Kendal's knees went weak with relief. At the same time he wasn't buying the story. "If you are so certain, then what the devil were you doing in there all this time?"

"Making sure," the doctor replied. "Making sure. He's more than a little overexcited right now, I'm afraid, but I don't want to give him laudanum to help him sleep."

"What do you mean, *overexcited*?"

"Well, not nearly so much as you, my lord, but he's talking more than is good for his throat. I expect he won't settle down until he sees you, so do calm yourself. While you are with him I'll give a few instructions regarding his care to Mr. Christopher. Or to the boy's nanny, if you prefer, although I place no great reliance on Miss Yallop."

Kendal had long since ordered the woman to her room and told her to keep out of the way. She was good only for wailing and wringing her hands. "You will stay the night, doctor. Kit, tell Geeson to have a bedchamber readied."

Pritchard rolled his eyes. "If I thought there were the slightest need—"

"*I* think there is. You are staying. If you wish to inform anyone where you can be found, riders will carry the messages."

"Oh, very well. I'll send word to my wife and my assistant. But I have a few orders for you, too, Lord Kendal. A few minutes, no more, with your son, and use most of them to encourage him to sleep. Someone should sit with him through the night, but not you. Understood?"

Gritting his teeth, Kendal nodded.

"Go on in, then. Don't let him talk too much. And when you come out, bring that damned puppy with you."

Stepping back, Kendal watched Pritchard separate himself from the clock and proceed down the passageway with Kit, shaking his head.

Then, heart in his throat, he went to the door and let himself into Charley's room. Only one candle was lit, placed on a sideboard where the light could not reach the boy's eyes. Kendal took it with him to the bed and set it on the night table. He had to see for himself that Charley was indeed *fine*.

Charley immediately tried to sit up. Kendal helped him, stacking pillows behind his back. In a white nightshirt, his hair still slightly damp, he looked infinitely small and frail. There was a wooden chair beside the bed and Kendal sank onto it, forearms resting on his knees.

His pulse pumped in his ears. He felt suddenly shy. Awkward. Words clogged in his throat, pushing to get out, but his thoughts were too jumbled to form a whole sentence.

"Are you mad at me, sir?" Charley asked into the silence. "Uncle Kit told me not to go in the race, but Ralph dared me, so I had to."

If he ever got his hands on Ralph—Kendal uncurled his fingers. "Nobody is angry, son. You gave us all a scare, though."

"I'm sorry, sir. I didn't mean to. It didn't look so far when I started, but then my leg hurted really bad and I couldn't kick anymore. So I stayed where I was and waved for help, like Uncle Kit taught me. Then you came out and got me."

Kendal took a deep breath. "That wasn't me, Charley. General Chirikov got there first."

"Oh. Well, I don't 'member what happened. I thought it was you, 'cause when I woke up, you were there."

Placing a hand on the boy's forehead, Kendal decided it was cool. It was hard to tell, what with the heat searing through his own body. "How do you feel now, Charley? Tell me the truth."

"Pretty tired," he admitted. "I swammed a long way. And my throat hurts a little, and my mouth tastes bad."

"That's because you drank rather a lot of Windemere Lake, I'm afraid." His fingers brushed down the boy's face, lingering

197

on his cheek. "Dr. Pritchard says you will feel much better in the morning. He wants you to go to sleep, though. Can you do that?"

"I'll try." Charley's eyes pleaded with him. "Will you stay with me?"

"Of course. For a little while, anyway. The doctor thinks you will talk more than you should if I am here, and he's given me strict orders to wait some other place until tomorrow morning."

"That's all right, then." Charley yawned. "He told me I'm oversited. And I guess you ought to take Wellington downstairs now. He keeps wiggling."

Kendal spotted a squirming lump near Charley's feet. Reaching under the blanket, he extricated the ball of fur and held it to the boy's face for a goodnight kiss. The puppy obliged enthusiastically, lapping at Charley's nose and chin, making him giggle.

That led to a coughing spell, not a bad one but enough to scare the devil out of Kendal. Snatching the dog away, he waited until Charley was breathing easily again. "You can see him tomorrow," he said. "We'll keep him in the house until then and take good care of him."

"I don't think he's had his supper, sir."

"Then I'll make sure he does. And Charley, when we are alone together, you needn't call me 'sir.' In company, it's polite to do that, but otherwise it isn't necessary."

The boy nodded. "Does that mean you will call me Charley? I like that."

"So do I. And yes, I will." One hand wrapped around the puppy, he used the other to rearrange the pillows and settle Charley on his back. Carefully, he adjusted the sheet and blanket. "Someone will be sitting with you all night, son. Not me, because the doctor says I can't, but if you wake up and don't feel good, say so right away."

"Yes, Papa." He yawned again.

"Good. And promise me you'll sleep now."

"I promise." His eyes drifted shut. "Cross my heart."

Kendal moved the candle back to the sideboard and tiptoed to the door, opening it soundlessly.

A whispery voice floated to him from across the room. "I love you, Papa."

Tears welling in his eyes, Kendal looked back at the shadowy figure on the bed. "I love you, too, Charley. Cross my heart."

He stood there a long time, listening closely until the boy's breathing grew deep and even with sleep. Finally, worried that the wriggling puppy might start barking, he moved into the passageway.

Kit was waiting for him, a plump young housemaid at his side. Before Kendal could close the door, she slipped past him into the room.

"That's Margaret," Kit said. "Doc Pritchard told her what to watch for, and she's a good sort. Charley likes her." He moved closer, his brows raised. "What's this, Jimmie? Tears?"

"Stubble it." Kendal handed him the puppy. "The dog is to stay in the house, in case the boy wakes up and wants him. See to it. Where's Pritchard?"

"Billiard room, last I looked. Chirikov is with him."

"Good." Suddenly fired with energy, Kendal headed swiftly down the stairs.

Pritchard regarded him without pleasure as he came through the door. "Just when we were about to start a game," he grumbled.

Ignoring him, Kendal looked around for Chirikov. The general, wearing loose-fitting cossack trousers and a full-sleeved linen shirt open to his waist, was selecting a billiard stick from the rack on the wall. He turned as Kendal approached him with his hand outstretched.

"I owe you an incalculable debt, sir."

"*Nyet.*" Chirikov took his hand and pumped it vigorously. "I vill not hear thanks to me. Iss gift from Gott. All childrens iss gift from Gott."

"To be sure," Kendal replied softly. "Even so, I trust—I hope—you will apply to me if ever I can be of service."

"Hah. You already giff me Mr. Wordsworth." Chirikov leaned closer, mustaches twitching. "Tell you truth, Kental. I understand nothing what he said. He talk too much, that whon. Better he write hiss poems and shut hiss mouth."

Kendal had not imagined he could laugh this particular night, but he did. Celia had been right about Vasily Chirikov. He was a rough-and-tumble fellow, but nobody's fool.

Chirikov clapped him on the back. "Maybe after Vienna meetink you come to St. Petersburk. We go for swim in Neva, where I haff swimmed many times. I swim good, hey?"

"Like a warrior, sir. And this afternoon, like an angel of God. But I'll not be traveling to the Vienna Congress after all. Pressing matters will keep me here at Candale for . . . well, for a long time."

"Iss good. Home is best place to be."

Pritchard cleared his throat. "Are we playing billiards or not, General?"

When Kendal glared at him, he shrugged. "You need to change out of those wet clothes, your lordship. Otherwise I really will have a sick patient requiring my attention. Have you satisfied yourself that young Paxton is recovering nicely?"

"No. And I think you ought to be with him."

"Females do better at times like this, you know. They have a gift for sitting quietly and focusing on a child. I repeat my injunction, Lord Kendal. Stay out of the boy's room. He's sturdy. Let his body do the work of healing, and that will happen best while he sleeps. You can play mother hen tomorrow, but only after he's had his breakfast. I've already dispatched orders to the kitchen regarding what he can eat, and I'll check on him a time or two during the night. So for God's sake, sir, stop worrying."

Kendal supposed the doctor wouldn't be playing billiards if he were the least bit concerned. Bowing to Chirikov, he returned to Charley's bedchamber and gingerly opened the door.

The maid was sitting in the near-dark room beside the bed. She looked up when he stuck his head inside the door and put a finger to her lips. Then she smiled, nodding toward Charley.

All was well, he presumed, but he wanted a closer look for

himself. After one step, though, the wet leather of his boots creaking loudly, he gave it up and backed from the room.

"Tsk, tsk," said Kit, joining him halfway down the hall. "You need to get hold of yourself, old son. You'll not do the child any good circling around him like a shark."

"And you're bloody damned cavalier, I must say. He could take a chill. Come down with a fever. Pneumonia. God knows what."

"Kids are resilient, Jimmie. And while you were in there with him I was putting Doc Pritchard through the wringer. He made a believer out of me. Keep in mind he delivered all three of us, and Charley, too. He wouldn't lie about this."

"Whatever you say." Kendal pushed open the door to his bedchamber. "Where the devil is my valet?"

Kit followed him in, grabbing the bootjack. "Most of the servants are having a meal, now that the crisis is past. Want me to ring, or can you do without him?"

"Just help me off with these boots, will you?" Kendal dropped onto a chair. "I'm officially banned from Charley's room until tomorrow morning, and damned if I can figure any reason for it. What's more, I don't know why I should take orders from Pritchard about where I can and cannot go in my own house."

"Well, for one thing, you're too overset. And stop glowering at me." Kit wrenched off a soggy boot. "And for another, Charley isn't used to you paying him so much attention. If he knows you're there, he'll try to stay awake so he doesn't miss a minute of it."

It made sense, in a painful, shameful sort of way. Charley had been exceedingly glad to see him. *Too* glad. Overexcited. Yes, the doctor was probably right about that. Kendal knew he would do as he'd been told, but he wasn't happy about it. "I'll feel a great deal better if you spend the night with him, Kit."

"I intend to." The second boot hit the floor. "And why don't you remove yourself from the house for a while? You're getting on everyone's nerves. Take a ride. Go visit someone." Kit gave him a meaningful look. "Need I mention any names?"

Kendal peeled off his coat. "Are you reading my mind, brat?"

"Like a primer, Jimmie, like a primer. It's a good idea, you know. She won't want to hear what happened secondhand, or read about it in the Kendal news rag. And if she gets the word elsewhere, it won't include the part about Charley being safe and well. Go tell her."

"It's late." Kendal removed his wet shirt and went to his dressing table, gazing into the mirror with disgust. "I need a shave. Likely she's asleep by now."

"So wake her up. Take my word for it, she won't mind. And yes, she's still at the Merry Goosegirl."

Kendal shot him a look. "Should I, Kit? I don't like leaving here, under the circumstances—"

"Do everyone a favor and go, dammit. Don't hurry back. If the boy has so much as a bad dream, I'll send for you. Now, do you want to shave and fancy yourself up, or should I tell somebody to saddle your horse?"

Now that he'd made up his mind, Kendal was in a hurry to be on his way. In the dark, it would take almost an hour to get there. He would use the time trying to work out what to say to her. "Horse. Ten minutes."

"Aye, sir." Kit snapped a salute. "You can thank me later. And Jimmie, she'll want to see Charley. Bring her home for breakfast."

Kendal spoke just before his brother reached the door. "Kit? I do thank you. And I meant to tell you earlier that I hadn't forgot about Charley's pony. It's being shipped from Ireland and was supposed to be delivered at Candale by this morning. I waited as long as I could, but there must have been some sort of delay. Finally, I went on to the picnic."

"Connemara pony?"

Kendal nodded.

"Splendid choice. Couldn't have done better myself. Well, I didn't, did I? Jimmie, old sod, I begin to suspect there may actually be some hope for you. But first, I'll see how things go with you and Celia tonight." He grinned. "One word of advice, though. Try not to behave yourself."

Chapter 19

Celia closed her book, placed it on the night table, and leaned back against the pillows with a sigh.

It must be well after midnight. The inn was quiet now, and from outside her window, she could hear the chirp of crickets and the distant *whooo* of an owl.

And so, what was she to do with herself until morning? Trying to read had proven a notable failure. She ought to be tired, and she was, but sleep was clearly out of the question.

In her own house, she would be free to wander downstairs and putter around, or take a walk in the moonlit garden. Really, she must come to a decision about a house. The agent had trolled her through several lakeside properties, all of them perfectly acceptable, but she continued to dither. Even Thomas Carver was growing impatient with her, although *he* got to spend his evenings in the taproom and take walks at night if he wanted to.

Mercy, now she was turning on poor Thomas! Such a vile mood she was in.

What she required was some means of working off her energy, perhaps a stiff wad of bread dough to knead or a heavy carpet to beat. Walloping a mallet across the back of Lord Kendal's head would nicely turn the trick.

Climbing out of bed, she straightened her nightrail and padded barefoot to the dressing table. The candlelight cast eerie shadows over her face as she sat on the spindly chair, gazing at her reflection in the mirror. Celia Greer, wealthy widow, no place to go, nothing to do.

She picked up the hairbrush.

Kendal would never let her see Charley again, that was certain. Not after what she said to him today. She wasn't the least bit sorry for it, though.

Well, perhaps the merest trifle, but if she had it all to do over again, she would. Only next time she would say it better.

As if words would have any effect on that blockhead! He must have heard them before, from Kit, and to no purpose whatever. Why would he listen to a mere female, especially one he neither liked nor respected? At the end of the day all she'd accomplished by her tirade was to deprive Charley of one of his few friends.

Too late now for second thoughts, Celia told herself, pulling the brush through her tangled curls. As usual, by acting without *first* thoughts, she had landed everyone in the soup.

The thing was, she could not bring herself to give up on him. She just *knew* that somewhere under that shell of ice was a good man, the one she had fallen in love with. But she was becoming terribly afraid that he had put himself beyond all reach. A man who could not love Charley was surely incapable of loving anyone.

A dog barked from the direction of the stable, and she heard the sound of hooves against the stone-flagged courtyard. Someone in search of a room for the night, perhaps, or a guest returning late. A few minutes later came muffled voices from downstairs and the closing of a door.

She listened intently, but the inn grew silent again. Rats. Any distraction from her gloomy reflections would have been welcome. Ah well. She went back to brushing her hair, which was practically standing on end. A storm must be on the way, she thought, glancing over at the window. She'd left it open against the humid July air, and the curtains had begun to billow as the wind picked up.

Double rats! A storm was precisely what she didn't need right now. If it kept her imprisoned in this room one single minute past dawn, she would likely take to gnawing at the furniture.

A distant rumble of thunder confirmed her fears. At about

the same time she thought she heard footsteps in the passageway. It must have been her imagination, because there was no sound of groaning hinges or the clunk of metal against wood as a door latch dropped. She was familiar with the night sounds at the Merry Goosegirl, especially those of a guest arriving, but she heard only a raspy snore from the cutlery salesman in the bedchamber next to hers.

Celia put down the brush, stretched broadly, and reckoned she could brush her teeth again. And wash her face again. She did both, using the last of her clean water, and wandered over to the open window.

A few drops of rain made plunking sounds against the windows, their casements swung wide against the walls of the inn. More drops pattered onto the wooden floor. She thought to pull the windows shut, but the wind and the electrified air felt stunningly cool against her overheated body.

Lifting her nightrail above her knees, she stood for several minutes, letting the rain dance onto her thighs and stream down her legs. A flash of lightning illuminated the distant fells and roiling clouds, followed swiftly by a sharp clap of thunder.

She knew these summer squalls, sudden, fierce, and like unfaithful lovers, quickly gone.

What was *that*?

She spun around, almost sure she had heard a thump against the door. It came again, louder this time, and then again.

Letting go her hold on the nightrail, she felt it clinging to her damp legs as she made her way across the room. "Who is it?" she asked softly when she reached the door.

Silence for a moment. Then, in a gravelly voice, "Kendal."

Oh my! Swallowing the hard lump that had jumped to her throat, she gingerly raised the latch and cracked the door. A tall shadow loomed in the dim passageway. She knew the shape of him, and even the smell of him. But what in holy heaven was he doing here in the middle of the night?

"May I come in?"

"That depends." She eyed him cautiously. "Have you come to throttle me?"

"Of course not." He curled gloved fingers around the edge

of the door and leaned closer. "The innkeeper is on the staircase," he whispered, "and I am nearly certain he has a musket aimed in my direction. He was not pleased to admit me, I assure you. He would not even accept the considerable bribe I offered him."

"Then how did you get this far?"

"I told him we were betrothed, and had quarreled, and that I'd come to make it up. For God's sake, Celia, let me in before he blows my head off. Or send me packing if you must. But please don't do that. I must speak with you."

Backing away from the door, she watched him slip into the room, lower the latch soundlessly, and turn. His eyes widened.

At that moment she became intensely aware of wet muslin clinging to her belly and hips and thighs. She felt the lamplight from behind her outlining her body. She was all but naked. Exposed to him.

And she was *glad* of it. This was exactly how she had always wanted him to look at her, with heated, barely sheathed desire.

Or perhaps what she saw in his eyes was merely a trick of the uncertain light.

Crossing her arms around her waist, she backed up to the bed and sat before her legs dissolved under her. "Why are you here?" she asked, her voice cracking like a wishbone.

"You make me forget," he said quietly. "Looking at you makes me forget. But I have to tell you something. Many things, if you will allow me, but first of all you must know what happened this afternoon." He took a deep, shuddering breath. "Charley nearly drowned."

"Oh dear God."

He moved closer, waving his hands in a gesture of denial. "He's fine now. Truly. Forgive me for frightening you. There was no harm done, or so the doctor assures me. At worst, the boy will have a sore throat from all the water he swallowed and threw up, but devil if I believe that he will get off so lightly. I was there when he was pulled from the lake."

He swiped a hand over his forehead. "Charley was in high spirits when I left, though, and Kit is watching over him now.

Dr. Pritchard agreed, under compulsion, to stay the night at Candale, but he ordered me to leave the boy alone so that he can get some sleep. I overexcite him, it seems. In any case, I was unceremoniously cast out. So I came here."

Charley. He was calling his son Charley. Not Paxton, which was one of the devices he used to distance himself from the child, but *Charley*. Once Celia had caught her breath, she began to take note again of the man who had begun to prowl her bedchamber.

When he failed to speak, she ventured a question. "Do you want to tell me what happened?"

He appeared relieved to be given a task. "There was a swimming race for the older boys," he said. "I did not see the first of it, and by the time I got in sight of the lake, the winner had already claimed victory. The boys were swimming to Belle Isle. It's about three-quarters of a mile from where they began. You remember it?"

"Yes," she said when he waited for an answer. "I remember the island."

He stopped at the open window, propping one hand against the frame, the wind-lashed rain pelting over his boots. "No one noticed that Charley had entered the race on his own. He told me later that he'd meant to prove he could swim as well as somebody named Ralph, who had apparently been tormenting him all afternoon."

Kendal glanced at her over his shoulder. "You were right. He has spent far too much time in the company of hired staff and has no idea how to deal with other children, let alone bullies. In any case, someone finally spotted him a few hundred yards behind the last of the racers, thrashing his arms. And screaming for help, I daresay, although I was just coming over the hill that overlooks the lake and scarcely knew what was going on. I could see only a dark shape in the water and everyone else running for the shoreline."

Kendal began pacing again. "Chirikov was after him immediately. He pulled off his boots and plunged into the water like a man possessed. But by the time he swam to where we'd last seen Charley, the boy had vanished underwater. Chirikov dove, and dove again. It seemed to take forever, although I'm told only a short time passed before he came up with Charley. Kit had just got there with the rowboat, and he brought him back to shore."

He turned to face her. "Charley wasn't breathing. I can't tell you how it was when Kit put him in my arms. He was so limp, and so terribly cold. Someday I might remember where I got the idea to do what I did. In any case, it worked. All of a sudden he coughed, and then he spewed out a great deal of water. We took him home, of course, and from all indications, he has come to no harm."

"Thank God." She folded her hands to keep them from shaking.

"Yes. Thank God. It has been a long time since I prayed, but I was begging for a miracle during the eternity that Charley wasn't breathing. I swear that fifty universes could have been created before he started gasping for air. It was a near-run thing, Celia. Had Chirikov not been there—" He gave her a wry smile. "To think I've spent the last two weeks wishing him to the devil."

His smile, such as it was, combed through the last of her fears. Kendal would not be making even a slight joke if he believed that Charley's health was in the slightest question. "Thank you for telling me what happened," she said, relief making her dizzy. "If Charley is feeling better tomorrow, may I visit him?"

Kendal exhaled slowly. "You needn't ask that. You will always be welcome. He'll be very pleased to see you."

She waited, but he said nothing else. He only stood in place, regarding her with an expression she could not decipher. Why had he come here *now*, when tomorrow morning would have done just as well? If she didn't know better, she might imagine he had acted as she so often did—on impulse.

He turned to the window again and looked out into the stormy night. "There are a great many things I wish to say to you, Celia, but I cannot think where to begin. Have you the patience to hear me out? Or the slightest interest in doing so?"

His voice grew husky at the end, even uncertain. She had a

misbegotten urge to rush across the room and wrap her arms around him. But she remained seated, pleating her nightrail between her fingers, sensing that he was better left to manage on his own. "Would you care to sit down?" she asked.

He shook his head. "I would have come to see you in any case, to thank you. What you said to me yesterday afternoon was intolerable to hear, and under ordinary circumstances, being somewhat mule-headed, I'm not certain how long it would have taken me to recognize it as truth. Weeks, perhaps, or months. When you left, I knew only that I could not bear to accept any of it. No man wants to look at himself and see a monster."

At that, she could not keep silent. "Good heavens, why must men always go to such extremes? You were wrong, my lord, and other things as well, but never a *monster*. How absurd."

"It has been a day of extremes," he said after a moment. "You showed me what I had become, and I knew that sooner or later I would be forced to deal with it. I want to think that I'd have come around, and realized how infinitely precious Charley has always been. But I've little faith in my judgment of late. It's possible I'd have retreated behind the walls I had constructed to keep him out.

"But then he nearly died in my arms." Turning, Kendal gazed at her from haunted eyes. "Without question I shall make many mistakes in the future, but not the same ones I made in the past. Charley is my son. Unequivocally. The wonder is that he loves me in spite of everything. I mean to be worthy of that love, Celia. I expect him to teach me how."

"I am persuaded you wil! learn quickly," she told him with conviction. And with love, too. It was swelling in her own heart, however hard she tried to contain it.

"I am also taking lessons," he said roughly, "in how to apologize. I've scarcely begun, mind you, except for the part where I realize that I *need* to apologize. Most of all to Charley, but I think he would not understand. Is that wrong? Should I—"

"Absolutely not. It would only confuse him. Concentrate on being what he already thinks you are." She smiled an apology of her own. "As if I've any idea what you ought to do, my lord.

I promise that you have heard the last of my insufferably self-righteous lectures."

"Give me leave to hope that you fail to keep that promise. But I will take your advice and confess none of my sins to Charley until the day, should it ever come, that he demands justification of my neglect all these many years. I hope he never does. There is no excuse for my behavior, to be sure, but there are reasons. And better they remain hidden, if that is possible."

He referred to Belinda, she was certain. And it was equally certain that one day Charley would hear the rumors about his adulterous mother. Celia could only hope that when he did, he would be secure enough in his father's love to forgive her. It would help if Kendal had forgiven her, too. She bit her tongue to keep from telling him so.

He moved a few steps closer to the bed, the lamplight shadowing the hollows in his drawn cheeks. Each time she had seen him since coming north, he had looked increasingly weary, as if he rarely slept. Tonight he was positively exhausted, she could tell, no surprise after the ordeal he had just endured.

"I have treated you badly," he said. "Abominably. You'll not credit this, but I have never behaved in such a fashion with any woman. Not even the only woman I had reason to despise, although that may be because I took care to put distance between us. I never even lost my temper with her, but I have seemed to do nothing else with you. I am sorry for it, Celia. Deeply sorry."

"Think no more of it," she said immediately. "I provoked you."

"Oh, indeed you did." He rubbed the bridge of his nose. "Not in the ways you are thinking, though. Well, not always. I've grown particularly fond of your sharp wit, and trust you'll not blunt it on my account."

"Oh, you may be sure of that. And I accept your apology, so long as you accept mine. As you reminded me on any number of occasions, I'd no right to interfere in your personal life. Which is not to say that I've the slightest regret about doing so, at least where Charley is concerned." She paused, flushing hotly. "Mercy me, what an abysmal apology *that* was. You must enroll me in the school where you are taking lessons."

"I will never cease to be grateful that you chose to interfere," he replied simply. "I am even more grateful that you have not long since ordered me from this room. It did not occur to me that you might turn me away until I reached the door. I stood there half a lifetime, you know, scratching up the courage to knock."

"Well, I'm glad you did. At risk of a musketball, too. Do you suppose that Mr. Grigg is still lurking on the stairs?"

He looked pained. "Does that mean you wish me to take my leave now?"

It wasn't what she had meant at all. Of course she wanted him to stay. She *always* wanted him to stay. She just couldn't figure why he wished to, after saying what he'd come here to say.

Unless there was more. Her heart made little fluttery jumps in her chest.

"Celia?" He moved closer to the bed.

She licked dry lips. "Yes, my lord?"

"There is something more."

"Yes, my lord."

"Will you marry me?"

Lightning flashed. Thunder shook the walls. For a moment a brilliant light passed over his face, and in that moment she glimpsed his deepest heart.

"Yes, my lord," she said. "Yes."

He raised stunned eyes. "Yes? Just like that, *yes*? Did you misunderstand? I asked you to *marry* me."

"My hearing is perfectly sound, Lord Kendal. Were you wishing for another response than the one I gave you?"

"N-no." He scratched his head. "But I certainly *expected* one. At the least I expected to spend hours or weeks or even years changing your mind. You told me once, in no uncertain terms, that you would never again take a husband."

"I changed my mind," she said with a dismissive wave. Her doubts had vanished so quickly that she never saw them go. "But had I the least suspicion you meant to propose to me, I

212

would certainly have advised you to lead up to it more . . . gently."

"I can do that," he said immediately. "I'll do it tomorrow, if you wish. I shall devise the most romantic proposal in history. Flowers. Musicians. Champagne. Only promise me your answer will still be yes."

"I promise." She smiled at the earnest look on his face. "But somewhere between the music and the champagne, my lord, will you get around to mentioning that you love me?"

Faster than a bolt of lightning he was beside her on the bed, gathering her into his arms, pressing urgent kisses over every inch of her face. Briefly, she was reminded of Charley's puppy. And then his lips met hers, and he whispered, "I love you," and she was lost in him.

After a long time he set her away with a shuddering groan, his hands gripping her shoulders. "I *do* love you, Celia. I suspect I fell in love with you under Lord Finlay's desk, the moment I first saw your face. And ever since, until tonight, I have been fighting it. I think you understand why, but I am sorry for being so damnably—"

She put her forefinger against his lips. "I do understand, you know. Some other time we can retrace our steps to this moment. I've a story of my own to tell, beloved, and I expect it will astonish you. For now, though, I want us to stop talking and go back to kissing."

"No." Carefully, he detached himself from her grasp and came to his feet. "That would be most unwise. I should leave now, while I still can."

"Whatever for?" Then she remembered. "You are worried about Charley."

"To be sure, although I am forbidden to see him until after he's had his breakfast. But that is not the reason. You put me beyond control, Celia. And it will be a week or more before I can send to the archbishop for a special license and have it in my hands. Three weeks if you prefer banns to be cried at the church, but I hope you'll not ask me to wait so long."

"I'm not asking you to wait at all. To the contrary." She

stood. "It's pouring rain outside, James. You cannot leave until the storm has passed."

His hot gaze swept over her body. "I'm well used to the rain."

Moving closer, she began to unbutton his coat. "All the same, I want you to stay. I insist on it. You owe me, sir. Was a time you left me alone in the bedchamber of an inn. You'll not do the same tonight. I mean us to finish what we started."

"And we shall," he said huskily. "When we are married."

"But it won't be the same, my love." Her fingers moved to the buttons of his waistcoat. "For more years than you can imagine, I have dreamed of a grand, glorious, passionate affair."

"I can safely promise you a lifetime of passion," he said, eyes widening as her hands crept over his chest.

"And I shall hold you to that promise. But it won't be the same, you see. It won't be . . . *shameless*."

"Y-yes it will. It will be everything you want."

She gripped handfuls of his shirt and pulled it from his trousers. "But I set out to take a lover, Lord Kendal. I want to have one."

"You will. Dear heavens, stop that." Her fingers had slid under his shirt and were dancing over his bare back. "I will be your lover. Soon."

"Soon isn't good enough," she murmured, raising her lips to his. "Soon isn't *now*."

With a raw sound, he wrapped his arms around her and kissed her long and deep.

"Mercy me," he said finally, breathlessly. "What am I to do with you, Lady Greer?"

She drew him inexorably to the bed. "Oh, I think you know, Lord Kendal."

He did.

Now available!

ISLAND OF THE SWANS
by Ciji Ware

In this resplendent love story, a dazzling era comes vividly
to life as one woman's passionate struggle to follow her heart
takes her from the opulent cotillions of Edinburgh to the
London court of half-mad King George III . . . from a famed
salon teeming with politicians and poets to a picturesque
castle on the lush, secluded Island of the Swans . . . an island
that can make her dreams come true or break her heart . . .

Published by Fawcett Books.
Available wherever books are sold.

Now available!

MURDER COMES TO MIND
by Joan Smith

In this fourth volume of the misadventures of the
Berkeley Brigade, the lovely Corinne deCoventry and the
dashing Lord Luten have finally announced their long-
awaited engagement. But with Luten's constant poli-
ticking in Parliament, Corinne fears they will never
make it to the altar. Fed up, Corinne accepts an invitation at a charming country estate and finds herself
embroiled in a mysterious murder. But the amateur
sleuth is in over her head, and Corinne's stalwart com-
panions must race to save this bride-to-be from her dangerous curiosity. . . .

Published by Fawcett Books.
Available wherever books are sold.

Coming next month . . .

THE BEQUEST
by Candice Proctor

When innocent, convent-bred Gabrielle Antoine arrives in Central City, Colorado, to receive an inheritance, she has no idea that what she is inheriting is a high-class brothel that was owned by a mother she didn't know she had. Gabrielle decides to reform these "fallen women," but her plan angers the wily Doug Slaughter, who wants Gabrielle's business for himself—and will stop at nothing to get it.

Gabrielle must turn to the handsome and rugged Jordan Hays, her mother's partner, for help. But who will protect Gabrielle from Jordan? And when Gabrielle finds herself irresistibly drawn to this enigmatic man who quotes poetry and can kill without batting an eye, who will protect her from herself and her own awakening passions?

Published by Ivy Books.
Ask for THE BEQUEST in your local bookstore.